THE
VAGABOND
CODES

J.D. STONE

To my students.

PART ONE

WORLD OF SHADOW

CHAPTER 1

LIGHTS OF BETRAYAL

At three o'clock in the morning, the fog finally rolled in from the coast. Silently, oppressively, it smothered the desolated city in a blanket of pale mist. For three nights straight, the fog had descended at midnight, but yesterday's setting sun stirred up a chill wind that kept the dark clouds hovering gloomily over the ocean.

Benedict Knight had prepared for a weather delay, but he didn't expect one this long. He was kneeling behind a self-driving Tesla; its windows were smeared with the bloody handprints of a small child, dried and flaking after a year exposed to sun and heat. He knew better than to look inside.

He glanced over at Danna, crouched twenty feet to his right behind an overturned ambulance. Half-shrouded in the mist, her eyes glinted as she nodded her head.

It was now or never.

Bracing himself, Ben pressed the handheld radio and whispered: "Alex, it's showtime — over."

Two blips in response. Five seconds later a shrill blast of music pierced the silence. One-and-a-quarter miles west to be exact. The range needed to be perfect. And so did the timing: two minutes, not a second later.

Old McDonald had a farm, e-i-e-i-o. . . .

Ben cringed. He pictured Alex snickering as he pressed the play button. He remembered singing that song in elementary school, but now it gave him the creeps.

And on his farm he had a pig, e-i-e-i-o. . . .

A minute passed.

Even with the far-off music, the silence was suffocating. Ben ran a hand through his hair and frowned. He felt Danna staring at him, but he kept his eyes ahead, watching for the slightest movement in the murk—and fighting off the reasons racing through his mind why this mission was a terrible idea. Even though it was his.

His stomach growled. He had a Power Bar in his tactical vest, but he knew it'd make him thirsty, and his tongue was already sticking to the roof of his mouth. He reached for his canteen then pulled back: if he dropped the cap he'd never hear the end of it.

He ventured a quick look around the headlights, wishing those *Things* would show up or that time would just freeze altogether—or at least long enough for them to get in and get out.

But the hands on his watch *ticked* onwards second-by-second until it *tocked* at his decision point — two minutes.

Time had run out. Mission abort.

Ben wiped his palms on his vest then raised the radio to his mouth.

Then he heard it.

Faintly at first but growing louder. The mechanical joints grating like rusted bicycle chains. The pneumatic actuators hissing like dry bursts from an aerosol can.

So familiar, that sound, and yet so alien. Ben couldn't help but shudder.

He peered around the front of the car. Three dark shapes emerged on the street, shuffling toward the music as if called by the Pied Piper. A minute later three more joined them.

Ben turned his head away and pressed himself against the car harder than before. He felt his heartbeat reverberating off the fender.

He counted to sixty then peeked around one last time, fingers crossed.

All clear.

"Alex, I've got visuals on six vagabonds," he whispered into the radio. "They're on their way. Looks like this is gonna work — over."

Blip, blip.

During his scouting expedition last week, Alex had spotted six vagabonds wandering around a two-block radius of the Carmel Hills Shopping Plaza. Now six plodded toward the music, their metal boots scraping the pavement in near unison. The math added up.

Ben pumped his fist. *Today is gonna be a good day.*

He heard Ron fidget behind him. The seventeen-year-old boy was sitting cross-legged on the damp concrete, clutching an empty black duffel bag like it was his teddy bear.

Ron had a round and pasty freckled face with a small, moist mouth and dewy, shifty eyes. He wore a large olive-green canvas coat, camouflage pants several inches too short, and a grimy pair of navy rubber boots that he'd stumbled upon several weeks ago while scavenging an abandoned dairy farm.

Ben studied Ron skeptically. *Three years older than me*, he thought, *yet he's like a child.*

Rolling his eyes, he crawled over to him and said flatly, "Ron, you're not ready."

Ron didn't respond. His ragged breaths were huffing and puffing into the chill air.

"Hey," Ben said, gently shaking the boy's shoulders. "You're gonna wait here, okay?"

Ron stared at the ground and nodded.

Ben darted a quick glance at Danna, who motioned to him to hurry up. He mouthed *I know!* and turned back to Ron.

"Do you have your radio?" he asked.

The boy fumbled around in his duffel bag and pulled it out.

"We need you to keep an eye out," Ben said firmly. "If you see *anything*, let us know. Channel four. Don't say a word; three clicks, that's all."

Ron licked his lips and nodded eagerly. He was relaxed now as if he'd been pardoned from a death sentence still pronounced for two others.

"Ron, which channel?"

"Ch-channel four," Ron finally replied. He took a deep breath and swallowed. "Three clicks. I got it. I'll keep an eye out."

Ben's eyes narrowed. "If we're not back in thirty minutes, take the car and get back to the retreat as fast as you can. *Don't* come looking for us."

He had a feeling that Ron wouldn't anyway.

Ron scuttled underneath a U-Haul truck with a picture of Mt. Rushmore on its side. He positioned himself to face Ben, who nodded approvingly. It'd be a good spot for Ron to keep watch, or at least to hide. It was also a straight run back to their car, which was parked behind a burnt-down 7-11 a quarter-mile back.

Ben tried to give him a reassuring smile, but he could only manage a thumbs-up. *He better not fall asleep.* . . .

He turned to Danna, who was strangling an imaginary neck with her hands. Ron had cost them precious time.

Scanning the street one last time, Ben gave the forward arm signal, and they slipped across the street, spread twenty feet apart. Their target was a Rite Aid pharmacy supposedly unscathed by looters.

Within seconds, they reached the door and flattened themselves against the side of the building.

Crouching low, Ben inched his way to the edge of the doorway and peered in through the glass. Empty like a tomb. He pointed to his eyes with two fingers and motioned Danna to look. She saw nothing too.

Time to get to work.

* * *

Danna pulled out a tension wrench from her bag and — rather theatrically — a bobby pin from behind her ear. She noticed Ben looking at her with a raised eyebrow. "I've always wanted to do that," she whispered wryly. "Just like the movies, you know?"

Ben rolled his eyes. With his back against the wall, he scanned the street for any sign of movement. Except for knives, they were unarmed. This mission required absolute stealth and silence. A firearm would be too tempting to use if things went south; the noise from a gunshot would be more dangerous than what would assail them.

Besides, no firearm smaller than a two-gauge punt gun could incapacitate a vagabond.

Ben cupped his ears. Not a sound except for the distant music and the slight scrape of the tension tool as Danna inserted it into the lock cylinder. Among her other skills once useless in that old safe and happy world, she liked picking locks.

Danna was slight of build for a girl of fifteen. She had shimmering, jet-black hair, tucked inside a baseball cap except for a high ponytail that gently bobbed as she moved. Her remarkably pale skin contrasted with her raven hair; and the only blemishes on her porcelain face were a quarter-sized birthmark under her left ear and natural, slightly dark circles under her large hazel eyes, which her mother said she got from her Italian side.

She moved gracefully like a ballet dancer, which contrasted with her fiery spirit and flair for the dramatic. Indeed, the group back at the hideaway learned quickly that it was a mistake to get on her bad side. A few of the younger kids were terrified of her, and she showered them with her wrath whenever they got in her way.

She always acted dumbfounded when told of her intimidating reputation, but Ben knew deep down she enjoyed it.

"We're super lucky," she whispered with a slight smile. "If this weren't a five-pin tumbler lock, we'd have to break through the glass."

Holding the tension tool with her left hand, she slid in the bobby pin and pressed her ear next to the lock. Listening carefully, she moved each lock pin one-by-one by rocking the pick until the pins finally clipped upwards in an unlocked position. She tucked a loose strand of hair behind her ear and grinned.

With a slight push, the door creaked open, and a faint *whoosh* of dry, musty air greeted them.

They peered into the empty expanse.

"Holy smokes," Ben whispered in awe as if he were standing on the threshold of a forgotten vault of unsurpassable riches. When the looting started, the pharmacies were the first to get hit. He shook his head in disbelief.

"People in this neighborhood sure got out of here quick," Danna said softly, with a slight tone of gratitude.

"Can we lock the door?"

Danna shook her head. "Any lock that's picked open must be picked to lock again. And don't forget that Alex said the back door was chained."

Ben nodded and took out a length of paracord, tied the door handles together, and gave them a sharp tug. Satisfied, he said, "Let's sweep."

They moved slowly, inch-by-inch, crisscrossing flashlight beams up each aisle. Not an item was moved;

everything was stacked neatly as if the pharmacy was merely closed for the night. Only a fine layer of dust covered the flat surfaces.

As they walked past the holiday decorations, Ben shone his light upward. A hideous witch leered at him with beady black eyes and a vacant, sinister smile. He jerked backward, and his flashlight slipped from his sweaty palm; but he caught it with his other hand before it clattered to the floor.

He let out a deep breath and shone the light up again. Halloween decorations were still up for sale. *How fitting for a haunted town*, he thought. He darted a look in Danna's direction, who was standing there with a mocking half-smile on her face.

"Don't worry," she teased; "I won't tell anyone."

Ben's cheeks flushed, and pursing his lips, he made an exaggerated motion to continue moving toward the back of the store.

"It's pretty ironic," Danna said softly, breaking the awkward silence, "that sick people had to walk all the way to the back of the pharmacy to get their medicine, but others could buy their cigarettes at the front counter."

"Yeah," Ben muttered under his breath. "Crazy world, wasn't it?"

The pharmacy's shutter window was open; and shining the light through it, Ben saw shelves of white pill bottles labeled and arranged neatly.

"Let's split up," he said. "I'll look for antibiotics in the back room; you find the medicine aisles. Grab as many ibuprofen and cold medicine as you can. Stuff your bag. We also need toothpaste . . . and toilet paper!"

He set his bag on the dusty pharmacy counter and hoisted himself through the window. Holding the flashlight with his teeth, he unfolded Katie's medication list and checked it over. He'd already memorized it two days ago, but he knew there'd be no coming back here. Not for a long time, at least.

Searching alphabetically, he plucked bottles off the shelves and dropped them into the bag. He smiled. *Today's a good day.*

A sudden crash of boxes coming from Danna's direction jolted him upward. He pulled out his knife and rushed to the window.

Danna's head popped up two aisles over.

"Sorry!" she whispered. "Somebody didn't do a good job stocking this shelf."

Ben shook his head, set his knife on the counter, and got back to work.

Ten minutes later, he'd mentally checked off every item except for the two he couldn't find. He hopped through the window and jogged toward the food aisle. More than anything, they needed protein. He knew what to get: beef jerky, pistachios, and trail mix. *Especially the beef jerky* — that was his favorite.

Danna met him in the center aisle.

"We good?" he asked, shining his light on the giant wall of refrigerators. The windows were stained with green mold. He could imagine the smell inside.

Danna shook her bags, which were stuffed full. "I even got gummy bear vitamins for Izzy."

"Okay, now we should—"

A thunderous crash rocked the front door.

For a moment they stood there, frozen. An item fell off a shelf and shattered.

"Could that be Ron?" Danna whispered.

Another booming crash.

"Is Ron wearing a coat of armor?" Ben asked wryly, flinging his bags to the ground. "Wait here."

"Yeah, right. I'm coming with you."

Ben shrugged and tip-toed his way to the front. He pressed himself against the wall and peered around the edge. Metal head, neon green eyes, that freakish metallic grin.

A vagabond. And it knew that they were in there.

Then Ben realized his mistake: it had seen their flashlight beams. He should've covered the lenses with red filters, which would've given them infrared vision without the bright beams. It was a stupid and costly mistake.

Ben rubbed his temples. *Today was supposed to be a good day.*

He pulled out his radio. "Ron, you copy?" he asked softly.

Static.

"Ron, are you there? Over."

No response.

"Why didn't Ron warn us on the radio?" Danna hissed. She grabbed Ben's radio. "Ron, do you—"

"You're wasting your time," Ben snapped. "He went AWOL." He shone his light on the aisle signs. "We need to find the tool section."

"I'll do it," Danna said. "You stay here and watch the door." She darted into the depths of the store, pacing the aisles once stocked by a high-school student just like her but long since dead.

"Toys, party stuff, school supplies, hardware — Ben, aisle seven!"

Ben snatched a Kodak disposable camera off a shelf and sprinted toward Danna. He dropped to his knees and tore the camera out of the box.

Another blow at the door. More items toppled to the floor. The door was smash-resistant, but the new guest was three hundred pounds of solid metal and well aware of its strength.

"It's coming through!" Danna cried.

Ben nodded his head, all but ignoring her. He flipped open the battery casing and popped out the battery. Then he pressed the flash button three times.

"What are you *doing*?"

"I'm draining the capacitor of any stored electricity," Ben replied, trying to sound calm.

"That's *not* what I meant," Danna replied, stomping her foot. "Ben, we have *got to go*."

"Yes, we do. But the back door is chained shut, remember? We're not getting outta here unless we take down that vagabond." He held up the camera. "This is gonna make that happen."

He wiped his fingers on his pants and cracked open the camera. Piece-by-piece he removed the circuit board, the flashbulb, and finally the film. His hands were shaking. He clenched his jaw and told himself to concentrate.

Boom! *Crack*!

Ben reached for a box of small screws and took out two. "Get me that electrical tape over there," he said. "And that roll of wire right next to it."

Danna handed him the wire, and he cut it into two four-inch lengths and stripped both ends with his pocketknife. He wrapped the wire around the screws and inserted them carefully into the slot that housed the film roll, with both screws sticking out like small, twisted spikes. He then wrapped the wire around the capacitor posts and mounted the circuit board back into the housing.

"How much longer?" Danna asked, rubbing her face with both her hands.

Ben didn't respond. He popped the battery in place and slid in a piece of film to keep the pack from touching the battery terminal post. That would prevent premature charging and keep the screws in place. He snapped the cover pieces together, leaving the film divider sticking out.

He held up the device and grinned. "Taser."

Slinging the duffel bags over their shoulders, they ran to the front, dropped the bags, and backed themselves against the wall next to the door.

"We need a diversion," Ben said as he tried to catch his breath. "Your turn."

"I'm on it." Danna reached up and grabbed a pack of Bic lighters from a rack next to a cash register.

She took out her knife, ripped open the pack, and popped open the plastic cover of one of the lighters.

Working quickly, she removed the striker wheel, flint, and the flint spring. She handed Ben the casing filled with the lighter fluid. Biting her bottom lip, she twisted the spring then wrapped it around the flint.

Ben was about to venture a glance when a metal fist punched through the door and began to rip off pieces of glass.

He turned to Danna. "How much longer?"

"Toss me the casing." She took out the other lighter, flicked it on, and began to heat the flint that was wrapped with the spring.

Not thirty seconds later there was a resounding smash.

The vagabond burst through the door, sending shards of glass in every direction. Ben winced as a piece stung his cheek.

The machine was an early version artificially intelligent android: six-foot-five with a fully exposed metal skeleton, unlike the recent models with synthetic skin. Its rusted cranium was human-sized except for a long protruding jaw that jutted down to cover its neck. The mouth was shaped into a gaping grin that stretched the entire width of its face like a demented clown from a gearhead's nightmare. Above its jaws were hollow, skull-like "nostrils" and beady green eyes that flickered like two trapped neon fireflies. And somehow stuck or glued to the top of its head was either a shredded blonde wig or the scalp of an unsuspecting victim left alive or for dead.

The vagabond was wrapped in a large, olive-green coat, the back seam split straight up the middle. Frayed thin ropes strung with brightly colored soda cans dangled from its neck like aluminum Hawaiian *leis*. Its spindly legs were covered with a pair of tattered blue trousers shredded to the knee, and its left foot was shoved into a filthy rubber boot.

The android was one of the "freaks," as his brother Cameron called them.

When the Surge hit, the electromagnetic pulse disabled the critical control function that kept the androids from developing personalities.

After the EMP had fried this control, the robots began to adopt peculiar human characteristics: attractions to vibrant colors, bright lights, extravagant clothing, retro music, and soft and feathery things.

Cameron loved to spook the kids by telling them that the Surge made the robots go insane.

While not all the rogue androids were pre-programmed with lethal capabilities, these "vagabonds" — as the group called them, for they wandered ceaselessly, seeking to amuse their fancies — don't have any value for human life, especially if a human has something it wants.

Like flashlights.

As soon as the vagabond burst through the door, Danna tossed the heated flint ten feet down the cosmetics aisle, and it hit the ground with a brilliant spark and flash.

The vagabond drew itself up and stomped over to the source of the flashing.

"Now!" Danna cried.

Ben pulled the strip of film from the taser; and in a fraction of a second, it was charged. He took two running steps toward the vagabond and leaped into the air.

Holding the taser high above his head, he came down upon the vagabond and drove the taser's screws directly into the back of its neck, sending a 9-volt jolt of electricity into its artificial nervous system.

An ear-splitting zap followed a faint pop, and the vagabond collapsed to the floor, shaking spasmodically.

For a moment, Ben stood there, his eyebrows raised, curious to observe the aftereffects of the shock.

"Ben, let's go!"

"Good idea," he said under his breath. He grabbed his duffel bag and followed Danna into the suffocating fog.

Ben stopped after twenty feet and pulled out from his bag an M67 grenade. The plan was to execute the mission unarmed, but as they left the retreat, he'd slipped the grenade in his bag. Just in case.

He flipped the pin and hurled the grenade like a four-seam fastball into the pharmacy.

So much for the beef jerky.

They took two running steps and hit the pavement, opened their mouths to prevent their lungs from collapsing from the imminent blast, and covered their necks.

The grenade detonated, shattering the rest of the door and setting off a ferocious firebomb; it must've landed near the flammable hairspray cans.

Coughing and out of breath from the grenade's pressure wave, they got on their feet, brushed themselves off, slung the bags over their shoulders, and hobbled hastily toward the car.

They didn't make it one hundred feet before they saw a person lying face down in the street.

Ben's heart sank. He knew it was Ron.

They dropped their bags and rushed to his side. His face was pale and slick, and he was missing his coat and one of his boots. A small stream of blood trickled on the black pavement.

Danna checked his pulse; he wasn't breathing.

Ben then heard the dull static of Ron's radio, still clenched in the boy's grimy fingers. He picked it up; it was set to channel three. Clenching his jaw, he hurled it down the street and watched it shatter into a thousand plastic pieces.

He tried to warn us, Ben thought. *He was brave after all.* He glanced at Danna, who was staring absently at Ron.

"We need to go," Ben said hoarsely.

"We're just gonna leave him?" Danna asked desperately, her porcelain face ashen with grief. She hovered over Ron's body protectively and looked up at Ben with tears streaming down her face.

But she already knew the answer.

"If we stay here any longer," Ben replied, firmly but reluctantly, "you know we're not gonna make it back."

Danna nodded her head and wiped her eyes.

With his dirty fingers, Ben gently closed Ron's eyes. Then they gathered what was left of themselves and limped to the car.

CHAPTER 2

THE STRANGER

Their car, an old Saab station wagon, was parked on the side of the road next to a burnt-out UPS delivery truck. As they approached the vehicle, Ben glanced over his shoulder. No pursuers. The fog was lifting, and their moonlit shadows followed them along the damp concrete.

They threw the bags into the backseat and jumped into the car. Ben reached for the keys to turn the ignition. No keys. He pounded the dashboard.

"Ron must've taken them with him," Danna said.

"I specifically told him to leave the keys in the ignition," Ben said, fighting back anger. "Who on earth is gonna steal a car at three o'clock in the morning in this graveyard?"

"There's no way we can go back and get the keys?"

Ben shook his head and got out of the car. "There," he said, pointing to an old Honda Civic parked on the other side of the road. "Grab the bags. And get the gun out of the glove compartment."

The Honda was unlocked. Opening the driver side door, Ben bent down and broke the plastic housing underneath the steering column.

"You think you're gonna hotwire this thing?" Danna asked skeptically as she got in the car.

"It's an older model Honda, so yes."

Ben yanked as hard as he could on the steering wheel, breaking the steering column lock and the lock cylinder from the lock body.

Next, he unclipped his multi-tool from his belt, flipped up the Phillips screwdriver, and turned the cylinder. With a choked whine, the car fired up.

Not a moment too soon. The car suddenly shook violently, followed by the piercing scrape of tearing metal. Ben turned around and watched in horror as a vagabond ripped off the trunk lid. Half of its head covering was torn off, and one of its neon eyes was missing.

Ben shifted into drive and hit the gas. The vagabond punctured the roof with its titanium alloy fingers and swung itself up to the front passenger side window. Its feet dragged along the road, sending up short trails of hot white sparks.

"Danna, duck!"

With its other hand, the vagabond punched through the window, sending a torrent of shattered glass into their laps. Danna leaned back just in time. The robot reset its approach, then edged its way into the window and reached for her neck.

Panicking, Danna fumbled around looking for a weapon. Her probing fingers felt Ben's multi-tool, and seizing it with her left hand, she lunged forward and jammed the screwdriver into the vagabond's remaining eye.

The robot's head exploded into a shower of neon sparks; and with a sudden jerk it reeled backward and slid off the car, grabbing and ripping off the side mirror as it hit the road.

Ben pushed the gas pedal to the floor and tore off down the road. Exhaling deeply, he glanced at Danna. Her hands and arms were covered with sharp pieces of glass, several of which were stuck into her arms.

"I'll be okay," she said weakly.

Far behind them, the vagabond lay in the middle of the road. For several seconds, its limbs twitched violently until a final flash of blue flame shot three feet upwards and then it moved no more.

* * *

For a while, both were silent. The car tires hummed dully on the road, and the wind rushed through the broken window.

Ben's thoughts turned to Ron.

Ronald Godfrey had been with the group since the beginning. He was a junior at Ben's school. Ben had never spoken to him before, but he'd known who he was; from what he heard, Ron was a class clown.

On the day of the Surge, Cameron had rushed to the school to pick up his brother and head straight to the retreat — to "get out of Dodge," as their dad used to say. As they were driving away, Ron lumbered alongside the van and begged to take the last seat.

Cameron had saved the seat for their cousin Dominic, but he chickened out at the last minute and decided that he'd be better off hiding under his desk until help arrived. But help never came, and Ben knew he'd never see his cousin again.

So Ron lucked out. Since they arrived at the retreat over a year ago, he had been practically useless; he'd just loaf around and watch the other kids work.

After a while, Ben finally decided to put Ron in charge of inventory in the food pantry, a menial job. It didn't take long for Ben to notice the missing packages of Ritz crackers and other snacks here and there. But he said nothing to Ron about it. Danna always said Ben was too easy on him.

Of the ten kids who'd escaped with Ben from school, Ron took everything the hardest. Sure, most of the kids were traumatized after losing their families — that was no doubt the worst thing about this whole mess. But Ron's dad split when he was ten, leaving Ron and his mom with a stack of bills and a beater car with an empty tank. Money was tight. They got close; they survived together, in a way.

After they'd all made it the retreat, Ron figured his mom was gone, but he never mustered whatever courage he thought he needed to go looking for her. Ben and Cameron never would've let him leave the retreat anyway: he wouldn't have survived the afternoon.

A few months ago, Ron decided that he wanted to get involved. Ben wondered if Ron wanted the younger kids to look up to him. He spent a day learning operational security, the retreat's defense protocol, and how to conduct patrols.

Ron wasn't allowed to carry a gun, however, because he neither received proper firearm safety training before the Surge nor, in the alternative, did he "graduate" from Cameron's haphazard gun lessons affectionately dubbed the "Warrior Academy."

Ben thought Ron was ready for supply runs; unfortunately, he was mistaken. To Ben, Ron represented a greater problem. The group was still too weak; too many were still afraid. *Not just afraid to die,* he thought. *They're afraid to live. And people afraid to live won't survive in this world.*

"How long till home?" Danna asked, breaking the silence. She forced herself to look out the window and not down at her bleeding arms. A couple of gashes were deep; she'd need stitches.

"Less than an hour. I took a different route home to shake any followers."

They moved into hillier terrain, where the fog still haunted the lowlands. Up above, the moon cast an eerie glow upon the dark land — a land without lights, without life.

Danna winced in pain. Ben leaned over and popped open the glove compartment. "Might be a first aid kit in here—"

"Watch out!"

Ben snapped his head up and saw a hooded silhouette standing in the middle of the road with its palms stretched outward, imploring them to stop.

He slammed on the brakes. The car swerved from right to left before coming to a screeching halt ten feet before the figure. With its hands now above its head, the figure stood there like a ghostly statue frozen in the swirling moonlit mist.

"Ben, let's go," Danna said warily, clutching her hands. "This isn't safe. Just drive around it."

Ben paused and leaned forward, squinting his eyes. He was about to drive off when suddenly he felt a dull, cold ache in his chest. And just as quickly, that ache began to wrestle with a strange feeling of warmth, like long lost joy, only reachable by walking blindfolded across a thin thread of hope.

He opened the door. "Stay in the car," he said to Danna blankly. "Whatever it is, it shouldn't be kept alive."

"Then just run it over!"

Ben shot Danna a sharp look then leaned over and pulled the handgun out of the glove compartment. He held it up as if to ask, "Better now?"

As he got out of the car, he thought: *Danna's right. What am I doing?*

"Stop right there," he said, pointing the gun at the figure.

Danna shone a flashlight on its face. It was a man. He had a gaunt face, ragged beard, and hollow, sleepless eyes. He wore a green, heavy-duty hooded poncho with a large military pack slung over his shoulder. Five feet behind him a large black garbage bag lay on the road.

In a steady voice, Ben said: "Set your bag down, take big three steps backwards, and drop to your knees."

The man did as told. "Please help," he said hoarsely, shifting from one knee to the other. He coughed. "My friends are dead, and I'm all alone."

"Welcome to the club," Ben said bitterly. As soon as the words left his mouth, his chest tightened with a pang. His father would've let him have it for speaking disrespectfully like that to an adult. *But I'm not a kid anymore*, he thought. *I should be, but I'm not. We're all equals now.*

Keeping the gun leveled at the stranger, he walked over to the man's pack and rummaged through it, searching for weapons. None. He slung the pack over his shoulder and stared at the man intently.

"What makes you think we can help you?" Ben asked. "Besides, you nearly killed us."

"It was the only way you'd have stopped," the stranger replied as he hunched his shoulders. "Besides," he added with a weak smile, "the thumbs-up sign doesn't work for hitchhikers nowadays."

Ben frowned. "We can't help you," he said. "Really, there's nothing we can do for you." Without taking his eyes off the stranger, he set the pack on the pavement and slowly got back into the car.

Danna's eyes were fixed on the man; her Ka-Bar fighting knife was on her lap.

The man let out a long, slow sigh and lowered his head. "Please, I beg you," he said, looking up again. "I don't need food or water; I just need shelter for the night — it's like they're hunting me."

Far, far away — miles perhaps — a single gunshot broke the silence.

"We're all being hunted!" Ben called out as he put the car in drive.

"Decided not to kill him, then?" Danna asked dryly.

As Ben drove past the stranger, who had gotten up and was walking to his bag, he was drawn to the man's hollow, distant face, a face without anger or malice, but one of kindness — and hope?

He wanted to hit the gas pedal. He knew he should. But he couldn't. He stopped the car. *Maybe I'm just out of my mind, and everything is finally getting to me. Dad said to trust no one. No. One.*

"Ben, are you *crazy*?" Danna snapped. "We need to go, like *now*."

"Where *are* you going, by the way?" Ben called out to the stranger. "There's nothing around here except death — and those who have caused it."

Wincing in pain, the man reached into his pack and pulled out a tattered map. "I'm not from around here. I started out — or *we* did — weeks ago." Tracing his finger along the map, he added: "I'm a half a day's walk to my destination if I'm not mistaken. I can set out in the morning if you put me up for the night."

"Are you going to a settlement?" Ben asked suspiciously, alarmed at the possibility of another group so close to the retreat.

"No, I don't think so," the stranger replied. "It's the summer home of an old friend of mine, Colonel Thomas Knight."

Ben and Danna looked at each other, stunned.

"Get in the car," Ben said roughly. "But first, take off that poncho and submit yourself to a search."

27

CHAPTER 3

THE RETREAT

Dawn was only an hour away, and Ben wanted to get home before sunrise. The home stretch was a two-lane highway that wound its way through ten miles of barren, boulder-covered hills before descending into a grove of oak trees and scrub brush.

The drive was slow. Every other mile he had to weave through abandoned vehicles on the road, many wrecked, flipped over, or smashed front first into the side of a cliff. Scavengers had ripped out the salvageable parts: pipes for weapons, side panels for armor, or tires for shoe soles.

Ben proceeded cautiously. Closer to the city, it wasn't uncommon for bandits to hide behind overturned vehicles and waylay unsuspecting travelers. But nobody travels on these roads anymore. Or at least Ben hoped.

They passed several houses a stone's throw from the road, all abandoned, or so they appeared. Of course, if anybody were living in one of those houses, they'd be smart enough to make it look deserted. The smallest flicker of candlelight would attract vagabonds; and no, the metal monsters don't ring the doorbell before entering. No doubt a lot of these homes were empty because people found that out the hard way.

As he drove by, Ben wondered if the mailboxes were stuffed with letters. Clothes catalogs, bills, a birthday card from a dear relative, never to be seen again.

Maybe he'd stop one day to see — they weren't far from home.

The road straightened for a half-mile as it cut through a large open space of old citrus groves surrounded by low-lying mountains plastered with massive boulders. The Martian Mountains, Ben used to call them.

It hadn't rained in a long time. A month ago, a brush fire ravaged the nearby hills, turning the sky into a filthy haze and dusting the earth with an unholy ash. Fortunately, the wind blew the fires elsewhere, to devour the empty cities and — Ben hoped — the ravenous deadheads that roamed the streets.

The road turned sharply to the right, avoiding a rocky outcropping, and descended into a small oak grove. Ben slowed down, pulled off to the side of the road, and stopped. Twenty feet to the right of the car were two fallen logs and an old, rusted-out minivan flipped over on its side.

Danna unbuckled her seatbelt, but Ben stopped her.

"I can get it," he said, hopping out. He ducked his head back in the car and glanced at Danna with a smirk. "I mean, seriously, look at your arms."

She gave a half-shrug and started tapping her knees with her fingers.

After looking both ways up the road, Ben walked over to the logs and dragged them to the side without a struggle. He then moved behind the minivan and lifted a tree stump, which, like the logs, was hollowed out.

Under the stump was a wheeled hand-crank attached to a chain. Ben cranked the wheel, and the minivan slid with a soft creak on a hidden track, as if on ice.

Within the minute, the minivan was moved to the side, revealing a two-wheel track that dipped and turned deep into the shadows of the grove.

As he got back into the car, he turned around to check on the stranger, who was sitting quietly in the back seat, blindfolded.

"I think he's asleep," Danna said softly, clutching her knife and the gun.

The stranger's head was fully resting on the back seat, his chest rising and falling in a gentle rhythm. By the looks of him, he must not have slept for days.

Ben pulled the car through the gate just past the minivan and stopped to reset the hidden cover. Two minutes later, after scanning the road one last time, he steered onto the pitted track and descended into woods.

The old trees hung low over the track, and their gnarled branches twisted together to create a murky tunnel that appeared to lead to nowhere. This place always gave Ben the creeps.

His dad said the grove formed a natural barrier to prevent an organized ground attack, particularly from large assault vehicles and troop transports.

Cameron used to scoff at their dad's schemes. But to Ben, seven-years-old when his father built the retreat, such defenses were critical to keeping the nasty people out — whoever they were.

He glanced at Danna, who was watching the Stranger in the rear-view mirror. She never took chances.

"It was stupid of us to use the flashlights," she said, breaking the silence.

"I know," Ben said, after a pause. "Live and learn."

"Except Ron didn't get to live."

"That's not on us, Danna." He gazed into her glistening dark eyes. "Ron's death is not on us. He had his orders; he didn't follow them."

Ben knew he was trying to convince himself just as he was telling it to Danna.

"Yeah, but if we never used those flashlights, then maybe that vagabond would have never shown up, and Ron wouldn't have gotten caught."

"Ron isn't the first one that we lost. You know that."

Danna pursed her lips and looked out the window.

* * *

Several hundred feet past the gate, the track ran beside a small, dried-up creek that wound through the middle of the grove. It followed the creek northward into the hills, curving and twisting, until it finally smoothed out and descended into a narrow ravine bound on both sides by abrupt cliffs fifty feet high.

After another half-mile, the track sloped into a flat, wide basin, about the length of three football fields and surrounded by sheer cliffs of various shades of gray, brown, and burnt orange. The flatland was scattered with cactus, tufts of wild grasses, and stunted, shriveled trees spurned by the rain gods.

At the far end of the basin loomed an isolated, otherworldly mountain several hundred feet high. The mountain face overlooking the basin was a two-hundred-foot vertical wall that dropped and crumbled into a steep mound of broken basalt.

The mountain was part of a volcanic vent created millions of years ago when lava had hardened inside the vent and caused an extreme build-up of trapped magma, which triggered a massive eruption that blew off half the vent.

The Spanish explorers who first discovered the area called it *la montaña embrujada* — the haunted mountain.

As Ben drove out of the grove, two grim-faced teens stepped out from nowhere. They were both wearing ghillie suits — camouflage garments covered by scraps of sand-colored material to blend in with the environment — and armed with semi-automatic rifles.

One guard stepped in front of the car as it came to a stop, and the other stood next to the driver's side door. Both leveled their rifles at Ben and Danna.

"Stop!" one of them called out sharply. Ben recognized the guard: Marcelo Apolito, his classmate.

The Stranger stirred in the back seat, awakened by the sound of the guard's voice.

Ben rolled down his window and stuck his head out. "Ben, Danna, and one pilgrim," he said, stony-faced. "Danna is injured, and the pilgrim is unarmed and secured."

"Driver, please exit the vehicle with your hands up and take two steps forward to be recognized."

Ben followed the order.

After circling the car, the other guard, Lena Martin, another classmate of Ben's, walked up to him and whispered, "Clipboard."

"Consequence," Ben whispered back.

"Supply run password is correct; proceed slowly."
Marcelo waved them through.

* * *

Ben turned into the basin. Past the sentry was a vast field of planted cactus and thorn bushes.

This area was a funneling defense system — natural barriers like cactus and thick brush would "funnel" attackers into a clear line of fire for the defenders. Here, the cactus field made it impossible to enter the basin except through the track or by descending the steep cliffs by rope.

Hidden among the cacti were several "spider holes," shoulder-deep dugouts covered by a camouflage lids, where two defenders could stand and fire.

Trip flares were spaced every fifty feet; one step would shoot off a flare two hundred feet into the air, all but eliminating a surprise attack. At first, the flares were a problem because deer and other animals would set them off unexpectedly during the night; but in the past six months most of the wildlife either had been eaten or had fled into the high deserts to die.

The retreat maintained two observation posts — OPs, as the group called them. At the highest points on the basin's western and eastern cliffs, they commanded a high ground and clear line of fire while staying protected from enemy sniper fire.

The OPs were rectangular holes, six feet deep and three feet wide. Inside, the defenders had the comfort and freedom to sit, stand, and shoot. Two feet to the front and sides of the hole were thick oak logs which formed a bullet-proof protective wall with openings cut in them through which to shoot.

On top of and across the OPs were more thick logs sealed with rain-proof material and covered with dirt and sand to provide shelter from the elements and protection from grenade or artillery fire.

To communicate with the retreat, the OPs had TA-1 military field telephones, which had built-in, battery-free pump action generators. For visuals, the posts were illuminated by two angle head flashlights with red, double-thick lens filters and armored binoculars. Most important, each post had a .50 caliber long-range sniper rifle that could pick off any intruder from any part of the basin.

As part of the duty schedule, each post was manned 24/7, with group members alternating every four hours. To prevent grumbling, those who were assigned the night shift in the OPs got an extra ration at dinner time.

The third and final lookout was near the mountain's summit, and it was accessible by a short climb aided by ropes and ladders. On cloudless days, the lookout offered visibility up to sixty miles in every direction, including the city, forty miles to the west, and behind it, the deep blue horizon of the Pacific.

For the first few sunsets after they'd arrived at the retreat, Ben and Cameron watched as human civilization burned in mayhem while the machines and the deadheads brought millions of people to their apocalypse. But they were far away. For now.

The retreat itself was partially constructed on the north side of the mountain thirty feet above the basin floor. Like an old adobe home, the walls were mixed from the local earth, making the building blend in seamlessly with the landscape. It was protected by a six-foot perimeter wall, which had several viewing holes that could fit a rifle for protected fire.

Only six windows were visible from the outside, all secured by one-inch iron plates that could open to allow in fresh air and sunlight.

The only way up to the building was a small steel staircase, carved and bolted into the side of the mountain and undetectable from the ground. The staircase ended at a two-inch titanium-alloyed door.

While small from the outside, the interior of the retreat was cavernous. The volcanic vent had bored several small lava caves, known as lava tubes, inside the mountain, particularly in the northwest side.

Ben's father discovered that the three largest lava tubes were stacked above each other, so he designed the retreat to have three levels joined by several shafts and fitted with light ducts for sunlight to shine deep into the lower levels.

Unlike the rest of the known world, the retreat maintained electricity after the Surge. Ben's father designed the building as a giant Faraday cage, capable of repelling electromagnetic charges by absorbing and distributing the charge around the cage's steel exterior. Thus, the cage kept the charges from frying the electronics; and when the EMP hit, the retreat was spared from the carnage except for the replaceable telecom equipment in the OPs.

To generate power for the retreat, a well was drilled into a geothermal reservoir of hot water one hundred feet into the mountain. Pressured steam was funneled into a small turbine, which generated an unlimited supply of electricity.

If the turbines failed, a colossal lithium air powered generator served as a backup, and the last resort was a one-thousand-gallon gasoline tank, which also fueled the vehicles.

The cave walls were naturally insulated to keep a constant inside temperature of 65 to 70 degrees year-round. To regulate the moisture in the air, which is a common problem with cave dwellings, Ben's father installed several large dehumidifiers, which produced more than one hundred gallons of water per day to supply the retreat's water needs.

There were three primary levels to the retreat, all connected by an elevator shaft and several ladder cases with fire poles. The top level, L1, was the only level with windows; and with its sweeping views of the basin, it served as the retreat's "command center" — or OPSEC room.

L1 also housed the retreat's main armory. Ben knew the armory's weapon cache by heart: ten Ruger 10/22 autoloading rifles; five Remington 870 Special Purpose Marine Magnum shotguns; five Bushmaster Carbon 15 M4 Carbine semi-automatic rifles; for the smaller and lighter people of the group, ten Kahr PM9 handguns; three Smith & Wesson Model 629 revolvers; and finally, two McMillan TAC-50 long-range sniper rifles.

All team leaders and those on patrol carried SIG Sauer P226 handguns. To round it out, the armory carried an array of silencers, scopes, night vision goggles, and two cases of M67 grenades.

L2 was the living quarters, which housed a small kitchen; a common area; four bedrooms, two for the boys and two for the girls, with bunks and extra fold-up cots as needed; two small bathrooms, one for the boys and one for the girls; and two utility rooms, one of which served as the retreat's infirmary.

Everything was military grade — sparse, metal, and grim. No doubt the quarters were tight, but everyone had a job to do, so only at nighttime did it get too cramped.

Except for those who had patrol or OP duty, the group always ate dinner together. Afterward, they would spend time playing cards or throwing darts. Some learned chess for the first time; others held marathon Scrabble tournaments, and a few discovered the lost joy of reading.

Boredom was perhaps their greatest day-to-day challenge, which is why everyone had jobs to do and why spending time together as a group was mandated. Ben's dad warned that boredom leads to bad decisions or depression, both of which pose serious internal threats to a functioning team.

L3, the lowest level, housed the supply rooms, another utility room, and the garage. The largest supply room was the green room, twenty by thirty feet, which held the indoor hydroponic vegetable garden. Under bright lights, the group grew tomatoes, carrots, broccoli, spinach, and a variety of herbs. There was even a small lemon tree.

The garden was designed to support no more than eight-to-ten people, so the fresh vegetable rations were meager, but somehow they'd been making it work.

Ben often pushed this part out of his mind, hoping the day would never come when someone would say the dreaded words: *We're low on food.*

L3 also housed the food pantry. Along with thousands of canned food items, including soup, meat, condensed milk, and fruit, the pantry was stocked with dozens of five-gallon buckets of wheat, oats, corn, and rice. Including the food brought from Danna's family's retreat, the group could feed fifteen people for nine to ten years.

The garage was the mechanical heart of the retreat. Besides an old Volvo station wagon and the van, it kept a John Deere XUV Gator, two Honda Rangers ATVs, the robotics workshop, a small armory, and Ben's power suit, HULC. The Saab, which Ben and Danna had used for the supply run, would now be marked as a loss.

Ben's father sunk his life's fortune into building the retreat. The family used to call it Rockburg, after the underground home in *Swiss Family Robinson*.

But it was more than that: it was a fortress. Fire resistant, earthquake proof, and virtually self-sustainable.

Ben's father built the retreat to be impregnable.

And so far, it had been.

Ben stopped the car ten feet in front of the flattest wall of the mountain. The retreat loomed twenty feet to his left and thirty feet up.

Once again, a camouflaged guard emerged from a hidden spot and yanked several shrub trees to the side, revealing a large, fortified door — the entrance to L3.

The door opened, sending a faint cloud of dust in the air. Two smallish armed guards stood inside an expansive, dimly lit garage, waving them in. Ben pulled in, stopped the car, and let out a deep breath.

The two guards, Joey and Cody, opened the back door, helped the Stranger out of the car, and sat him down on the garage floor.

Katie Chiang, the group's medic, was already at Danna's side.

"Did you get everything I put on the list?" she asked.

"I think so," Ben replied as he got out of the car. He paused. "We were a little rushed at the end."

"Where's Ron?" Joey asked.

Ben hefted the bags out of the car. "Didn't make it."

CHAPTER 4

THE REVELATION

Later that morning, the group leaders gathered in the OPSEC room. The room was long and narrow with a low-slung ceiling; one main wall was hewn rock, the other was lined with control panels and television monitors and tacked with 3D maps of the basin and the surrounding area.

Ben sat at the rectangular table in the middle of the room next to Tomás, his best friend since elementary school and the retreat's tactical officer, and Aiden, who handled logistics.

Ben rubbed his face. He hated these "debriefs." After a month, he concluded that being a leader wasn't his thing, but he wasn't a follower either. Maybe somewhere in the middle. Or maybe not on that spectrum at all. A black sheep? Hardly. He didn't know.

He'd only been at Sierra Madre for two weeks before the Surge hit. Still the new kid, still trying to figure out his place in the pecking order. Then *It* happened. And suddenly kids who never even said hi to him are piled into his family van and the next thing he knows, he's in charge of guys that are bigger and older than him and girls who probably think he's a loser.

They never say anything, but he wonders what they think of him. Whether they really respect him or trust in him. Whether they talk behind his back and laugh about how he's weak or stupid.

All their lives, they were told what to do, what to say, and how to act. Then suddenly the world collapses, and that's all gone. But it hasn't been a year-long party: after the first couple of deaths, they realized that a world without adults had its downsides. And they still weren't necessarily *free*.

Not as free as Ben, though. In reality, *he* can do whatever he wants. It's *his* place. His family's place that is. He doesn't rub it in, but they actually have to follow his orders. If not his orders, then Cameron's.

But Cameron has been gone. Ben is the boss. He hates it, but he wouldn't have it any other way. Not here. Not now. It's not his fault his family prepared for the end of the world.

And what if someone stops listening to both of them? Would he and Cameron have to kick that person out? He hadn't figured out what to do if that ever happened.

Ben looked up as Danna walked in, followed by Katie.

"Where's Alex?" Aiden asked, sitting up. He was the tallest and burliest member of the group, a stereotypical jock: blonde, tightly curled hair, chiseled jaw, Roman nose, and ears pulled close to his square head. True to form, Aiden was Sierra Madre's star football player and the only sophomore in school history to be voted captain of the varsity football team.

"How am I supposed to know?" Danna replied sharply, holding up her bandaged forearms. She also had a small Band-Aid above her left eye.

"You were part of the team," Aiden pressed. "We all need to keep an eye on each other, especially when we're *out there*."

Danna's eyes flashed. "At least *I was* out there," she hissed.

Ben smiled inside as Aiden slouched ever so slightly in his chair.

"I think the issue is whether Alex followed the plan," Tomás asked, his eyebrows scrunching in thought.

Tomás was short and gangly, with deep caramel skin that was unhealthily pale, as if he'd never spent more than two hours outside in his life, and a matted mop of wavy brown hair fell over his narrow and angular face. His dark, intelligent eyes were quick, although he'd often stare at a single object for long periods of time while he was lost in thought in his "alternate dimension." Snapping one's fingers in front of Tomás' face was a running joke at the retreat.

Tomás was the smartest kid at their school. Although he was a freshman, he could've gotten his college degree before his driver's license. He never made a big show of his intelligence. Unless someone at school would hand him a Rubik's Cube. Then a crowd of kids would huddle around and watch him solve it in seconds. Afterward, he'd just smile and give it back as if it were nothing.

By the time he hit fourth grade, he was programming advanced software. But when augmented reality — or AR — began to replace the "real" reality of hundreds of millions of people around the world, his parents pulled the plug and enrolled him at Sierra Madre, one of the last schools that rejected universal virtual learning and actually assigned paper books to read.

Surprisingly, Tomás never pouted about it; he just quietly pursued other interests, like differential equations and mechanical engineering. But once the Surge hit and things got bad, something switched in his brain, and a new Tomás emerged: a cunning leader and a strategist.

"If he deviated by any means," he said, "he might've compromised himself."

"He obviously started the music," Ben replied, scratching his head. "Which means he must've hidden his bike two miles from the speakers, and—"

Aiden cocked his hand condescendingly. "Which means he should've been halfway back to his bike by the time the vagabonds reached the stereos."

"Maybe the vagabonds didn't make it all the way to the stereos?" Katie asked softly, twisting a dainty gold necklace around her fingers. "And they somehow caught him?"

"Unlikely," Tomás said. He had that distant look on his face as if mechanical gears were operating in his head. "His return route was in the other direction."

"We should go look for him," Aiden said bluntly, standing up.

"Let's give him another hour or so," Tomás said quickly. "If he's not back by then, Danna can put together a search party."

"Why?"

Ben looked at Aiden and frowned. "Because it's too dangerous," he said shortly. Saying that felt like a punch in the gut. One of their own is out there, and it'll be his fault now if something happens. *C'mon, Alex, come home. Don't do this to us.*

"Where's the Stranger?" Danna asked.

"He's downstairs resting," Ben replied. "Got him oatmeal and let him take a shower. He's fine."

Danna rested her bandaged arms on the table and pressed her lips into a fine line.

Aiden, reading her expression, said: "Yeah, it looks like we're gonna be operating a Hilton Hotel for the next few days."

"Don't worry about it," Ben said, brushing him off. "I'll care of it."

"Why do we keep calling him the Stranger?" Katie asked. "Isn't he gonna tell us his name?"

"*He* said it wasn't important," Danna replied tersely, wrinkling her nose and giving Ben a side glance.

"I guess it's not important *at the moment,*" Katie said, smiling at Danna. "We can find out later."

Danna and Alex discovered Katie Chiang hiding in the back of an In-N-Out Burger during a supply run two months ago. She told them she was in nursing school before the Surge, so they welcomed her into the group to serve as the retreat's medical officer.

At twenty-years-old, she was the oldest of the group; and because of her cheerfulness and sweet demeanor, the younger children looked to her as a mother figure.

"We've sorted out what you brought," Tomás said, ready to move on. "You really scored for us."

"The antibiotics are going to be huge," Katie added.

"I saw that my poor buddy here didn't get his beef jerky," Tomás said, giving Ben a soft elbow.

They laughed for a moment, but quickly fell silent, as if laughing was an unutterably profane sacrilege. Ron's death was heavy in the air.

"There's no way we can go back for his body?" Katie ventured. "For a proper burial?"

Ben shook his head. "There's too many of them. Alex counted six vagabonds. We were attacked by two, but the second one could've been the one I jammed with the taser. I only hit it with nine volts of power, so the least it could've done was paralyze it for a minute."

"But then again you tossed in the grenade," Tomás said. He shook his head and grinned. "Boy, would I have loved to have seen that."

"I have to admit," Ben said as he leaned back and stretched, "it *was* pretty cool."

Danna snorted.

"Go ahead and roll your eyes, Miss Pull-a-bobby-pin-out-of-your-hair."

The other group members looked at each other, confused.

"*Anyway*," Danna said. "We know for a fact the second vagabond is gone. I made sure of that after this." She held up her bandaged arms.

"So, there's definitely four, possibly five vagabonds left," Aiden said. "And we know they settle in groups, so they've probably been back there for a while."

"It sounds risky," Tomás said, raking his hands through his hair.

"But to just leave him there?" Katie asked.

"We have to balance the risk against the reward, so to speak," Tomás replied. "Sure, we can put a small squad together and make a run for him, but we could lose somebody else while doing it."

"The only way we could pull it off is HULC," Danna said, glancing at Ben.

"As much as I'd love to take those freaks out with HULC," Ben said, "I just don't see it happening. It's over thirty miles away, and I've never taken HULC past the farmhouse."

They were silent for a moment; everyone was lost in their thoughts.

"So, we all agree that we can't get Ron?" Aiden asked.

"What about Cameron and Alex?" Katie asked. "Should we wait for them before we decide?"

"They're not here, so it's our call," Aiden said. "We all know we can't do it. We can't keep letting people get killed. We've lost three in the last month, not including Robby, who just bolted in the middle of the night. Nineteen is getting low."

Ben clenched his fists. *Letting people get killed? Let?* He felt an overwhelming desire to break that Roman nose. But a soft elbow nudged his arm, and out of the corner of his eye, he saw Tomás shake his head discreetly.

"To survive, our strength is in numbers," Aiden said in a patronizing tone.

"Wow, I never thought of that before," Ben muttered.

After a final vote, everyone agreed that they couldn't retrieve Ron's body. Instead, they'd hold a memorial service for Ron when Cameron and Alex returned.

If they returned, Ben thought.

Aiden leaned back into his chair and crossed his arms. "So, is this *Stranger* going to be Ron's new replacement?" he asked, with a touch of sarcasm. "Can't afford to have a freeloader around here."

Ben narrowed his eyes on Aiden. Their moms were roommates back in medical school, so he was kind of a family friend, even though Aiden ignored Ben at school. Even so, when Cameron roared into the parking lot at Sierra Madre on the day of the Surge, finding Aiden was a priority.

He knew that Aiden wanted to lead the group and that it ate at him that Ben, at fourteen-years-old and two years younger, had the final say on things — even though it was Ben's family's retreat. For the most part, Ben ignored it, but lately Aiden had been stepping out of line, especially since Cameron has been going on his hunting expeditions. They were just trivial things, but still. . . .

"He's not staying here permanently," Ben said assertively. "We agreed to let him stay for one night and then he's out tomorrow morning."

"And what makes you think he's gonna wanna leave tomorrow morning?" Aiden asked, crossing his arms.

"He said he's on his way somewhere important," Danna said icily, rising to Ben's defense.

Ben shot her a quick glance of appreciation.

"Whatever," Aiden replied. He yawned noisily. "Can't imagine someplace important enough that'd be worth being out there. Everybody's mother and their cow is dead."

Everybody looked at Aiden and frowned.

"Sorry, not what I meant," Aiden muttered, leaning further back in his chair. He paused. "Did this *Stranger* at least have anything useful on him?"

Tomás reached over and lifted the Stranger's backpack onto the table. "A knife, binoculars, an emergency thermal blanket, a small tarp, a can of peaches. And this." He held up a small black plastic device that looked like an old flash drive. "Found it in his pants pocket."

"Weird," Aiden said, taking it from Tomás. "Looks pretty sturdy. Wonder what he's doing with it."

"It's a military-grade HVD," Ben said. "Holographic virtual disc. It crams data onto layers of tiny holograms. It's titanium encased and secured by a biometric lock, like a fingerprint, eye scan, or a voice wave. Virtually unbreakable."

"Should we get him to open it?" Aiden asked.

"For what?" Danna replied. "It's none of our business."

"Maybe it's something really important," Katie said.

Ben took the device from Aiden and put it in his shirt pocket. "I'll ask him about it."

"So, what are we gonna do with this guy?" Aiden asked. "I don't believe he's just gonna stay one night."

"We have more than enough food," Katie said. "If the Stranger is as harmless as he seems, then I think he should stay here as long as he needs until he regains strength. I looked him over, and he could use some rest. And perhaps he'll tell us about that thing before we even have to ask him."

"I agree with you, Katie," Tomás said. "But nobody is *harmless* nowadays. Everybody has an angle. Everybody is dangerous." He glanced at Aiden.

* * *

Ben didn't want to talk to this so-called Stranger. At least at the moment. Instead, he wanted to lay in his bed and sleep. He had four hours until his next duty: perimeter patrol. A four-hour nap would be perfect.

Standing outside a utility room, he hesitated, then gently knocked on the thin metal door. Without waiting for a response, he unlocked the door and pushed it open with his left hand. His right hand was next to his holster.

The Stranger was stretched out on his cot with his hands behind his head. He offered Ben a warm smile.

"Thought you could use some more," Ben said, setting a water bottle on a small table.

"Thanks," the Stranger replied, rubbing his eyes and sitting up. "It's been awhile since I've had water that wasn't taken from unsavory sources." He motioned Ben toward the single chair. "Please, sit."

Ben gave a half-shrug and sat down.

The Stranger, having now showered and eaten, looked like a new man. He was in his early-to-mid-thirties, tall and slim, yet well built, with a narrow face, high cheekbones, and a sharp nose — all marks of an upper-class family heritage. His large blue eyes were thoughtful and intense, yet friendly; and his short, wavy dark hair was receding slightly and streaked with gray on the sides.

The Stranger took a long sip from the water bottle. "So, let me guess: you're Colonel Knight's youngest son, this is his 'summer home,' and you're here to ask me how I know your father."

"He goes by Dr. Knight now," Ben said. "Or *went* by. He switched to his Ph.D. when he went civilian."

"Well, he'll always be Colonel Knight in my eyes," the Stranger said warmly. "I once met your older brother when he was a little boy. Cameron, right? He probably doesn't remember me."

"Probably not," Ben replied flatly.

"Is he here?"

"Maybe."

The Stranger sighed. "Look, Ben, I understand you're suspicious, and you have every right to be." He leaned forward and put his hands together. "But now that I made it, it's going to happen. It has to."

"I don't understand what you're talking about," Ben said with a frown. But then he remembered. Reluctantly, he pulled the holographic disc out of his pocket and held it up. "Does it have anything to do with this?"

"I think you know the answer to that," the Stranger replied gravely.

Ben rubbed his forehead then crossed his arms. "Look, I need to know why you're here right *now* because everybody thinks I'm crazy for letting you in."

"I can't tell you everything until your brother gets here."

Ben rolled his eyes. "Seriously?"

The Stranger hesitated, then said: "But I *can* tell you that I'm here because your dad asked me to."

Ben's chest tightened, and he dug his fingers into his palms. "My parents are dead — neither one of them made it out." He leaned back in his chair and stared into the Stranger's eyes. "Are you saying they're alive?"

"Unfortunately, I don't know. I hope they are."

Ben sat there stiffly, his mind racing. His dad sent one video message on the day of the Surge. He was at DARPA headquarters in Washington, DC, presenting test run findings of his prototype JU-G1 assault mecha to senior military command.

His dad called him during the middle of class. That was unusual, so Ben snuck to the bathroom and replayed the message.

The transmission was garbled, but Ben could make out the deeply lined wrinkles on his dad's forehead that would appear when he was ticked-off or deeply concerned. He was standing in a bunker, and people were running behind him.

He told Ben that his brother was on his way to pick him up at school and they were to drive to the retreat at once and without stopping. He said not to worry about Mom and that she'd be okay. He told him he loved him, was proud of him, the usual dad stuff.

Then he got serious. His last words, barely understandable: "*If things get bad, don't trust anyone—*"

After that, the message cut out.

Ben called him back, but the connection was dead. Not two minutes after he got back to class, the power went out. Two minutes after that, a Boeing 747 crashed into the neighborhood across the street and the classroom windows shattered. After that, seventy-two hours of screaming, panic, and death.

"Hey, Ben?"

Ben looked up sharply at the Stranger, who was watching him patiently. "Maybe you *did* know my dad," he began, "but it doesn't matter, because the last thing he said to me was to trust *no one.*"

The Stranger chuckled. "I'm not just anyone."

Ben shot him an absurd look, and his eyes flashed in anger. He abruptly stood up, and the aluminum chair fell backward. "This is all really messed up; you know that?"

"Look, just hear me out—"

The Stranger was suddenly cut off by a piercing, high-pitched tone.

The perimeter security alarm. It had never gone off before.

Ben felt a rush of adrenaline. "Sorry, but this is gonna have to wait," he said quickly. "I'll unlock the door, but Katie is gonna keep an eye on you. And remember: we all have guns."

The Stranger nodded gravely, but Ben was already out the door.

CHAPTER 5

Gypsy Danger

Ben burst into the OPSEC room. "Who hit the panic alarm?"

Tomás and Danna were standing at the security monitors, watching CAM 1, the camera by the sentry gate where Marcelo had stopped them in the car.

"It was Aiden," Tomás replied, squinting at the screen. "Up in Eagle-West."

"Any idea what's going on?"

Suddenly they heard a loud mechanized whine and several distant gunshots. Ben grabbed a pair of binoculars and rushed to the window.

It's finally happening, he thought.

A dozen men on dirt bikes were at the entrance to the basin, all armed to the teeth. Their pierced and tattooed faces were painted red as if they were a vicious tribe of psychopaths having arisen in this new world of death.

Ben focused the lenses. Closer to the sentry gate stood an enormous beast of a man, his long gray beard twisted into a greasy braid that dangled at his collarbone, his filth-ridden hands black and deformed, and two red dragon tattoos wrapped around his scarred bald head. His one hand clutched the neck of a sandy-haired boy; the other hand held a gun to that boy's head.

"They've got Alex!" cried Danna, who was standing next to Ben.

"Tomás, you're the tac officer," Ben called out over his shoulder. "We need a plan — now!"

"Just give me a second!" Tomás snapped. He was trying desperately to page Marcelo, who was on duty at the sentry gate, over the radio. After two more unsuccessful attempts, Tomás pounded his hands on the table.

"You okay, man?" Ben asked.

"Of course!"

Tomás turned the channel on his headset. "Adobe Group," he called out, his voice trembling with excitement. "We have Gypsy Danger at the sentry. We're upgrading to Hammer Strike. This is not a drill. Get to your assigned stations and prepare for assault." He gave himself a self-assuring nod of approval.

With his Sig Sauer in his hand, Ben unbolted the front door and slipped out onto the outside walkway. It was blistering hot out and windless, and the blood sun baked the basin like a filthy stone bowl on fire. Danna came out and handed him a radio headset. Putting it on, he squinted through the holes in the side of the wall. Sweat dripped down his face and stung his eyes.

The tattooed skinhead threw Alex to the ground and stuck out his chest. "We know you punks are up there!" he roared, his voice echoing against the cliffs. "We know y'all got a lot of food and beds. Y'all let us in and stay for a while, and we'll let your little buddy here keep his brains!"

Alex sat up slowly and wiped the blood off his face with his sleeve. He had a black eye and a gash on the side of his head.

The man took two steps forward and hollered: "You have two minutes to show your face and let us in, or I'll put a bullet in his head and holy hell in your hidey-hole! I swear to the devil above that those who die will be the lucky ones!"

"Aiden, if you can hear me, you gotta take out the leader!" Tomás called out over the radio. "Just like we practiced!"

"Copy that, Adobe."

Up in Eagle-West, Aiden wet his finger and held it to the wind. None. He settled in behind the McMillan sniper rifle and flipped open the scope covers. Zeroing in on the biker leader, he said: "Target in range."

"Eagle-East," Tomás called out. "Cover Aiden. Lena, if he misses, you take that scumbag out."

"Copy that, Adobe."

For the last moment for a long time, all was silent.

* * *

The dragon-faced man stood next to his dirt bike like a defiled statue, his bulging eyes never wavering from the direction of the retreat. After a moment, he spat on Alex, cocked his handgun, and pointed it at the boy's head. "This is your last chance, you brats! Come out now or—"

The bullet, traveling faster than the speed of sound, hit its target with a sharp wet smack. The gunshot followed a half-second after, and it echoed across the basin in a deep, mournful boom. Aiden's shot struck the dragon-faced man in the upper thigh, and he fell to his side, screaming the worst profanities and inventing new ones.

Propping himself up on one elbow while clutching his thigh with his left hand, the man raised his handgun at Alex, who was crawling slowly into the brambles. Before he could pull the trigger, another bullet hit him in the right shoulder, sending him sprawling backward. A half-second later, Lena's shot reverberated across the cliffs.

Then everything happened fast. As soon as the man tumbled over, Alex scrambled over to his body, picked up his handgun, and tumbled down into the creek bed. Howling for blood, two bikers opened fire on Alex, and the rest revved their dirt bikes and roared into the basin.

Machine gun fire suddenly ripped out from a hidden spot among the cactus and rocks, spraying the first three bikers with a barrage of bullets and sending them crashing to the ground. Two bikers swerved to avoid the collision and lost control and flipped over. One biker, wearing only jeans and a sleeveless shirt, was catapulted into an enormous saguaro cactus.

"Marcelo's in one of the spider holes!" Tomás called out, pumping his fist.

The remaining bikers sped toward the mountain. Ben and Danna, now armed with semi-automatic rifles, opened fire, hitting two instantaneously. The bikers split formation, and the two sides moved in a wide semi-circle to close in from the east and west.

Pairing up, each unslung his rifle — AK-47s, from what Ben could see — and with one hand gripping the handlebar, returned fire. Ben and Danna dropped to their knees as a round of fire blasted the wall six inches from their heads.

"This day has just gotten *so* worse," Danna said, blowing a strand of hair from her face.

Several shots rang out from the OPs, missing their marks.

"Tomás, what's the situation?" Ben said into his headset.

"The jerks are just cruising around firing randomly," Tomás replied, his voice crackling over the radio.

"We can't keep shooting at them — they're moving too fast! We're gonna run outta ammo by the end of the day."

"Maybe that's what they want," Aiden called out. "It wouldn't matter anyway; there's no way they could get in."

"Well, they don't know that yet," Danna replied. "And I think they wanna make this place their permanent residence."

Danna barely finished her sentence when they all heard a loud *vroom* and a deep crack of machine gun fire on the far side of the basin. An old pickup truck had burst out of the wood and was barreling toward the retreat.

The truck was painted black, and at least ten six-foot-long jagged spikes stuck out from holes drilled into the sides like a rabid metal porcupine. Several human skulls were crudely nailed to the truck's front grill. And mounted on the truck bed was an M2 Browning machine gun operated by a tattooed skinhead with his finger on the trigger and another man with a one hundred round ammunition belt slung over his shoulder.

"Incoming technical!" Lena yelled over the radio.

Multiple shots rang out from the OPs, striking the side of the truck. The truck opened fire again, this time at the retreat.

Ben and Danna hit the deck. A barrage of bullets struck the wall above them, sending down a rain of rocks and dust.

"Get in here, guys!" Tomás hollered.

Ben and Danna placed their rifles through the cracks and unleashed several more rounds. Then, crouching low and covering their heads, they scrambled back inside.

"Tell Aiden and Lena to stop firing!" Ben barked as he rushed into the OPSEC room. "They'll spot them!"

A thundering blast hit the side of the mountain, sending a shudder through the retreat, and several objects fell from shelves and smashed to the floor.

They had grenades.

Handing his gun to Danna, Ben started for the elevator shaft.

"Where are you going, Ben?"

"We can't just let those guys have their way down there," he replied over his shoulder. "The only way to wipe them out is fighting them face-to-face."

"And how are we going to do that?" Tomás asked nervously.

Ben popped his head around the corner. "Not *we*," he said with a grin. He pointed to himself. "*Me.*"

"You mean HULC!" Danna called after him. "There's a difference!"

* * *

The elevator door opened to the dimly lit garage and Ben walked out to see Joey Nguyen and Cody Frank, both twelve years old, standing there dressed in oversized Kevlar military body armor and carrying semi-automatic rifles with extra magazines strapped to their vests. Their faces were nervous but grim.

Ben had planned to ride out alone on HULC, but he quickly changed his mind. "Okay, here's the deal," he said as he grabbed his exosuit body armor from his locker. "You guys remember two summers ago when we went paintballing and destroyed those older kids?"

"Yeah, that one dude was pretty much crying for his mommy," Cody replied with a grin.

Joey didn't answer. He took off his helmet and wiped the sweat from his brow.

"Look, it's gonna be the same thing," Ben said. "But this time you'll be on the ATVs, and as soon as we open the garage door, you start unloading on them." He caught his breath and continued: "Once you're out, Joey, you've got left; Cody, right. I'll be right behind you, guns blazing with HULC."

"Who's covering the garage?" Cody asked.

"Nobody — I don't wanna risk getting shot from behind. That's why we need to get out fast. The last thing I want is them getting in."

"Okay, then what?"

"You each drive straight to the rock markers at the foot of the OPs. Get down and use your ATV for cover, and take down every scumbag you see."

"Lena and Aiden will cover you," Tomás added over the radio.

Another blast shook the retreat.

Ben gazed sharply into their eyes. "This is it, guys."

Joey and Cody nodded their heads. They were brave kids. Ben had known them since fourth grade, and all those years they had never backed down from anything or anyone. If they were scared now, and they probably were, they didn't show it.

"Let's do this," Joey finally said, his jaw clenched.

They held their hands high and bumped their fists.

* * *

For a short period after Ben's father resigned from the military, and before he was hired as the advanced robotics and artificial intelligence director at DARPA, several corporations contracted him to design prototypes for exoskeletons and mini-mechs.

Upon hearing of the sudden and shocking retirement of Colonel Thomas Knight, one of the world's foremost experts in the field, companies like Lockheed Martin,

Caterpillar, and John Deere scrambled to get his expertise and ideas to become the first manufacturer to sell powered hard-suits to nonmilitary customers.

Ben's dad sold his services to Lockheed and developed a prototype large-scale exosuit called the Hybrid Universal Load Carrier. Or, as Ben affectionately called it, HULC. Larger than an exoskeleton but smaller than a mini-mecha, the seven-foot-tall HULC was the first exosuit to be powered by kinetic energy and supported by a beyond state-of-the-art lithium air battery.

Designed for heavy industrial labor such as mining and factory work, HULC was outfitted with sensors that reacted to the operator's movements and added substantially more power to whatever move the operator wanted to make.

As Ben's father put it, HULC transformed the operator into a superhuman. For example, it had the power to flip over a truck or break through a brick wall and still protect the driver from muscular and skeletal injuries.

Most exoskeletons and mini-mechs must either be tethered to a power generator or have minimal battery power. However, both HULC and its subsequent prototypes designed for DARPA could operate for weeks, if not months, depending on the project or mission.

For over six hours in a remote part of eastern Oregon, Dr. Knight had demonstrated the HULC prototype to

Lockheed Martin, which wanted to manufacture exosuits for the new Mars colonization mission. Afterwards, the corporation offered him five million dollars for the design.

Dr. Knight never told Ben or Cameron why, but he turned it down, and instead joined DARPA to lead the government's top-secret research in robotics and artificial intelligence.

Dr. Knight brought HULC to the retreat to help with the final stages of construction, such as building the OPs. Just three weeks before the Surge, he and Ben — who adopted HULC as his own and thought he knew it even better than his dad — outfitted it with an M240 machine gun and custom-made RPG launcher. Ben once asked his father where he got all the weapons. With a wink, he just replied: "I'm not supposed to remember."

As Ben ripped the dust cover off HULC, he realized that his father's decision to weaponize HULC and bring it to the retreat might save many lives.

Ben flipped HULC's main power switch, and the large upper body helmet-hatch hissed open. Outside in the basin, Ben heard the enemy's machine gun exchanging fire with the group's defenses. He wondered about Alex.

Ben stepped into the footbeds underneath his boots and fastened the straps around his thighs, waist, and shoulders. He grabbed the augmented-hand controls and ran a system check. Within a millisecond, the foot pads' sensors connected to the onboard microcomputer, which initialized the electrohydrostatic actuators.

Gritting his teeth, Ben closed the helmet-hatch, and his visuals were transformed to a digital interface projecting through a helmet-mounted display. He then attached the body hatch to his armor and checked both the machine gun and RPG launcher as well as the riot shotgun, which was strapped in a side compartment.

Joey and Cody pulled up next to him on Honda Ranger ATVs, rifles in hand. They both gave him a thumbs-up.

Ben flicked on HULC's radio. "Tomás, this is HULC, do you copy?"

"10-2, HULC, signal is good."

"Any word from Alex or Marcelo?"

"Negative, HULC. Heavy fire down there. Danna, Tess, and Vic are holding down the porch."

Ben pursed his lips. He increased to full power and locked and loaded the machine gun. "Okay, guys, let's form up," he said in a low, steady voice. "Joey, on the left; Cody, on the right."

"Copy that, HULC."

"Adobe One, open the garage door," Ben said. "All units cease fire."

The garage door opened, and the blazing morning sun lit up the vast concrete space like a lantern casting forth unwelcome light into a hidden catacomb.

* * *

The men were forty feet away when they saw L3's door open. Two were reloading the truck's machine gun; another two were on dirt bikes and arguing with the driver; the location of the others was unknown.

For a moment the men paused, gaping into the garage, probably wondering why it opened and whether the "punks" were surrendering. Within a second, the driver popped the clutch, spun the truck into a semi-circle, and slowly idled toward the entrance. The two bikers signaled to the driver and followed.

Hidden in an angled shadow at the entrance, out-of-sight from the men, Ben launched the RPG for the first time in his life. The screaming grenade tore through the dust and hit the ground fifteen feet in front of the pickup truck and exploded, shooting chunks of broken rocks and a great cloud of dust high into the air. As exhilarated as he was, he had missed the truck.

The two bikers swerved off course and accelerated to loop back around for another attack.

"Now!" Ben barked into the radio.

Firing their rifles in one hand, Joey and Cody roared out of the garage in the ATVs and broke off in opposite directions.

As soon as they were out of view, Ben stepped out into the entrance, held up his right arm and pulled the machine gun trigger, firing thirty rounds at the cloud of dust.

He heard bullets hitting metal, and then saw the flash of the truck's machine gun. Blinded by the suffocating blanket of dust, the gunner wildly returned fire. One bullet struck HULC's two-inch glass helmet, leaving a small chip near the top.

Ben gasped and jerked his head backward. His body stiffened, and the color drained from his face. He stepped back into the shadows for cover and unbuckled his left arm and reached over to slide another cylinder grenade into the launcher. The second-to-last one. Clasping his arm back into place, he waited.

Several bullets hit inside the garage, shattering one of the overhead lights.

"Adobe One, this is HULC," Ben said into the radio. His heart was pounding hard. "Can you see anything?"

"Negative, HULC," Tomás replied. "No visuals, your blast sent up a huge pile of dust."

Ben closed his eyes, gathered himself, and stepped back out.

Ten feet away, two armed men were cautiously approaching the garage. Looking up, they saw HULC for the first time, and terror engulfed their faces.

They stumbled backward and raised their AK-47s to fire, but Ben was faster. He cut loose with the machine gun, shredding fiber and flesh and sending them sprawling on their backs. They did not move.

"Adobe One, two guys down," Ben said, his voice trembling.

I just killed two people, he said to himself, as if it were the first time. He shook his head and blinked. Sweat was still pouring down his face. *Note to self: if you survive, install an A/C unit in HULC.*

The dust was settling, and Ben could make out the shape of the pickup truck. A plume of dark smoke billowed from its hood: the engine was on fire. The gunner was still in the truck bed trying frantically to load an ammunition belt into the machine gun's feed tray.

Aiming slightly high and to the left, Ben fired the grenade. This time it hit its mark. The blast lifted the truck three feet off the ground, and as it landed a fireball erupted followed by an explosion and a billowing storm of dust, rocks, spikes, and skulls.

With his finger on the machine gun trigger, Ben stomped toward the truck. "Adobe One, confirmed three dead. I can't tell if there's anyone else out there."

"I don't think so," Tomás replied. "Eagles, can you see anything?"

"Negative," Aiden said. "Just Joey and Cody at the marker points."

"Me neither," Lena added. "But I saw Joey take down one of the bikers."

"Wait, I see the other one," Aiden said. "He's heading back to the woods."

The biker, a shirtless pig of a man, must've realized that he was the lone survivor. And with his dirt bike at full throttle, he almost escaped the "haunted mountain" and its arena of death.

But four rounds fired from a hidden enemy cut him down as he approached the sentry gate, and he tumbled over his bike like a sack of rotten potatoes and slid belly first into a flowering prickly pear cactus.

Marcelo, still in the spider hole, had hit his mark with three out of the four shots.

Ben felt a surge of relief.

"Cody and Joey, make a perimeter patrol around the cliffs to see if any more are hiding out," Tomás said. "Eagles, keep your eyes on the scopes."

"Guys, I see people coming out of the woods," Lena said.

"Is it Marcelo or Alex?" Tomás asked.

"No, it might be more of these guys," Aiden replied. "I see 'em too. Five at least."

Ben zoomed in his sights. Five figures wearing blue and gray camouflage jackets and light blue caps were marching into the basin.

"Birnam Wood marches to fight us," Lena muttered, barely audible over the radio.

"What?" Ben asked.

"From *Macbeth*, remember?" Danna interjected, sarcastically. She was still standing out on the walkway, rifle in hand. "We were in the middle of Act 4."

Ben smirked and shook his head. He was just an ordinary freshman at Sierra Madre when the Surge hit, sitting through another boring lecture in English class. "Must've been doodling during that part."

He checked his ammunition. One belt left. "Okay, Aiden and Lena, hold your fire. We'll take them out. Joey and Cody—"

"Adobe One, these guys are acting strange, over," Aiden said nervously. "They're plowing through the cactus like it's nothing."

At that moment, a trip flare whistled out of its hidden spot and burst into brilliant red streaks of potassium nitrate and sulfur two hundred feet in the air.

CHAPTER 6

THESE METAL MONSTERS

Biting her bottom lip, Lena lifted her sniper rifle and squinted into the scope. Her face paled.

"Guys—"

"Vagabonds!" Aiden called out sharply, cutting off Lena. "Five of them."

"All the noise must've gotten their attention," Tomás said. "Eagles, you gotta take them out. Aim for the eyes or the neck."

"Not a chance, guys," Ben said, adjusting his target displays. "Not even with a .50 caliber."

Two shots rang out across the basin.

"I need an update, guys," Tomás said sharply.

"Those weren't from the Eagles," Lena replied. "They were coming near the sentry gate."

Ben refocused the lenses, and he saw Alex spring from a hidden spot and sneak up behind one of the robots. *It's going to kill him*, he thought. *I'm watching Alex die.*

Alex fired two quick shots in the vagabond's cranium and then dove into the bushes. The robot fell face first into the dirt.

Ben threw back his head, dumbfounded.

Inexplicably, the other four vagabonds ignored their comrade's termination and marched forward with precision, like metal corpses oblivious to the living world.

"Did you see that, guys?" Aiden called out.

Ben's mind was going blank, but then it clicked. "Close the garage door! There's something in there they want. They *always* want something." He wondered if they saw the Honda, their getaway car.

"10-4, HULC," Tomás replied. "Good thinking."

Alex, seeing that the other vagabonds had ignored his attack, grew bolder: gun in hand, he dashed up to another one. But this time a vagabond swung around and struck a blow across Alex's face, instantly knocking him unconscious. He hit the ground with a thud. The robot turned and resumed its march toward the retreat.

A furious shout that sounded like Marcelo's voice echoed throughout the basin, and gunfire instantly erupted from the north spider hole.

"Adobe One, a vagabond just hit Alex pretty bad," Ben said. "I need to get out there, but Marcelo is shooting like crazy. Still can't reach him on the radio?"

"No," Tomás replied. His voice cracked. "He's on his own."

Fortunately, at that moment the gunfire stopped.

Ben zoomed and studied the approaching vagabonds. The camouflage uniforms were military issued, but he'd never seen them before. Being a military brat, he knew his fatigues. He looked closer at the vagabonds' shirts: a patch above each left pocket read *Global Federation*.

Ben shook his head in disbelief. *Is there even an America anymore?*

"What's your status, HULC?" Tomás called out.

"I gotta get out there and get Alex, Adobe One," Ben said, clenching HULC's metal fists. "I'm moving in, guys."

"If you do, you're on your own against four vagabonds," Danna said uneasily. "Marcelo knows it's suicide if he comes out of the spider hole."

Ben didn't respond. Scanning the burnt-out truck one last time, he stomped out to meet the metal monsters.

* * *

Ben was within fifty feet of the approaching vagabonds when he realized he forgot to reload the RPG launcher. Coming to an abrupt halt, he unbuckled the operator's harness and reached for the last grenade.

At first, the vagabonds calculated that the advancing machine was simply an industrial-use automaton. But as soon Ben lifted the helmet-hatch to reload the RPG launcher, they identified a living human and initiated termination protocol. Picking up speed, they commenced their attack.

Ben was desperately trying to insert the tiny bomb into the tube, but his sweaty fingers couldn't get a firm grip on it. He wiped his hands on his shirt and tried again. These grenades detonated upon impact, not by a four-second timer like most grenades, so if he dropped it. . . .

Up at the retreat, Tomás, Danna, and the others watched in alarm as HULC suddenly came to a stop just as the vagabonds initiated their attack.

"What the heck, Ben!" Tomás cried over the radio. "They're right on top of you!"

Once again, Ben didn't answer. He looked up.

They were ten feet away.

He panicked.

The grenade slipped from his fingers.

In that millisecond, Ben watched in horror as it fell and hit the ground with a dull thud. He closed his eyes and waited for the explosion and his death. In that briefest of moments, he thought about his mom, about his dad, and whether he'd get to be with them now.

Two milliseconds.

He opened his eyes, and a burst of oxygen surged into his lungs.

Not today. Not yet.

Ben narrowed his eyes, and with beads of sweat streaming down his cheeks — or maybe it was tears — he dropped the helmet-hatch over his head and strapped his arm back into place. He didn't have time to reattach the harness.

The first vagabond went straight for the helmet-hatch, but with a furious jerk of his right arm — HULC's right arm — he swung upwards and struck a mighty blow at the vagabond's head.

The head snapped backward, dislodged from its socket, and it dangled on the vagabond's back, held by a few crackling wires still attached to the neck. It stood there motionless.

Ben stepped back and cocked his shoulders to release the weapon locks on each arm. The RPG launcher and M260 slid back to expose HULC's titanium four-fingered, crab-like claws.

The claws were designed to lift steel beams and heavy machinery, but Ben was confident they'd be good for a fist fight. He was about to find out.

He knocked the beheaded vagabond to the ground, and at once the second and third robots latched onto each claw, trying to rip them off.

Ben didn't know their full capacity strength, but as the androids pulled backward, he felt the joint actuators on HULC's shoulders strain and creak in reaction. *Now I know*, he said to himself.

With HULC's right arm, Ben backhanded the vagabond on the right and flung it six feet to the ground.

The robot got up on one knee, but at that moment Cody drove in full throttle and struck its side with the ATV's front brush guard.

Cody let out a triumphant *whoop* as the vagabond staggered and dropped to one knee, and he turned around to make another pass.

The vagabond locked sights on Cody and stepped in his direction. But then Joey ran into it head on, sending the robot to its knee again, but also his out-of-control ATV front first into a small ditch.

Joey shifted the ATV into reverse, but it only spun its wheels. The vagabond limped toward him, its blazing neon eyes flashing rapidly like seizure-inducing strobe lights.

"C'mon!" Cody shouted as he roared up to Joey.

Joey hopped on the back of the ATV and Cody hit the throttle, just barely escaping skull-crushing fingers.

"Go get Alex and take him back!" Ben hollered over the radio as he yanked at the other vagabond that clung to HULC's arm. He knew that they'd get slaughtered if they stayed to fight.

Joey gave a thumbs-up, and the two boys sped off to where Alex lay unconscious.

Ben was surrounded. The vagabond latched to HULC's left claw ripped the Bowden cable that powered exosuit's entire left arm, and Ben felt it go limp. Surprisingly, the robot let go and took several steps backward, forming up with the other two.

Ben knew that each vagabond had just calculated millions of various attack strategies with the highest likelihood of success for the desired outcome — Ben's death. All three have reached the same prediction, as if they foresaw the future like mechanized prophets of woe, heralding the death of *he whose heart still beats*.

The three separated into a tight semi-circle: one in front, one to Ben's left, and the last one behind him. They determined his left arm was disabled and therefore the primary weakness.

In a fading corner of his mind, Ben could hear Tomás paging him over the radio; but his pulse was pumping in his ears and he was going to die right now and he should have been dead already. No more talking. He was here, and they were there.

And here they are, these metal monsters. These freaks. *Look at them*, Ben thought. *How can they make those stupid faces? They are angry now. For what? They can think — my dad said so. Can they talk? Should I ask them to stop? Do they like to kill, or do they have to kill? Can they really think?*

Once again, his dad came to his mind, and how he was right all along about everything, how he gave up his career and a chance to be a decorated general because of his never-ending struggle to warn the powers that be about what could happen. What would happen. What *did* happen.

Everyone had laughed at him, Ben thought. *Even the President!*

He remembered when his dad got home from the White House, early in the morning, and they asked him how it was and he just smiled and said it was wonderful and told them to pack up the truck because they were going fishing for the rest of the day. It was a Tuesday. . . .

Ben blinked sharply. For a moment, he'd blacked out.

Time to fight. Like yesterday. And the day before that. And forever, it seems, before that.

HULC's left arm was useless. He held out the right arm and unlocked the machine gun and slid it back into firing position with the hundred-round ammunition belt hanging underneath. Stepping backward to face the vagabond in front of him, he fired thirty quick rounds. Most of the bullets missed, five bounced off its shell, and one of them hit its exposed left shoulder joint — a sweet spot.

An arm for an arm, Ben thought, with a slight smirk. He turned to the vagabond to his left and opened fire. He managed only fifteen rounds before he heard a loud *click*. The gun had jammed!

The vagabonds were upon him. They leaped onto HULC's back and ripped the power cords. Ben knew a critical malfunction could send a surge of power to the sensors and electrocute him.

At this point he had only one choice: he had to get out. He popped the head-hatch and reached down and unlocked the sensor casings on his legs. Just as he was breaking free, the vagabonds pulled HULC to the ground. He rolled out before he was crushed under the weight of the exosuit.

A shadow fell over Ben; the third vagabond was standing there in its tattered, half-ripped camouflage jacket, blocking the sun and waiting for him with an eerie smile (or so he thought) on its rusted face. The robot had calculated this scenario.

Ben jumped up and lunged toward the vagabond. Not predicting the human's maneuver, it extended its arms to clutch the human's skull and crush it; but as it did so, the human dove beneath its legs, resumed bipedal position, and accelerated.

Ben was faster than the androids, which, as far as he knew, weren't programmed to sprint. He'd made his escape.

But he made it no more than forty feet toward the retreat when he landed awkwardly on a rock and came crashing to the ground.

Clutching his ankle, he winced and let out a cry of agony. He got up and took one hop before he fell to his hands and knees. Spinning around, he saw the three vagabonds in pursuit, the one with the rusted face twenty feet ahead of the other two.

Wiping the sweat from his eyes, Ben crawled toward the retreat. In the distance, the Gator roared out of the garage, his friends coming to his rescue. *They're going to die, too*, he said to himself. *Idiots.*

Then he came upon the grenade, half buried in the dirt, two feet in front of him. He stretched out and grabbed it, and turning around on his back, he hurled it as hard as he could.

A deafening blast shook the earth, and a vagabond's leg landed right next to him followed by a shower of small rocks and metal fragments.

Ben started to crawl again. His lungs burned. His limbs were jelly. He clenched his jaw and dug deep. The Gator was fifty yards ahead, coming in fast. The other two vagabonds were nearly upon him.

He finally collapsed in anguish.

Yet with all of his will, all of his heart, and with every fiber of his being, he stuck his arm out and pulled himself forward; then he pulled his knee up to his side; then the other arm; then the other knee. His fingers dug into the earth, pulling, scraping, pulling.

Then he heard the dull, commanding steps. He curled into a ball, covered his head with his hands and squeezed his eyes shut.

Suddenly, he heard the sharp whine of a dirt bike, then two brief pops like two cracks of an electric whip, then another two pops, then a strange, split-second sound, unlike anything he'd ever heard before, like a hyper-charged magnet thrown into an electric power grid.

The dirt bike shut off. People shouting. Footsteps. Someone shaking his shoulders.

"Hey, buddy, you're good," a familiar voice said. "You're all right."

Ben turned over and wiped his eyes with his sleeve. Kneeling next to him was his big brother, face covered in sweat and grime, and a prototype plasma railgun (!) slung over his shoulder.

Just before everything went black, Ben saw many hands lifting him off the ground.

CHAPTER 7

HEAVEN SENT

Ben's eyes fluttered open. He was back in his room, lying on his cot. He squinted his eyes and saw Cameron sitting on a stool, cleaning his fighting knife with a white cloth. He hadn't seen him in three weeks.

Once neatly trimmed for military school, Cameron's choppy brown hair fell across his deeply tanned face, the result of countless days wandering under the Southern California sun. His chestnut colored eyes were both bright and dark, depending on his mood, and always watching, observing, aware. His nose, narrow and sculpted, gave him a refined appearance of a soldier born to lead; but it was also crooked, the result of a fight outside a bowling alley a few years ago. His thin lips always seemed to be half-smirking, which made it impossible to tell whether he was taking something seriously or not. Much to his delight, that smirk used to drive his teachers nuts.

On his forehead, above his left eye, was a small, pale scar from an accident when he was thirteen. He had staggered home late one night with a blood-soaked bandage on his forehead, blubbering to Mom and Dad that he'd slipped and fallen while exploring a sea cave with friends as part of a biology class assignment.

Two months later, however, Ben overheard him telling the bridesmaids at their cousin's wedding that an ocelot slashed him when he and his friends had broken into the zoo during the middle of the night. Over the next couple of months, Ben had blackmailed Cameron out of at least fifty bucks.

Cameron looked much better than Ben thought he would after such a long trip. He was dressed in his military academy t-shirt and the same olive-green tactical pants he always wore, but now they were tucked into a new pair of brown, rugged combat boots. Curiously, Ben also noticed that he was wearing a new Luminox wristwatch, the one worn by Navy Seals.

Cameron saw that Ben was awake. "Hey, look who's alive," he said.

"Not funny," Ben replied with a groan, rolling on his back. "I swear that I was dead."

Cameron handed a water bottle to his brother, who gulped it down. "Mom wouldn't like you swearing, bro," he said with his half-smirk. "But yeah, you looked like toast."

"Where did you get that dirt bike?"

Cameron's dark eyes flashed. "Some scumbag was sitting on it at the road gate. I heard all the shooting start a couple miles out, and I was just about to cross the road when I saw him chilling there with an AK-47. Figured he was bad news, so I took him down."

"You killed him?"

"Well, not exactly. I invited him to my doll party and poisoned his sweet tea." He snorted. "Of course I killed him. Didn't you take out like ten dudes yesterday?"

"Yesterday?"

"Yeah, you've been passed out for almost a day."

Ben shot his brother a worried look.

"Katie said you were cool though," Cameron said reassuringly. "Just tired and shocked is all."

Ben threw off his blanket and rose out of bed; in an instant, a sharp pain exploded in his ankle. He grimaced, plopped back onto the cot with a groan, and lifted his bandage-wrapped ankle off the bed.

"You should've seen it yesterday," Cameron said as he set his knife on the table and stretched. "Looked like a purple baseball."

It all flashed through Ben's mind. So much had happened, and yet he felt like he'd missed everything. "How's Alex? And Marcelo? Anyone else get hurt?"

"Alex got a little roughed up, but Marcelo is fine. In fact, he's out right now helping to drag the bodies."

"The bodies?"

"Dude, slow down with the questions. Yeah, the bikers. The ones you guys toasted (good work!). Joey and them are digging the graves."

Ben carefully sat up and ran his fingers through his hair. His stomach growled; he hadn't eaten in over a day.

Cameron got up and walked out to the hallway, bringing back a pair of crutches. "Here," he said, leaning the crutches against the cot. "Figured you don't wanna be stuck in bed all day. Alex is in the infirmary; he'll be happy to see you."

Ben had a blasting headache. A million questions raced through his mind. He stared at Cameron, wondering what he'd seen on his trip and if there was any news. Of Mom. Of anybody.

The Stranger. He'd forgotten about him.

"What about the guy we picked up?"

Cameron sat down, stretched his legs out, and put his hands in his pockets. "Yeah, *the Stranger*, that's what everyone is calling him." He paused for a moment and stared blankly at the wall. "He said you weren't too trusting of him, which is probably not a bad thing. . . ."

"And you do? You trust him?"

"I don't know. But I think his being here right now is what Mom used to say was a 'God thing.'" He chuckled. "Remember that?"

"Yeah, I remember," Ben replied quietly.

Whenever something really good happened, like when the family randomly won a vacation to Disneyland after their dad got back from deployment, she'd say it was heaven sent. She always believed everything happened for a reason, even the bad things. *Would she still think like that today*? Ben wondered. *In this world?*

"Anyway," Cameron went on, "I told him that once you're feeling better, we'll sit down and talk about what's going on."

Ben furrowed his brow. "*What's going on*? I thought this was it, you know? Life. Everything."

Cameron handed Ben the crutches and helped him up. "You'll see."

* * *

Ben hadn't used crutches since he fell out of a tree and twisted his knee when he was eight-years-old. Even though he just had a sprained ankle, he felt paralyzed: if there were another attack, he'd be useless. Everything would be lost.

When they arrived at the infirmary, Katie was standing at the counter making a fresh ice pack. She looked up and smiled.

Alex was sitting up in his cot, half of his face wrapped in a large bandage. He lifted his hand slightly to wave, but his eyes squinted in pain.

"Dislocated jaw," Katie said, giving Alex the ice pack, "and lots of bumps and bruises. He's a brave kid. I had to use my thumbs to put it back in place." She glanced at Ben and said: "Luckily, you got anesthetics from the pharmacy. It really helped to relax the jaw muscles."

"Can he even open his mouth?" Ben asked.

"Only a little bit," Katie replied. "He'll have this wrap on for at least six weeks. It's the only way to stabilize the jaw."

"Hopefully he likes applesauce," Cameron said.

"What happens if he yawns or sneezes?" Ben asked.

"Then he could dislocate it again, and we'd be back to square one."

Cameron clicked his tongue and patted Alex on the shoulder. "Good luck with that, buddy."

"If he can't talk," Ben said, "then it looks like we're not gonna know about this biker gang for a while."

"I asked him some yes or no questions earlier," Cameron said as he moved a thumb up then down. "From what I could get out of it, he saw a campfire in the woods on his way back, and he had the brilliant idea to sneak up and check it out. Didn't get within fifty feet before the guard caught him. He shot that one, but they caught up to him on their dirt bikes."

"So that explains that one gunshot me and Danna heard that night," Ben said. "You're lucky they didn't kill you then and there!"

Wincing, Alex nodded his head.

Cameron continued: "So after he got caught, they forced it out of him who he was and where he was from." He gave him an understanding nod. "Must've been rough, bro."

Ben glanced at Alex, and he could see even through his bandage-wrapped face he was ashamed. Ashamed for giving up the retreat, ashamed for his betrayal.

"On the bright side," Cameron said quickly, probably sensing Alex's embarrassment, "a dozen fewer psychopaths walk the earth. A couple of them still had tethers on their ankles, so I bet they escaped from a nearby prison."

"After the Surge hit, would you call it escaping?" Katie asked.

"Good point."

"All in all, a broken jaw and a sprained ankle," Katie added cheerfully. "Not a bad price."

"Eeezy 'or you da zay," Alex croaked. He dropped his head back into his pillow.

Katie's cheeks flushed in embarrassment. "Sorry."

"HULC got beat up a little bit, too," Cameron said quietly.

Ben glanced sharply at his brother. "He's wrecked?"

"I don't think so, but there's a lot of ripped wires and broken hoses. Dad built *it* to bust rocks on Mars — I wouldn't worry about it."

"I'll try not to," Ben muttered, lying. His headache was getting worse.

"All right, guys," Katie said, ushering them out. "Let's give him some rest."

"Alex, hang in there," Ben said, giving him a thumbs-up. "I'll stop by later, okay?"

Alex tried to move his thumb upward. Instead, he just closed his eyes and turned away.

* * *

Ben stepped outside the infirmary and leaned the crutches against the wall. "Don't need 'em," he told Cameron, who was looking at him with a raised eyebrow.

He tested his ankle and found he could walk. *If Alex has a broken jaw, then I'm not using crutches.* Stepping gingerly, he went back to his room, grabbed his gun and baseball cap, and headed to the stairway.

Cameron was keeping a safe but watchful distance. "You're not gonna take the lift?"

"Nope."

Cameron shook his head and shrugged. "Fine," he said, walking toward the lift. "I'm gonna check out those freaks; they're still laying in the dust."

Ben nodded and continued his descent. As he passed L2, he heard giggling down the hallway. He paused for a moment as if shocked by a sound long since forgotten. Curious, he stepped into L2. Danna was leaning against the doorway to the garden room with her arms crossed.

Noticing Ben, she beckoned to him with a nod, and Ben limped toward her. When he was two feet from the door, she motioned for him to stop and she held her index finger to her mouth and gave a slight nod for him to peek inside the room.

He stuck his head around the corner; and there on the bench in the middle of the garden room was the Stranger and Danna's sister, Izzy. She was picking out the names of the vegetables to him. Handing her penguin to the Stranger, she ran to the corner of the room and brought back a tiny clay pot with a seedling popping through the soil.

Ben had never seen Izzy smile before, nor even talk to anyone other than Danna. He cocked a bemused eyebrow at Danna. She crossed her arms again and gave a half-shrug.

They both peered back in the room.

". . . but Penny doesn't like to get dirty," Izzy explained to the Stranger with an air of importance, "which is why she always stays on the bench."

"So, she has never *once* helped you plant flowers?" the Stranger asked, holding up the stuffed penguin.

Izzy giggled and shook her head.

"Yet she likes roses," the Stranger said, rubbing his chin. "I think Penny's making you do all the work here."

Izzy giggled again. "Here, let me show you—"

She looked up and saw Ben and Danna watching them. She froze, as if turned to stone, and her cheeks flushed.

The Stranger immediately stood up, and giving Ben and Danna an understanding wink, he cleared his throat.

"Well, Isabel and Penny," he said in a playful yet formal tone, "I must be going now. I hope you'll invite me back soon." He pretended to shake the penguin's fin, and then he gave it back to Izzy.

She clutched the penguin and held it close in her arms, not taking her eyes off Danna and Ben.

The Stranger knelt in front of her and gazed deeply into her eyes. "Thank you," he said. For a moment, Izzy matched his gaze but then looked down and nodded.

With one last smile, he stood up and walked to the door.

"Bye, Mr. Theo!"

He turned around. Izzy stood tip-toed, holding still as if in breathless expectation.

"Bye, Isabel," he said, giving her a nod.

Danna shook her head in disbelief.

* * *

"I'd like to help out," the Stranger told Ben and Danna as they walked down to L3.

"You just did," Danna said. She shook her head in disbelief. "I don't know how you did that."

"I have — or *had* — a couple of nieces about her age," the Stranger replied. "I tried to be their favorite uncle, so I developed some tactics."

"Well, thank you," Danna said. "I really mean that."

"She's basically been a shell since it all happened," Ben said. "She's seen everything. *Everything.*"

"Poor thing," the Stranger said. "She truly deserves the world."

Ben followed them into L3, where Joey was towing HULC into the garage with the Gator. One glance at HULC and Ben's shoulders curled forward like his chest was caving in.

"Ouch," Danna said, scrunching her cheeks.

Ben limped over to the power suit.

"We were extremely careful," Joey said with grave reverence.

"No worries," Ben replied woodenly. "I appreciate it."

He worked his way around HULC, inspecting every inch. The damage wasn't as bad as he thought it'd be. The vagabonds ripped several Bowden cables, and the belt-screw drive and possibly the controller might need to be replaced. His face grew sour. He might not have the proper parts.

"Everything all right?" the Stranger asked. He stood a few paces back, hands in pockets.

"Yeah, we'll see," Ben mumbled. "Not sure yet."

"It truly is a magnificent machine."

"He did his part yesterday, that's for sure," Ben muttered. He wanted to kneel and start moving things, but he held himself back and headed outside.

The day was hot like yesterday but cloudier, and Ben could see the wind rustle through the oak trees on the far side of the basin. The burnt-out truck had been towed to the side of the crumbled rock mound, out of sight from the basin's entrance.

Two group members, unsure who exactly, were exchanging duty shifts in the east OP. Cameron was two hundred yards out crouching next to the vagabonds. To his left, Aiden and Cody stood at the far south side of the basin holding shovels. He went that way.

"Hey, guys," he said. "Need help?"

"From you?" Aiden asked, wiping sweat from his brow. "You should be resting that ankle."

"Actually, feels good," Ben lied again, straightening his shoulders.

Over ten fresh graves had been dug, each a rectangular mound topped with jagged black rocks. To the left of the graves was a blue tarp with two long shapes underneath.

"Two more to dig," Aiden said. "And these guys stunk even before you ripped 'em up. Rigor mortis set in too; heavy as logs."

Ben wondered whether Aiden was really that desensitized to death or if he was just putting on a tough-guy show.

"Pretty sad what happened to HULC, right, Ben?"

Ben turned around and saw ten-year-old JB McGuire's sunburnt face staring up at him. He was one of the youngest at the retreat. He timidly picked at a callus on his hand.

"Really sorry."

"Yeah, thanks," Ben mumbled in reply. He couldn't take his eyes off the graves. Directly behind the freshly dug graves was a row of tiny white crosses stuck crooked in the rocks.

"Friends?" the Stranger asked, coming alongside Ben. "The ones with the crosses?"

"Yeah, friends," he repeated. He paused as if thinking for a moment. "We've all been together from the beginning, you know? Except for Katie; but she's no different, I guess. We're kinda like a family now. All our parents are gone. Grandparents. Cousins. Everybody. We just have each other."

"And I heard about Ron," the Stranger said somberly. "I'm sorry."

Ben watched the pebbles crumble down the grave mounds like miniature black avalanches. A slight breeze swirled in the basin. Looking once again at the shapes under the tarps, he turned around.

"We got this," the Stranger said, nodding to Danna. They both held shovels.

"I'll keep at it, too," Aiden added.

Cody and JB were pleased.

"You gonna start fixing HULC right now?" JB asked eagerly.

"No," Ben replied, rubbing the top of his forehead. "I'm going back to bed."

CHAPTER 8

THE FIRE

"Ben, wake up."

He awoke to his brother standing over him. Ben rubbed his eyes and squinted. "What time is it?" he asked groggily.

"Midnight. Let's go."

"Go where?" Ben looked past his brother, and for a moment he thought he saw his dad standing in the doorway. He blinked twice. It was the Stranger, wearing one of his dad's parkas.

The man nodded gravely.

Cameron tossed Ben's coat on his cot. "We're going outside," he said, reaching for the crutches.

Ben waved away the crutches. "Nah, I'm good," he said as he stood up and stretched. "Feel great."

"Yeah, I forgot you've always been a quick healer," Cameron said. "Darnedest thing."

Ben and the Stranger followed Cameron up the stairway to L1. Aside from whoever was on duty in the OPs, everyone was asleep, and all was dark except for the dull secondary lights that ran in a single line above the hallways. Ben could hear the slight hum of the geothermal energy lines.

Holding a lantern, Cameron led them down a little-used passageway carved into the volcanic rock, which ended abruptly at a steel rung ladder. He climbed until only his boots were visible, and Ben heard a metal pop then felt a gentle rush of crisp night air against his face.

Cameron came down two rungs and reached for the lantern. "Can you climb?" he asked, pointing to Ben's ankle.

Ben nodded and tested his ankle. Some soreness, but not too bad.

"Okay, well watch yourself."

Ben knew about the secondary escape hatch, but he'd never used it before. It opened to a small outcropping on the north side of the retreat and joined the barely visible pathway leading to the mountain lookout.

He climbed up and out. All was silent except for the tiny rocks crunching and breaking under his boots. He looked down. Beyond the edge of the outcropping was a twenty-foot drop.

Someone grabbed his arm.

"Be careful," Cameron said with a smirk.

Ben rolled his eyes. He followed his brother and the Stranger twenty feet up the pathway until they reached a small cave. It was about six feet deep and high enough for them to crouch in and sit comfortably.

Cameron set the lantern down at the mouth of the cave and clambered out. After a minute, he returned with an armful of firewood. Not long after, a healthy fire flickered in the cave, casting dancing shadows on the walls.

"One of my favorite places here," Cameron said, letting out a deep breath.

"Can't somebody see us up here?" the Stranger asked.

"Nah, we're too far high and too far in. But we still have a good angle to look out below. Geometrics and all that."

They sat on the cave floor, which was a blanket of fine black sand. Cameron took out his knife and whittled.

Ben looked out upon the barren, rocky landscape. The night was dark, but the stars were out, sparkling like diamonds scattered across infinity. He'd never learned the different constellations and planets; he could only identify the Big Dipper, Mars, and possibly Venus or Mercury — he didn't know which one. He'd asked for a telescope for Christmas. Well, the last *real* Christmas, two years ago.

Looking up at the bright dot of Mars, he imagined those small colonies of brave families on that red planet, trying to survive, trying to live, and now, perhaps, forever cut off from the rest of humankind. Maybe that made them lucky. Maybe, like him, they escaped. He felt like he could understand.

A chill breeze gently blew across his face, and a trace of salty ocean air mingled with the wood smoke. He shuddered and inched closer to the fire.

"Hot chocolate," the Stranger said, handing him a thermos.

Ben pursed his lips. He didn't want to accept anything from this guy as if by doing so he'd be obligated to trust him or even be his friend.

Mind your manners, he heard a familiar voice say in the back of his mind.

Ben took the thermos and mumbled a "thank you." The hot chocolate steamed his face as he opened the thermos, and he took a sip. Delicious. He muttered another thanks and gave the thermos back to the Stranger.

They were silent for a moment as if they all knew this was the very moment for which they gathered in the middle of the night.

"Well, we've got a lot to talk about," Cameron said, breaking the silence by saying the obvious. "Better get to it."

"I've already spoken to your brother a little bit," the Stranger explained to Ben, "but we'll start from the beginning because obviously, this involves you, too."

Cameron looked at Ben with that look that only a big brother gives. "You okay to talk about this?"

"I'm fine," Ben replied curtly, annoyed by the look that Cameron was giving him. But he realized this would be a mature conversation, so he swallowed his pride.

He turned to the Stranger and asked coolly: "Who are you and how do you know my dad?"

The Stranger smiled apologetically. "Truth be told, I don't *personally* know your father."

Ben paused, taken aback. "What are you, then, a con man? Are you making this all up?" He looked at his brother, who stayed stone-faced.

"Ben, chill," Cameron said calmly. "Let him go on."

Ben crossed his arms.

"Do you know why your father resigned his commission from the military?" the Stranger asked.

"Because they weren't listening to his doom and gloom warnings. He'd say all the time" — Ben imitated his father's voice — "there's nothing a human brain could do that couldn't be done by a computer. And once it got to where AI could imitate us, they could become more powerful than us." He scoffed, then added: "He also said he wanted to spend more time with us."

The Stranger leaned forward, and the shadows from the fire shifted and illuminated new contours on his face. "The year he resigned, the government took your father's robotics and AI research — all of it — and handed it over to the United Nations."

Ben blinked. He'd forgotten about the United Nations. Heck, he'd forgotten about countries. Didn't matter anymore.

"The deal was that the UN would let America build more defense systems in Eastern Europe if we fork over Dad's research," Cameron explained. "Top secret."

"Install twenty nuclear warheads in Poland and the Ukraine, to be exact," the Stranger said.

"So what?" Ben asked. "Didn't that stuff happen all the time?"

The Stranger's face darkened. "You see, the government never told your father about the UN deal. In fact, they hid it from him."

Ben shrugged. "Big deal. It's not like they had to tell him." He raised an eyebrow. "How did he find out?"

The Stranger picked up the thermos and unscrewed the cap. "A top military official — a good friend of your father's — was involved in the deal. He told him what happened."

"And so Dad resigned," Cameron said, snapping his fingers. "Just like that."

The Stranger took a sip, then said: "Afterwards, your father took the teaching position and then focused his research efforts on mechanized hard suits."

"Like HULC," Ben said. "As well as larger ones — mini-mechs." He ran his hand through his hair. "I get all this. He met with a bunch of companies, and I think it was Lockheed that offered him like a billion dollars for HULC. He said no."

"Yeah, but Dad never told us the *real* reason why he turned them down, right?"

"It wasn't because DARPA wanted Dad to manage the AI and robotics research?" Ben asked.

"To an extent," the Stranger said slowly.

"So, I guess it has something to do with why Dad resigned, then."

Cameron gently elbowed Ben on the shoulder and said: "This is where our Stranger here cut me off from the story, just when it was getting good."

"I thought that what I'm going to tell you would be best told just once," the Stranger said gravely. "This is bigger than all of us."

"The suspense is leaving us trembling in anticipation," Cameron deadpanned.

The wind picked up a little bit, clouds moved in, and the smell of rain touched the air for the first time in months. Ben looked for lightning on the horizon. He loved thunderstorms. But there was only dark, swirling sky. Another disappointment.

In the distance, he made out a tiny yellow dot. A campfire. He wondered who they were, where they were from. He hoped that they'd make it through the night.

Ben glanced expectantly at the Stranger, who was watching the embers from the fire crumble into themselves.

Finally, the man let out a deep breath and said softly: "Your father joined DARPA for one simple reason. He needed access and funding to write a code."

"Code?" Ben asked, his eyes narrowing. Now things were getting interesting.

The Stranger nodded, then said: "*The* code. One code that could disable or control every AI processor that he helped design in the last fifteen years."

He leaned his head against the rock wall and rubbed the bridge of his nose. *How can this be?* he asked himself. He wanted to close his eyes and *think*.

A million things flashed through his mind. He'd have to dive back into old memories and gather the clues, anything that'd back up what this guy was saying. Things his dad said, the way he acted, where he was on certain nights — this was going to take a lot of time, and he needed a clear head and to be alone.

But one thing was sure. . . .

"It was the UN deal that did it for him," he said, speaking up. "When the government handed over the research. *His* research."

Cameron grinned and clapped his hands once. "He totally would, right? That would be his *ultimate* preparation for his doomsday, even greater than this castle." He chuckled and poked at the fire.

"To an extent," the Stranger said. "When your father discovered that the government had made the UN deal, one project concerned him in particular. An important one."

"They were all important," Ben said with a shrug. "His scientist friends would always come up to me and say how *your Daddy's* research on sensors and neural electrodes helped thousands of people see, feel, touch, and walk again."

"Wasn't he the Einstein of AR too?" Cameron asked. "Great going on that one, Dad."

"Really?" Ben shot back, prickling. "His work was the opposite of AR."

"Same difference."

"No, moron, it's not." Ben took a deep breath. "In AR, when a person wants to do something, he can just *imagine*, and the neurons in his brain will send signals to that artificial world where the person can do whatever he wants. But in the real world, someone can *think* something, and the electrodes implanted in his brain will pick up that electrical pattern generated by the neurons and transmit it somewhere else. *That* was Dad's work."

"What do you mean *somewhere else*?" Cameron asked.

"Anywhere. For example, if each signal can be translated into a command code for controlling a robot, then that person can control that robot just by *thinking*. In the field of robotics, it's called telepresence."

"I get it," Cameron said with a fake yawn. "So, instead of moving your body and having the robot mimic what you're doing, you can pretty much think what you wanna do, and the robot responds. Boring stuff." He tapped his knees impatiently. Unlike Ben, Cameron couldn't care less about their dad's work. As far as Ben knew, his brother's only interests were girls, shooting things, and living in the wild.

The codes! They were getting off track.

"What was the project?"

"Super soldiers," the Stranger replied, leaning back. "AI-enhanced."

Cameron whistled.

Ben rubbed his forehead. "Did the government know what Dad did?"

The Stranger paused. "No," he said slowly. "It was undercover."

Ben's face darkened into a frown. "So, what he did was illegal?"

Silence. He already knew the answer.

"But why would he do that?" he pressed. "Why would he break the law?"

Cameron rolled his eyes. "C'mon, Ben, it didn't matter whether it was legal or not. He did it to protect us, protect everyone."

But our dad? Ben thought.

"It's treason," he said with a tinge of disgust. "No different from that military officer."

The Stranger looked up at him impassively.

"Look, I get why he did what he did," Ben continued, "but that makes Dad a criminal. *Our* Dad. A criminal."

Cameron scoffed. "Look around you, Ben," he said sharply, motioning across the basin. "You think Dad bought all of this stuff? The weapons, the supplies, the military-grade features? He's been backdoor dealing with his fellow doomsday buddies in the military for years. It was probably just as good that he resigned before they caught him."

Ben had never thought about it that way before. He grew up with so much advanced technology and prototypes of so many different things that his dad brought home.

But everybody respected Dad, he thought. *They respected his honesty. His honor.*

"Dad is no saint," Cameron said flatly, crossing his arms and shaking his head in condescending disbelief.

Pushing it out of his mind, Ben looked at the Stranger. "That's why you're here, isn't it? You have the codes."

The Stranger pulled the holographic virtual disc out of his shirt pocket and held it up. "In here. As far as I know, it contains the codes, your dad's research, the UN files, everything we talked about."

He handed the disc to Ben. "You can check for yourself. It recognizes both yours and your brother's thumbprints."

"How did you get this?"

"When your dad finished writing the codes, he made a master copy of everything and downloaded it into this disc. It was arranged that it should be kept with me for safe keeping."

Ben cocked his head. "Why not with us?" he asked skeptically. "Why not here?"

"Your father didn't want to take a chance of it being discovered in his possession. I live on a farm in the Santaluz Mountains, quite remote and far from prying eyes. The arrangement was simple: I'd keep it safe, and in the event of 'zero hour,' I'd get a message from your father telling me to activate the next step. And that's what happened: I got the message from your dad on the day of the EMP."

"The next step was to get it here," Cameron said.

"Right."

"But this was over a year ago," Ben said. "Why didn't you come sooner?"

The Stranger looked at him intently with his piercing blue eyes. "I tried."

"Fair enough," Cameron said, slapping his knees lightly. "You're here; you brought the codes — what's next? We punch numbers and all the robots go boom-boom?"

Ben glared at his brother.

"Not quite," the Stranger replied. "It has to be done by satellite."

"But there's no electricity now," Cameron said. "How can that work?"

"Satellites are still up there orbiting space," Ben explained. "If the electrical grid fails, that doesn't mean they stop working and come crashing down to earth. In fact, you can still broadcast signals by satellite, but you need a charge as well as access to the satellite you wanna use."

"Leading to what I was going to say next," the Stranger said, smiling. "According to your father, the only way to transmit the signal is at this one particular DARPA facility. A laboratory or military center here on the West Coast."

"You don't know where it is?" Ben asked.

"That's the thing," the Stranger replied with a hint of irony in his voice. "I don't."

Ben and Cameron both gaped at him.

The Stranger held his hands up. "Let me explain. Your father *intentionally* withheld the location of the outpost. He thought separating the codes from the facility's coordinates would be another fail-safe in case the disc was to ever fall into the wrong hands."

"So, what now?" Ben asked, laughing. "The codes are useless!"

"Just wait," the Stranger said, holding up a finger. "Let me finish. Right before your father's message cut out, he was trying to give me the coordinates. However, he must've recognized that he was losing the signal, so he quickly said: 'at my house, on my desk, the—' Then that was it."

"That's it?" Cameron asked abruptly. "Really?"

The Stranger nodded. "As part of the original plan, I wasn't allowed to contact him, so I didn't call him back."

"*On my desk. . . .*" Ben mumbled to himself. He perked his head up. "He must've meant that the *location coordinates* are on his desk."

"Nice work, Sherlock," Cameron said, brushing off a spider crawling on his boot. "Of course that's what he meant. Probably on a sticky note, collecting dust." He paused and bit at a fingernail. "That is if the house wasn't toasted by fire."

"I certainly hope not," the Stranger said, rubbing his chin. "That'd put a damper on things."

Ben stared at him. "You're gonna go?"

The Stranger looked at him and nodded his head gravely. "I made an oath. To my father. To yours. It must be done."

"And you know where my parent's home is, right?" Cameron asked. "Practically in the middle of the city. Probably a hundred thousand deadheads and a thousand vagabonds stand between us and there."

"He's right," Ben said. "There's no way you'd make it there."

"Speak for yourself," Cameron said. "And that's not what I said. I'm going."

Ben laughed incredulously. "Seriously? That's insane, Cam. *Insane.*"

"What's *insane* is spending the rest of our lives in this hole, cooped up like a bunch of flea-bitten rabbits. Eventually, we're gonna run out of food. People are gonna get sick with a disease, whatever. I'm not gonna sit around and wait to be wasted by those freaks. It's war."

"Not to mention the death and destruction that these machines are causing," the Stranger added carefully. "Many millions have perished."

Ben didn't think that many people were still alive in this world, but he knew that the Stranger was including the deadheads in his estimation. He scoffed and looked out upon the dark lands.

Far away, a half-dozen gunshots pierced the cold wind.

The Stranger looked up, alarmed.

"No worries," Cameron said. "Far away."

Ben looked for the distant campfire. Nothing but damp darkness.

A raindrop hit the dust, triggering a steady drizzle. The soggy earth would make the climb back down from the cave difficult, especially with his ankle.

"Time to head back in," Cameron said. He threw dirt on the fire and stomped it out.

The Stranger moved to stand up, but Ben stopped him.

"So, you're going? Both of you?" He looked at them with incredulous eyes, not sure whether to feel terrified, encouraged, or embarrassed at his lack of desire to embark on this suicidal mission.

"I'd like to leave tomorrow night," the Stranger said solemnly. "Cam, I assume is coming. I think you should come. And one more, too."

The Stranger extended his hand to Ben to help him get up. Ben took it.

On Dad's desk lies the key to the survival of humanity? Is this for real? Ben knew he'd be lucky if he slept that night.

CHAPTER 9
To the Unknown

The vagabond stood in the middle of the garage, clutching a Bowden cable in its left hand. An overhead fluorescent light flickered and buzzed like insects flying into an electrocuting flytrap. The elevator lift hissed as it reached the open floor, and the first thing Ben noticed when he walked into the garage at noon the next day was Tomás rummaging through his dad's tools.

"You're outta your league, Tomás," Ben called out. He walked over to the towering robot, and crouching at a slight angle, he tugged at the cable in its grip.

"Wait," Tomás said, holding a custom-made tool that looked like a screwdriver with a cross-shaped head. "I already yanked at it hard, but this should work." Licking his lips, he inserted the screwdriver into a socket in the vagabond's wrist; with a pop, the hand opened, and the cable dropped to the floor. "Out of my league?" he asked. "I even got the thing to stand up: some sort of gravity stabilizer in its torso."

"Nice," Ben muttered. "At least I can still throw a baseball further than you."

"Farther."

Ben snorted and picked up the cable and handed it to his friend.

"Pretty crazy couple of days."

"Tell me about it," Ben replied, carefully examining the markings on the side of the robot's skull. "The Stranger shows up, and suddenly we have a mission to save the world."

"Well, you know I can hold down the fort here," Tomás said, wiping the screwdriver on his shirt. He gave a quick look around, then leaned in. "As long as Aiden behaves."

"I'm not too worried about him," Ben replied. "Danna will keep him in his place."

Tomás looked at him quizzically. "Wait, she said she was going with you guys."

Ben cocked his head to the side. "Going with us?"

"Yeah," Tomás replied, his eyebrows furrowing. "She probably didn't say anything because she knew you'd try to talk her out of it."

"What about her sister?"

They heard a shuffling of feet. "Izzy's just gonna have to suck it up." Cameron strode out of the L3 armory holding a small ammunition belt. "We're gonna need her big sister's secret agent skills."

The Stranger had wanted another person. *Did he already have Danna in mind?* Ben thought. *Why wouldn't he ask me first if she could go with us? This is my family. Not his. I should be the one to decide.*

Ben turned around and walked toward the stairs.

"Where you going?" Cameron called after him.

Ben didn't answer.

* * *

Ben tapped lightly against the door to the girls' room. "Danna?"

"I'm going with you!" came a muffled reply.

"So I heard," Ben replied. He leaned his head against the door. "You sure?"

The door opened suddenly, and Ben fell forward half a step. Danna was adding a final few things to her rucksack. Izzy was sitting on her cot, holding her legs and knees close together. Her eyes were red, and she was trying not to sniffle.

"Do *you* even wanna do this?" Danna asked, giving him a probing gaze.

Ben crossed his arms and studied his dirt-caked fingernails. "No, not really."

"You're afraid?"

Ben scoffed. "Of course not," he said, looking up. "But we're safe here, you know. I mean, I know we gotta do this, but think about it—"

"Wait." Danna set her pack down and motioned Ben to move out into the hallway. Glancing back at Izzy, she whispered: "I don't want her listening."

Ben stiffened. Lowering his voice, he continued: "I mean, realistically, there's no way we're all gonna make it back. I just—"

"Need to find out about your parents," Danna said, finishing his sentence.

Ben nodded.

"You don't care about everything else? The codes?"

"I *do* care, but what chance do we have? Besides, the Stranger doesn't even know where that place is."

"Yeah, he told me about that," Danna said. She tugged on a strand of hair, then said softly: "He asked me to go, you know."

Ben shrugged half-heartedly. "*Tsk*, why wouldn't he?"

"Because I'm a girl?" Danna asked, with a self-deprecating but slightly uneasy laugh.

"Yeah, right," Ben replied dryly. "It's *pretty* obvious that you could take on anyone here."

"Even you?" She gave him a playful nudge.

"Not if I got HULC."

They both fell silent.

"But seriously," Danna said, her dark eyes studying every movement on Ben's face. "Do you want me to come? I know this is about your family."

"C'mon, Danna, you know I do."

Ben realized he meant it. He just wished the Stranger didn't go behind his back. This was *his* place. *His* rules. Even Cameron seemed to let the Stranger do whatever he wanted.

Danna's face brightened. "Good."

"But what about Izzy?" Ben whispered.

"Katie is gonna look after her," she replied. She tugged on a couple of strands of her hair. "She can't just live her whole life here, right?"

"If it's safe, then why not?"

The air circulation vent suddenly hissed, and Ben felt a gentle puff of canned air against his face.

"I think everything happens for a reason," Danna said. "And this is it — this is our moment."

"I hope so."

Ben put one hand in his pocket and held the other one up to the air vent, feeling the stale air breeze through his fingers.

He wasn't afraid. But he'd weighed the pros and cons. *What would happen to the group if none of us makes it back? What if people get sick? Or something happens to Katie? Or if they're attacked again? What if. . . .*

He suddenly heard, as if for the first time, the tinny voices of people upstairs and their footsteps on the steel gangways. A sudden pang of guilt hit his chest as if he and Cameron were abandoning the group, abandoning the place that their dad made for them for times like these. As if . . . they were throwing it all away.

What would Dad do? What would he want?

Time was running out. He had a sudden desire to run somewhere, somewhere hidden, and alone, where he could just think. He felt like the decision to abandon the group was his, and the entire mission rested on his shoulders. And if they failed, and came back to discover the retreat in flames. . . .

"Hey," Danna said, throwing little boxing punches in the air. "We're gonna do this."

"I know." Ben's muscles tightened, and he pushed away his doubts. "I know," he repeated resolutely.

Cameron popped his head around the corner of the hallway. "You guys ready? We're in the armory."

Danna looked at Ben.

He nodded.

* * *

Cameron and the Stranger were waiting for them in the armory.

"Let's get to it," Cameron said, taking off his jacket and rolling up his sleeves. "We're gonna rough it in the woods as long as possible. Stay away from the city as much as possible."

"So, extreme camping?" Danna asked.

"No, more like bushcraft," Cameron replied. "There's really one fundamental principle: you can camp anywhere and in any weather if you got the 'five C's.'"

"The five what?"

Cameron planted his feet in a wide stance and feigned shock she wouldn't know such sacred terms. "The five C's: cutters, cover, combustion, container, and cord!"

"It's an old bushcraft saying," the Stranger explained to Danna. "Cutters, knives or some other blade; cover, like a tent or blanket; combustion, that's fire; containers for water and food; and cord, like rope."

"How do you know that?" Cameron asked quizzically.

The Stranger gave a sly grin. "Spoilers."

"Can you believe this guy?" Cameron asked Ben and Danna. He shook his head and chuckled. "Anyway, the five C's form the core of what you need to pack when you're in the wild."

"But it's not exactly like we're going into the wilderness," Danna said. "It's less than a three-day hike to your old house."

"Well, you need — or we *all* need — to look at this like we're gonna be in the wilderness. We have to plan like we're not gonna find any food, water, shelter, or safety. If we let our guard down one bit, it's over. Got it?"

Ben and Danna nodded. Both of them, of course, grew up learning how to camp in the outdoors; but Ben knew that keeping Cameron in a good mood was essential for this trip to work, so he advised Danna to play dummy.

"Okay, folks," Cameron said, rubbing his hands together. "Let's go shopping."

Cameron led them into a small supply room attached to the armory, which was lined on three sides with shelves stocked with a vast assortment of gear. Rucksacks and backpacks, heavy-duty outdoor clothing, military fatigues, body armor, helmets, belts, tents, sleeping bags, bivvies, blankets, tarps, pots and pans of various sizes, packaged food rations, hatchets, machetes, and fishing rods.

Under each shelf were dozens of drawers filled neatly with an assortment of knives, compasses, lighters, tactical gloves, candles, cord, repair kits for tools, fishing tackle, and various other gear and supplies.

"Impressive," the Stranger remarked, glancing at Cameron.

"This room is in case we ever need to bolt," Cameron said as he pulled a large Bowie knife out of a drawer. He handed the knife to Danna. "Let's get started."

"Actually," Danna began, handing the knife back to Cameron, "my Ka-Bar is better than this one."

"Debatable," Cameron replied, putting the knife back into the drawer.

"So where do we begin?" the Stranger asked.

"We all need to be outfitted with the same gear; that way, our supplies won't be affected if something happens to one of us."

Ben winced.

Cameron handed them each a USMC ILBE military pack and a wool blanket. "I'd keep extra supplies in here like this."

He knelt down and unrolled a wool blanket until it was folded in half lengthwise, then he laid it on the floor. Next, he unfurled a small blue tarp and placed it on top of the blanket, then he said: "You can put extra clothes, another blanket, and even some spare tools in here, then you roll it back up and tie with some cord."

"And most importantly?" Ben asked, shooting a quick wink at Danna.

"Socks," his brother replied gravely. "Always pack extra socks."

Cameron opened the drawers. "So, we're each gonna pack a knife, compass, light, magnesium fire rods, tarp, ax, candles, repair kits for the blades, sewing stuff, Israeli military first aid kits, and a cooking pot."

"Each one of us has to carry a cooking pot?" Danna asked, skeptically.

Cameron nodded eagerly. "Definitely. This one famous bushmaster (can't remember his name) once said he could survive an entire winter out in the wilderness with nothing but a cooking pot. No knife, no tent, nada. Couldn't do it without a pot though."

"A pot it is for each of us!"

"I presume we'll all be wearing the same military fatigues?" the Stranger asked, eyeing the stacks of clothing.

"Yeah, we all need to match in case we're ever separated. And black: it's the color the vagabonds are least attracted to, at least that's what Ben says. Should be sizes for all of us."

Cameron stood there for a moment scanning the shelves, mentally checking off the essential items. He crossed his arms and gave a small nod. "Okay, let's get packed up; it'll be dark before we know it."

* * *

The garage door opened, and Ben stepped outside into the night. It was very dark. He could barely make out the towering cliffs, but he could see the blue haze of the atmosphere on the horizon, pushing back against the eerie glow of the moon rising behind the mountain.

He closed his eyes and inhaled the night air through his nostrils as he listened to the familiar sounds of his last four hundred nights: the whistling wind etching new lines of music into the sandstone and the branches of withered trees rubbing against each other like wooden boats grinding against a battered dock. He exhaled.

"Okay," Cameron said, coming up beside him; "we're packed."

"So, we're set with the route?" Ben asked, looking out across the basin.

"Yep," his brother replied, running his hand through his hair. "We're heading ninety miles north to the San Jacinto gap. Tomás will drive us to the old mission, thirty miles from here. We're going by foot the rest of the way."

"Why so far north?"

"It's the only mountain gap into the city that doesn't have a freeway running through it. We need to avoid major roads at all costs. After that, depending on how things look, we'll either work our way back down the foothill range or head for the coast and go down from there."

"You sure the coast isn't dangerous?"

"The Stranger came down that way; he said it's pretty low key. But I'm thinking we need to stay in the hills as much as possible."

Ben nodded as he kicked at a few bits of gravel. "Looks like this it."

Behind them, the station wagon fired up, sending a bluish-gray puff of exhaust into the garage. It was an older model Volvo, faded white, with a roof rack now tied down with extra gear for the journey. Danna, Tomás, and the Stranger were already in the car.

Cameron grabbed the back of Ben's neck and shook him playfully. "I'm glad we're doing this together, bro," he said with a big smile.

Ben cringed and stepped away, not before swatting at Cameron's hand. "You're actually pumped up about this, aren't you?"

"Heck, yeah," his brother replied in mocking disbelief. "Now that I got the railgun, I don't have to bolt at the first sign of a vagabond."

"Yeah, well, I have a feeling things aren't gonna be as peachy as you think."

"I'm not saying everything's gonna be peachy," Cameron replied. "But we'll make it through. That's how Dad raised us: we're survivors."

Ben wanted to scoff at him. *Not all of us*, he thought. *Mom and Dad didn't survive.*

He took one last look around the garage in an absent-minded check for anything they'd missed. Nobody was there to say goodbye; everybody was asleep, having said their farewells hours ago. His eyes settled on HULC, leaned up against the wall by the workshop. *Take care, buddy.* He followed Cameron to the car and squeezed into the backseat next to the Stranger and Tomás.

Danna, who was sitting in the front seat, turned around and glanced back at him. She smiled. Ben returned a half-smile and looked out the window. Cameron backed the wagon out of the garage, shifted into drive, and then they were off.

Up above in the OPs, Marcelo and Naomi watched the wagon rumble across the basin and pass into the oak grove like a midnight wraith.

PART TWO
WORLD ON FIRE

CHAPTER 10

INTO THE WILD

They were ambushed within thirty minutes.

After twenty-one quiet miles down the old county highway, Cameron rounded a sharp curve and came upon an uprooted eucalyptus tree that had fallen across the road. He came to a slow stop and shut off the headlights. "Now what?" he asked, tapping his fingers on the steering wheel.

"Can't we just take the other way?" Ben groaned, rubbing his eyes. He'd dozed off.

"It's too dangerous," the Stranger replied. "Brings us too close to the city."

"So, we're just stuck then?"

Cameron shifted in his seat and glanced out the window. "A little way back there's an old logging road that I'm pretty sure twists up into national forest land before meeting up with the highway."

Tomás unfolded his paper map and traced his finger along the county road. "The logging road is just a tiny squiggly line," he said, holding the sheet close to his face and squinting. "But, yeah, it seems like we'd be on it about twelve miles or so before it reconnects with this one."

Cameron nodded crisply. "Sounds good to me. Everyone else?"

There were no objections. With a whistle, he shifted the car into reverse.

They found the logging road a mile back, nearly hidden between two craggy boulders. It immediately climbed into a chill gray mist, and towering, pale pines loomed above.

"Ugh," Danna muttered, biting her lip.

The road was a rutted, potholed track that clung to the mountainside in a series of switchbacks with intermittent turns into the forest. It seemed to have been used more than once recently, which assured Cameron that eventually it'd intersect with the county road.

After a bone-shaking quarter mile, the road condition suddenly improved, and Cameron accelerated to take advantage of the smoother surface.

Up ahead was a particularly tight bend, and as soon as Cameron maneuvered it, they suddenly came upon two pickup trucks blocking the road.

"Watch out!" Danna cried, putting her hands on the dashboard.

Cursing under his breath, Cameron slammed on the brakes. He fought the skid and nearly lost control as the car swerved toward the precarious edge. With a hard jerk, he yanked back the parking brake and the car came to a sliding stop just inches from the brink.

In an instant, loud whooping cries fell upon them from above, and dozens of torches engulfed the car.

Danna shrieked as a blue and white painted face pressed against the glass. Then another. And another. Hands splattered all over the car windows, rocking the car back and forth.

As the cries grew to a feverous pitch, Ben leaned his head back and groaned in dismay.

Shadowy shapes barely illuminated by the torches circled the car in a continual motion as if in a mad sacrificial trance.

One savage, wearing only tattered pinstriped dress pants, clambered on the hood and beat his chest so violently that Ben thought he was going to break open his rib cage.

"Any ideas?" Danna shouted, unbuckling her seat belt. "Someone? Anyone?"

The Stranger cocked his pistol and said coolly: "Lock and load."

"Wait!"

Tomás held up his hand then reached into his pack and pulled out an EG18X military smoke grenade.

He cracked the window open an inch. Dozens of pale, grimy fingers rammed into the gap like writhing maggots.

"What are you doing!?" Cameron roared.

Tomás opened the window another inch, pulled the pin ring with his teeth, and dropped the grenade alongside the car.

"Roll it up, roll it up!"

With a flash, a billowing cloud of blue smoke erupted and enveloped the car. The fingers pulled out of the window amid terrible fits of coughing. The hood crumpled as the chest-beating savage jumped off.

"Go!" Ben cried.

"I can't see a thing!" Cameron said, shifting the car into reverse.

Tomás leaned forward, grabbing the front headrests with each hand. "Pull forward until you bump into the trucks, and back up from there so you have a bearing."

"Forget this," Danna said. "Cover your ears!" Cocking her pistol, she rolled down her window and fired off five quick rounds into the blue haze.

Ben's head exploded with the high piercing whine of his eardrums protesting the sound of the gunshots. He closed his eyes and clutched his face, but the Stranger gave him a quick elbow, and he jerked back to alertness.

Cameron pulled forward until he could make out the shapes of the trucks then shifted into reverse, then forward again, and the car was turned around. Shifting into drive again, he plowed into cloud and crowd.

A torch-bearing brute immediately rolled over the windshield, snapping like a matchstick. The bumper hit another savage low and hard, launching the body across the hood and off the edge to whatever murky depths lay below. The front right tire hit a large mass, bones crunched, and the right side of the car lurched upwards.

One last crack on the rear windshield and suddenly they were through the smoke and pealing down the gravel road.

Ben clenched his fists. *Is this how this 'mission' is going to be? Why are we doing this? What difference does it make?* His head swirled, and his ears felt like they were bleeding.

"What's *that?*"

Ben snapped his head up.

Not fifty feet ahead a half-dozen barbarians stood in the middle of the road; all clutched spiked baseball bats except for one — he was swinging a medieval mace.

"They're the cut-off group," the Stranger said calmly. "I got this."

Bracing himself, he rolled down the window and lifted himself through it until he sat on the edge. With one arm holding onto the driver's headrest, he aimed his Glock 9 mm and fired seven rounds, dropping five.

"The other one should jump out of the way," he said as he slid back into his seat.

Ben and Tomás gaped at the Stranger, then at each other in wide-eyed, *"Did you just see that!?"* amazement.

The savage, however, a skeletal long-haired boy of about sixteen, stood his ground. As the car bore down on him, he sprung up and down frenetically, gnashing his teeth and pounding his hollow, rib-lined chest.

"He's not gonna move," Danna said, leaning back in her seat and bracing for impact.

"C'mon, dude, move," Cameron muttered under his breath.

The cadaverous boy didn't budge.

Cameron waited for a half-second then stepped on the accelerator.

The car struck the boy head on, and he flipped up and landed on the windshield, causing a shattering spider web of cracks. Cameron yanked sharply on the steering wheel, and the boy rolled to the right and tumbled off the edge of the road.

Ben glanced up at Danna; her face was ghostly pale. She had pulled in her legs and sat curled up in her seat. Next to her was Cameron, who was white-knuckling the steering wheel and glancing compulsively at the rear-view mirror.

"They put that tree across the road," the Stranger said, leaning forward. "We walked right into it."

"Drove, rather," Tomás said flatly.

Ben laughed bitterly. "This is insane," he said hotly. "We're not going to last one day out here. *Not one.*"

"Relax," Cameron said. "It's not as bad as it seems."

"Maybe for one person. But all of us?" Ben turned to the Stranger. "Even *you* said your friends couldn't make it. How do you expect *us* to live?"

"Because we will," the Stranger replied calmly, ignoring Ben's callous remark. "Because we *have* to."

"Yeah, you keep saying that," Ben muttered. "Sorry for being afraid of getting my head ripped off by a mace."

"Did you think that was actually going to happen?"

"I have no idea. That's why I'm saying this is crazy. I mean, look at Danna right now. And, Tomás, no offense, you look like you're going to throw up."

Tomás swallowed, took a quick breath, and waved his finger at Ben. "Fear's not a bad thing, you know."

"You're right, Tomás," the Stranger said. "In fact, it can be a good thing. It makes us careful; keeps us from making stupid decisions."

"If that's the case," Ben said spitefully, "then we should've been afraid of turning onto that road."

Cameron slammed on the brakes and came to a stop. He whipped around, and his eyes blazed at his younger brother. "You wanna go back to the retreat, Ben?" he snapped. "You *really* wanna go back?"

Ben crossed his arms and stared blankly out the window.

"Then *shut up*." Cameron glared at his brother in the rearview mirror a final time before shifting into drive. "Seriously."

A long period of silence followed, broken by the scraping sound of the right bumper, which had been partially torn off and was now dragging alongside the front tire. But the car soon hit another large pothole, and the bumper snapped and fell to the side of the road to sit there for all eternity.

* * *

Five bumpy minutes later, they reached the county road, and Cameron pulled off to the side. He unbuckled his seatbelt, and after cocking his pistol, he opened the door and stepped out. He looked around, then slid back into the driver's seat.

"Look," he began, waving away the lingering smoke in the car. "We need to go on foot from here."

"But we've got a hundred miles to go," Ben protested. "It'll take us forever to get there." He looked at Danna for backup, but she absently stared out the window.

"Can we find another way?" she asked quietly.

"There's no point," Cameron replied. "We'll just get ambushed again. I said all along it was a bad idea to drive."

The Stranger nodded silently.

"So, what are we going to do?" Ben asked, unscrewing his water bottle to take a sip.

Before the bottle reached his lips, Cameron turned around and grabbed his wrist.

"Save it," he said sternly. He looked at the others. "We leave here by foot, and Tomás takes the car back. We know it's clear back home from here."

"I think that's wise," the Stranger said. "We're too easy to spot on the road."

"It's going to take three times as long," Ben said, eyeing his water bottle.

"Two, maybe three days more," Cameron replied. "Nothing we can't handle."

The Stranger looked at Danna. "Thoughts?"

She gave a half-hearted shrug. "I'm down with whatever."

"Okay, then," Cameron said, glancing out the window again. He uncocked his pistol. "Let's unload and get prepped to move. Tomás, keep watch."

Ben stepped out and gazed upon the moonlit countryside. It was three o'clock in the morning; and, as Ben noted, nearly four days since Ron died and the Stranger appeared.

The car was parked next to a wire grazing fence that bordered the road as far as a hill crest farther down the road. The other side of the road was lined with large eucalyptus trees spaced far apart enough for him see the rolling fallow fields beyond.

Cameron came up next to him and lifted him his rucksack. "Look, I know that was a close call," he said quietly.

Ben nodded and gazed downwards. At his foot was a broken white mileage post half buried in the wild grass; he poked around it with his boot, trying to make out the number. "Thankfully we had guns, and they didn't."

"Some kind of tribe?"

"Cannibals," the Stranger said over the roof of the car. He came around and popped a fresh magazine into his pistol. "I've no doubt."

"We should've brought some rat poison with us," Danna said. A little color had returned to her face. "Next time I'll take a swig before they get me so I'll get the last laugh when they roast me for dinner."

"The only ones they'll be roasting for a while are their dead," Cameron said with a grunt as he slung the railgun over his shoulder.

Ben grimaced; he had a light stomach. He pursed his lips and tightened the pack straps across his chest and around his waist. Giving them a quick tug, he then pulled out his handgun from the holster strapped to his thigh and made sure it had a full magazine. He knew there was, but it was a habit. *A good one too.*

Five minutes later, they gathered in a circle next to the car. Gearing up seemed to have settled their nerves a little. All was quiet except for the tiny pieces of broken glass crunching under their boots and the soft idling of the car.

"Good to go?" Tomás asked, crossing his arms over the driver's side door.

"Should be," Cameron said. He gave Tomás a bear hug and tousled his shaggy black hair. "Keep an eye on things for us, eh amigo?"

"You got it."

Ben gave him a fist pump. "I know you got it. And make sure Izzy's okay."

"And HULC, too," Tomás said with a sly grin. "C'mon, admit it."

"And HULC, too," Ben said, smiling back.

Danna came up alongside him and nodded. "Thank you," she said, giving him a warm hug.

Tomás, who had a bit of a crush on Danna, blushed at first, but then straightened up. "I'll protect her like she's my own sister."

Ben gave Tomás a knowing grin. "So that makes Danna your sister too?"

"Shove it."

The Stranger patted his shoulder. "Tomás, you're a good man."

"Thank you, sir," Tomás replied, standing tall. He got into the driver's seat and adjusted the mirrors. "Well, guys, good luck," he said, fastening his seatbelt. "It's already been a crazy night. And I'm not lying when I say that I'm glad to be heading back."

Ben felt a shot of envy, but then he realized that he'd have a better chance out here than Tomás ever could. *It is what it is*, he said to himself as he waved goodbye to his friend.

Tomás shifted the car into drive but then stopped. "I almost forgot," he said, reaching into his bag. "Here's an extra flash grenade. Remember to pull hard." He handed it to Ben then drove off with a lurch.

"Does he even know how to drive?" Cameron asked, squinting his eyes.

"Well, I know for a fact he never took driver's training," Ben said.

"Neither did you, Ben," Danna said with a laugh. She looked at Cameron. "You should've seen your brother drive the other night; I was more scared of him than that robot."

"What's your deal?" Ben said, giving her a slight push on the shoulder. "Always busting my chops."

"Can't help it," she replied with a smirk, pushing back. "You're easy prey, Mr. Serious."

"I gotta admit, Ben," the Stranger said with a smile. "It *was* a little rough on the road the other night."

"You should've just called a cab, then," Ben shot back. He shook his head and watched Tomás drive erratically but surely down the road, bathed in the pale moonlight until it passed over a slight incline and was seen no more.

Suddenly Danna chuckled and held something up in her hand. "Well, how about it — a quarter." She slipped it into her pocket.

"Well, what in the world would you need that for?" Cameron asked.

Danna opened her mouth to reply, but then she stopped abruptly and smiled sheepishly. "Oh! I forgot there's nothing to buy anymore."

"I'd keep it anyway," the Stranger said lightly. "For luck."

* * *

As soon as Tomás disappeared from view, the Stranger gathered them together. Ben studied him keenly. He wasn't the same pathetic person he and Danna had picked up three nights ago. He saw a fire in his eyes and a grave intensity that magnetized the group to trust him, even with their lives. Cameron was strong-willed and independent, but Ben knew his brother felt it too. It was as if the Stranger gave them hope — and courage.

"From here on out, we'll have to be 'busting bush,'" the Stranger said plainly. He retightened the Velcro straps of his tactical gloves. "It was stupid of me to allow us to get ambushed."

"How can that be your fault?" Danna asked.

"It just was," the Stranger replied shortly. He paused for a moment as if he were replaying in his mind all that had happened within the past hour. "But it's over now. From here on out we'll march as a patrol; you all know the drill."

Ben nodded confidently.

The Stranger paused again, then softly said: "No doubt it's Providence that your parents taught you this stuff." He put his hands on his hips and shook his head lightly. "Truly extraordinary."

"Well, Dad's big gamble paid off," Cameron said. "For us, at least."

Cameron had thought their dad was crazy, and Ben would never forget his own humiliation when some kids at school had called his family "doomsday kooks." Now, more than ever, he wished his parents were alive if only to tell them thank you. He glanced over at Danna, and he could tell she was thinking the same.

"In the woods," the Stranger continued, "we'll march spaced apart, probably fifteen feet between each of us. On the mountain paths, we'll walk single file together, but still with enough distance so two people won't get hit by the same bullet."

Ben grimaced at the Stranger's words. "You're expecting snipers out here?"

"Hey, no need to take chances, right?" Danna said as she shifted the weight of her pack.

"And we gotta be *quiet*," Cameron added. "They used to say back in military school that when marching, you gotta act the way you would if you were—"

"Sneaking up on a deer," the Stranger said.

"How come you're always cutting me off? You're getting worse than Danna."

The Stranger looked up and grinned. "I don't know . . . but it sure is fun."

Ben chuckled and shook his head. He could already tell this was going to be an interesting adventure.

"But Cameron's right," the Stranger said. "We've got to march as silently as possible." He paused and set his gear down. "When you walk, carry your body weight balanced on your rear foot, then lift your forward foot high enough to clear any brush or logs, then lower your forward foot *gently*, toes first; *then* lower the heel of the forward foot slowly and transfer your body weight to that foot. It sounds complicated, but we've got another quarter mile or so before we get into the woods, which should be enough time for us to practice."

Ben nodded and took two awkward steps, but he was interrupted by Danna's laughing.

"You look ridiculous," she said, snickering.

"How about *you* do it, and *I'll* stand here and laugh?"

"I already know how to walk on patrol," she replied, making a pantomime of steps. "My dad taught it to me a long time ago. Comes from the special forces."

Ben scoffed. "Anything else you need to teach me?"

"Not *Danna*," the Stranger said, carrying on. "But I do, even though I wouldn't necessarily call it teaching."

"More like commanding."

"Let's call it 'solemn suggestions,'" the Stranger replied with a smile. "At all times, Cameron will be twenty feet ahead of us as the scout; I'll be at the rear. That way there'll be no surprises. Every forty minutes or so Cam will halt the patrol and do a quick recon of the area."

"At that time, you guys can take off your packs for a minute or two and get a drink of water," Cameron said. "When we need to stop for a while longer, I'll spot us a good place to lay low, and we'll set up a small perimeter."

"We can rotate eyes if we need to," the Stranger added.

"Just remember that no one stops unless we *all* stop," Cameron continued. "Not even to take a sip. People get lost easily once we get into the hills."

"These aren't exactly the Himalayas," Ben said dryly; "but whatever."

"All right, then," the Stranger said, surveying the surrounding area. "Let's move out, shall we? Take the lead, Cam."

Suddenly the reality of it all hit him. Ben's mind and body had been on such an edge from the ambush that he'd almost forgotten that they were about to begin a hundred-mile trek. In full combat gear.

Just then he was thirsty. He clutched his canteen like it was forbidden fruit. He hated the feeling of wanting something so badly that's not possible to have until one must do a lot of hard work first. He remembered a time when his friends were hanging out at the beach, but his parents made him study for three hours for an upcoming literature test before he could go.

He forced his mind away from his canteen. But then he thought about the weight of his pack, how it seemed so much more, and now his back ached, and he wished he could take it off.

Mumbling under his breath, he shuffled after his brother, rifle in hand, trying to walk like the special forces soldier that he'd never be.

The night was at its coldest now, stinging his nostrils with the scent of eucalyptus leaves and dewy grass. In the distance, a coyote yelped. Ben was surprised that a living animal still dwelt so close to human habitation. He numbingly watched Cameron march, twenty yards ahead; and he could feel Danna watching him from the same distance behind.

Despite the company, he felt exposed and unprotected, far away from the retreat. *From the last home in the world*, he thought, *now invading the realms of cannibals and killer robots.*

* * *

The moon grew brighter as they passed stealthily down the country highway. Miles away, a truck suddenly roared to life. Perhaps the savages had regrouped to mount a pursuit, or maybe they'd found new victims. They were in open view, and everyone was tense.

Ben suggested they should just make a run for the woods, but the Stranger replied that a patrol should never run unless they're under fire.

The dull grind of the distant engine split the silence. Ben glanced over his shoulder to check if there were headlights, but there were none. At any rate, they arrived at the edge of the forest; and wary of another ambush, they left the road and at once plunged into the woods.

The air was colder than it was out in the open, and Ben wished he'd brought a knit cap. *No complaints*, he thought. *I'd take cold over rain every time.*

Up ahead, Cameron paused. Ben pumped his fist, hoping that they could rest for a moment. But his brother moved on, and Ben found himself following once again like a mindless sheep.

There was no sound except for the repetitious *crunch-crunch* as he stepped on the layers of dead leaves and twigs. Fortunately, the moon still shone brightly into the woods, and he spent a great deal of effort watching for cactus that grew in small batches here and there.

After five minutes of tromping through the woods, they clambered down a low rocky shelf and into what Ben thought was an old irrigation canal that ran parallel to the road fifty meters from the left side.

Cameron's plan was to follow the highway — or at least use it as a guide — until it intersected with a county road in Wynola Springs, a small mountain town known for its apple orchards that drew thousands of tourists every autumn.

Once they reached the junction, they were to take a left and follow the new road along the western ridge tops for fifty miles until it met with the state highway that split the San Jacinto gap. From there, they'd descend on the city and make straight for home.

After several hours of hiking, with a few short breaks in between, Cameron called for a stop. Ben unsnapped his pack and slung it to the ground. After checking for spiny plants, he collapsed to the ground, leaned his back against a fallen tree, and let out a deep sigh.

He was surprised that he wasn't thirsty; instead, all he wanted to do was curl up in his sleeping bag. He yawned and closed his eyes.

Not a moment later, he felt a hard push on his shoulder. He jerked upwards and snapped his eyes open to see his brother looming over him.

"I signaled for a listening halt," Cameron hissed. "Not to unload and paint your nails!" He stomped back to the head.

Ben rolled his eyes. He had mixed up the signals. *Idiot!* He stole a glance over at Danna, who was standing fifteen yards away, arms crossed and smiling smugly.

He slowly got back to his feet and lifted up his pack, and he thought he heard Danna and the Stranger chuckling, but he didn't dare turn around.

Is this for real? Ben kicked at a half-buried plastic bucket; and for the next hour, he burned with silent anger toward the Stranger.

* * *

They hiked until dawn, and then they set up a hide site to rest for a while. Cameron had signaled for another listening halt, which Ben followed this time, and he led them down into a dense thicket. One-by-one he ordered them to crawl into the thick patch of brambles, which had a small clearing in the middle about the size of a pickup truck bed. For an hour they relaxed, ate, checked each other's packs, and planned their next move.

During the stop, Cameron and the Stranger rotated security shifts every fifteen minutes; Danna applied a fresh bandage to one of her cuts, which had opened again; and Ben put a Band-Aid on his left leg where his boot had been chafing against the skin.

By this time the sun had risen, and the forest awakened with the melodies of birds and the hum of insects as they danced in the morning wind.

Ben smiled as the first ray of sunlight warmed his face. His anger at the Stranger hadn't lasted long, and he didn't mean it to begin with: he was only frustrated at his brother. He wasn't one to hold grudges, and he was always a quick forgiver — except of himself.

Shortly after leaving the hide site, the terrain steepened, and they trudged up the side of a rocky, thickly wooded hill. It was mid-morning when they drew near to the top.

The Stranger signaled for them to stop and gather together.

"Don't go up to the summit; silhouettes create an outline that makes for easy spotting."

"Never thought of that," Cameron said pensively.

"I'm shocked!" the Stranger replied with a broad smile.

Fifty feet below the crest, Ben looked northward. A hazy range of wooded mountains curved far to the northwest; and between them and the most northwesterly distance on the horizon were barren hills separated by ravines and small canyons, with small pockets of homes and farmland.

The climate was milder here than at the retreat, which was on the eastern side of the range and cut off from the ocean breezes.

"I think we should head down to lower ground," Cameron said, pointing to the hills. "The road runs along the top of the range, and after what happened last night I'm not too sure about staying so close to it."

Ben agreed. Being that close to a main road would increase the chances of running into enemies — flesh or metal.

"I'm not sure about the road down," Danna said, crossing her arms. "It seems exposed; somebody could spot us easily."

Ben took out his binoculars and glassed the lands below, then zoomed out to follow the northwest mountain range. Turning west, he focused on the distant haze. Underneath it sprawled the dead city, and in a quiet neighborhood at the end of a cul-de-sac, his house.

His *old* house. Then the thought came to him that it's still very much his family's house. *But not my home.* He remembered his bedroom and his robotics bench and the rough draft of that English essay due the day after the Surge, still laying on his desk. *Maybe it's all burned down; or maybe somebody else lives there, who knows?* He wasn't too eager to find out, except for that gnawing curiosity that just maybe his mom. . . .

Ben put away his binoculars and straightened his pack. "I say we go down," he said, taking a swig from his canteen. "We can cut in and out of the woods when we need to."

After talking it over, the others agreed with Ben. *I could get used to this*, he thought.

* * *

Their way down into the lower hills was easygoing, the momentum lightening their steps. After seven miles, they came to the edge of a narrow, winding ravine with magnificent shades or rock.

Ben blinked in surprise. Each layer was made of a different color: pale grays, leather browns, smoky blacks, burnt oranges, and chalky whites. He liked geography just like his brother — one of the few things they have in common —, and he was surprised that he never knew about this place.

Looking down, he grimaced. The floor of the ravine was filled with scrub brush and shale and hiding places for all the venomous creatures that Ben hated most about living in Southern California.

"What do you want to do?" the Stranger asked Cameron.

"Well, the ravine runs north and south for a little bit, so we could follow along the bottom as far as we can."

"You think it's a good idea to walk in a ravine?" Ben asked. The thought of walking through tight spaces within a snake's biting range didn't sit well with him. "Doesn't that make us easy targets from above?"

"It *can*," Cameron replied. "But having a good feel for this area, I think we'll be okay as long as we stay sharp."

Having agreed to use the ravine as a shortcut, they spent quite a while finding a place that would allow them to climb down. After trudging north along the top of gully for at least half a mile, they came upon a large dirt slide, caused by erosion from the recent heavy rains. The clumps of dirt were still moist, which meant they could climb down without ropes.

Once they reached the bottom, Ben caught his breath then looked up. Several vultures circled ahead. He shook his head and blinked. *There's no such thing as bad luck.*

The passage through the ravine was slow. As Ben expected, they stumbled across more than one rattlesnake; but all of them were just seeking shade under nearby rocks, their unnerving rattle only an uncomplicated warning to stay away. Still, Ben wished he had a hiking stick as a defense.

After an hour of trudging through the gully, Ben heard trickling water. Peering through the thick scrubby undergrowth, he made out a small stream that flashed as the pale sunlight danced and glimmered on the ripples.

Cameron motioned them to halt and signaled that he would move forward to check out the stream. Ben crouched to one knee, and he watched his brother move deftly through the brush, hacking off a bough here and there with his machete.

Cameron paused at the brush line and carefully surveyed the banks, up and down the stream, and the tops of the ravine. After a minute, he stepped toward the water bank, and scanning the landscape another time, he knelt and ran his fingers through the water. He stood up, wiped his hands on his pants, and signaled the group to form up and meet at a large, split boulder next to the stream.

"It's a seasonal stream from all the rain," Cameron explained once they gathered. "It'll dry up after a couple of weeks."

"Safe to drink, right?" Danna asked.

"You can drink pretty much any water as long as you have purification tablets," Cameron replied, tapping his pack. "Even so, we can boil it and it'll be good for sure."

"I knew that," Danna replied saucily. "I was wondering if we can drink it fresh *without* the tablets."

"I wouldn't, but—"

"So, we're gonna stop?" Ben asked, cutting them off. He was hot and wanted no more than to splash cool water on his face.

Cameron looked at the Stranger, who nodded in approval. "All right, then," he said, setting his pack against the rock. "Couple of minutes."

"I'll keep watch," the Stranger said as he took off his ball cap and wiped the sweat from his brow. He picked up his rifle and climbed to the top of the sunbaked boulder.

Ben's boots squished softly as he stepped into the mucky bank. He gazed into the stream and watched leaves and blades of grass drift along the rippling surface in a swirling waltz. He crouched and scooped cool water into his face.

He heard a splash next to him as Danna jumped into the stream with a soft squeal of delight. She was barefoot; her pants were rolled up to her knees.

"Cameron said I could," she chirped. She kicked water at him. "Why don't you come in? It's not even ankle deep."

Ben paused for a moment then thought *why not?* Hopping on one leg, then the other, he unlaced his boots and pulled them off, and then his socks. After a quick roll of his pants, he stepped into the stream, feeling the pokes of sharp rocks under his bare feet. He looked up at Danna, who was tip-toeing around a protruding rock in the middle of the creek.

"I don't see any minnows in here," she muttered under her breath.

"Like Cameron said, it's only a seasonal creek."

"Still, it'd be cool." She stuck one leg out to feel around with her foot. "I haven't seen any fish in a long time."

Ben remembered the last time he'd seen a fish; a pet Betta in his English teacher's classroom. *Poseidon the Betta*, he recalled. It died the day before the Surge.

He splashed more water on his face and then sunk his filtered canteen into the stream, watching the bubbles float out of the hole like a plastic squirt gun in a swimming pool.

"You guys ready?" Cameron called out. He wiped his brow with his arm and smiled.

"No!"

"That's alright," he replied. "I'm gonna check out what's upstream and see if there's a good spot to set up camp."

"Okay, cool," Ben replied. His brother's words were music to his ears. He looked up at the Stranger, who held his rifle tightly but also had a small smile at the corner of his mouth.

The afternoon seemed to last forever. Ben hadn't enjoyed himself this much since he beat Aiden and Lena in target practice a few weeks ago. They were warming themselves on the rocks and chewing on beef jerky when Cameron appeared around the bend with his rifle slung over his shoulder. He'd been gone for over an hour, and Ben forgot he'd even left.

"I found a good spot for the night," he said, catching his breath. "A half-mile up the ravine, an incline leads up to a really cool pocket of forest. Never seen anything like it. It's not an easy climb, so I think we'd be safe from the freaks."

The Stranger stood up and clapped his hands once. "Let's do it then," he said cheerfully. "Good work, Cam."

Ben and Danna glanced at each other, knowing each other's thoughts. "Can't we just set up camp around here?" Ben asked.

Cameron scoffed. "Next to a water source? The local hotspot for all the predators of the night? Nah, it's good to camp with a water source *nearby*, but never next to it."

"Yeah, yeah, I know," Ben grumbled in reply, lying flat on his back with his hands behind his head. "I — *we* — just don't feel like moving another inch." He stretched and yawned.

The Stranger extended his hand and helped Danna to her feet.

"Like your brother said, it's only a half mile," he said. "Think of the delicious can o' baked beans that awaits us tonight!"

"Well, geez, let's get moving!"

* * *

The afternoon sun blazed overhead as they hiked upstream. Large boulders and patches of cactus and other thorny bushes slackened their pace. Ben could tell that Cameron wished he'd cooled off in the stream when they'd stopped before.

Ben uneasily looked up at the sharp cliffs on both sides, awash in the hot light, and squinted. He couldn't see over the edges; for all he knew, they could be in the middle of a camp of deadheads (if they even camped). The Stranger, meanwhile, quietly held the rear, which gave Ben an uncomfortable sense of security.

After fifteen minutes, they came to a slope of jagged rock shelves formed like steps rising thirty feet high. A small trickle of water laced down the side of the rocks and into the stream. Looking up, Ben could make out a row of dense treetops which seemed like coastal redwoods.

"Here we are," Cameron announced, holding his hand to his forehead to block the sun as he looked upwards.

Danna frowned at the unstable slabs of bare-faced rock. "I was picturing something a little bit easier to climb."

"Well, feel free to pitch a tent down here, Danna," Cameron replied with a hint of iciness. With a hop, he grabbed onto the lowest rock ledge and pulled himself above it; then, finding secure footing, he repeated the motion until he was over the ledge. "But," he called down, catching his breath. "Since I'd worry about you all by yourself down here, I'll tie some cord around this here tree and drop it down for you."

"Save it for the packs," Danna replied. She dropped her rucksack, walked up to the ledge, and after giving it a quick look over, she pulled herself upwards. Within a minute she was up and over the top and gloating at Cameron.

Ten minutes later, they pulled the last of their packs up with the cord and moved cautiously into the woods. The walk was rougher and steeper than it looked from below, and several times Ben had to grab on to a tree to steady himself. The air was getting thick, and he was surprised that such a dense wood grew in this arid climate.

"Pretty cool, isn't it?" Cameron said, looking up at the tall treetops. "When I saw this place, I couldn't believe it."

"Is this the only way in and out?" the Stranger asked.

"As far as I know," Cameron replied. "The site is straight ahead: the ground levels off about twenty meters up and there's a nook that I think would make a good campsite."

The crunch of their footsteps and the distant buzz of a cicada echoed across the forest. Ben watched as the sunlight filtered through the trees and danced on the fern fronds and moss-covered logs. His feet hurt and he had a headache, but he found this hidden corner of wilderness bearable, if only for its mysteriousness.

After picking their way through the woods, they arrived at a rocky outcropping surrounded by tall trees and bound on three sides by immense fallen trees.

Cameron made a sweeping wave with his hand.

"Perfect," the Stranger said. He unstrapped his pack and swung it to the ground. "We're all clear?"

"Safe and sound," Cameron said clearly. "Won't get better than this."

At Cameron's words, both Ben and Danna dropped their bags and collapsed to the ground in relief.

"What about water?" Danna asked, holding up her empty canteen. "I can't imagine climbing back down to the stream."

"There's a spring twenty feet that way," Cameron replied, pointing south. "Go upstream for getting water and downstream for washing up. But remember: nobody goes *anywhere* unless we're all on alert."

Ben scratched his head and gazed deep into the woods. The air was thick and stuffy; not a leaf moved. "Are you sure this place is clear?" he asked abruptly. "I'm not getting the creeps, but. . . ." His voice trailed off as he looked around.

The Stranger, who had begun to set up the camp layout, shot Ben a sidelong glance. "Cameron?"

"I was planning to do another patrol anyway before I set the traps," Cameron said, slinging his rifle over his shoulder. He turned to Ben. "Why don't you come with?"

Ben looked at Danna, who was sitting cross-legged on the ground and pulling little twigs out of her hair. She was unusually quiet. He was about to ask her if she was okay, but he thought the better of it.

"Sure," he replied, after a short pause. He groaned as he got up stiffly: his feet were like dead weights. He grabbed his rifle and followed his brother, who was already ten steps ahead of him and who rarely waited for him for anything.

* * *

Cameron took a left from the bivouac and follow southward along the crag to its end, then circle back around east toward the ravine and back to camp. All was still but for the massive trees that creaked in the soft breeze.

Ben gazed wide-eyed at the forest, lost in wonder, and, for just a moment, in time. Patches of pale white flowers grew among the ferns, twinkling like tiny lamps set alight by the filtered rays of the sun. He craned his head and traced the thick strips of rough bark on the enormous tree trunks zigzagging up into the canopy far above them and meeting the cracks of blue sky. He inhaled through his nostrils and scented the sharp smell of redwood and wild mint.

As they waded silently through the greenery, Ben glanced at his brother to see if he was experiencing the same thing, but he couldn't tell. He could never tell. In fact, he hardly knew anything about his brother.

They'd pressed on for ten minutes when Ben caught sight of a dark structure fifty feet to his right. He stopped dead in his tracks and signaled to Cameron.

"What is it?" his brother whispered, coming up to him.

"Look," Ben said under his breath, pointing with his rifle.

Cameron squinted toward the building. "Looks like an old cabin. Doubt anybody's using it."

"We have to check it out," Ben said warily. "Should we go get Danna and the Stranger?"

"Nah," Cameron said. "We'll be fine." He elbowed his brother gently. "Lead the way, bro."

Ben pursed his lips and nodded. Creeping closer, he saw it was a small cabin made of mud-chinked logs with windows on each side and a front door that led out to a ramshackle porch. The roof was covered with dead leaves and branches; it drooped a little, but it seemed intact.

His brother motioned him to circle the cabin and approach from the other side. He gave a thumbs-up; and crouching low he moved slowly from tree to tree, taking care not to step on anything that would snap.

The cabin sat in a small, sunlit glade twenty feet from the tree line. Ben knelt behind a large fern and plotted his next move. Insects buzzed around his face, and he fought the urge to wave them away.

Ben frowned — he'd have to make a run for the side of the cabin. *Déjà vu.*

He braced himself, and keeping his rifle tucked into his shoulder, he sprinted out into the clearing. He reached the cabin and pressed against the logs, and inching slowly, he peered into the filthy windows.

Beyond the dead flies and curled up wasps on the windowsill, he could make out a table and a chair and a small cot covered with blankets shredded to bits by vermin.

He was suddenly startled by a loud hawking caw of a crow, and in a flash he felt like a thousand hiding eyes were watching his every move — waiting. A chill shivered down his spine, and he held his rifle close. *Maybe this is a creepy forest, after all*, he thought.

His back against the logs, Ben slid his way around the corner to the front porch and came upon Cameron crouched next to the door with his knife in his hand and an index finger to his lips.

Ben nodded and stepped onto the half-rotten porch, and the floorboards protested with a thick, damp groan. He cringed, but his brother motioned that it was okay.

Cameron sneaked another look into the window then tried the doorknob. It was unlocked. He twisted the handle and pushed, but he felt the resistance of buildup and dirt caking the warped door frame.

"Cover me," he whispered.

Ben took a quick look around the clearing then stood to the left of his brother, his rifle held high.

Cameron stepped back and then pushed forward quickly, driving his shoulder into the door. It burst open with a rain of clumpy crud and Ben followed his brother inside, finger on the trigger.

In the center of the one-room cabin was an old wood-burning stove bearing a single dented kettle covered in cobwebs on top. Stacked on a plywood shelf next to the stove were a couple of rusted soup cans and a knocked over box of macaroni with a chewed-out hole in its side. Everything was covered with dust and animal droppings.

And then Ben saw the dead man.

The corpse sat in an old rocking chair with his rifle laid across his lap. By the looks of him, he could've been dead for well over a year. Ben thought that dead people quickly decomposed into skeletons, but here before his very eyes was a mummy.

His face was pale gray and shriveled like thin, sinewy strips of leather pulled tightly to the hollow eye sockets. His open mouth revealed an accordion of brown teeth, one of which had a silver filling. Long wisps of gray hair fell neatly across one side of his head, which leaned slightly onto the left shoulder. He wore tattered denim overalls and a black and red checked cotton shirt.

Over a year ago Ben might've freaked. But now, after seeing so many dead, he wasn't afraid; he just couldn't take his eyes off the corpse.

"We don't have to stay here," Cameron said quietly. "C'mon."

"Hold up," Ben said. He took a slight step forward. "There's something in his hands."

Indeed, the man's bony fingers clasped a faded sheet of paper, likely ripped from the blank pages of a book. Ben walked over, and gently lifting the dead man's arm, he pulled the paper out and opened it up.

In faded pencil mark: *Passing through nature to eternity. Be back soon.*

Ben looked up at Cameron, who was watching him with an amused look on his face. He scowled at his brother, then gently raising the man's arm again, he slid the paper back into his fingers.

He straightened up and said, "Let's go."

Stepping out onto the porch, and with one last look inside, Ben pulled the door shut as far as it could close.

"You're really gonna worry about closing the door?" Cameron asked, cocking an eyebrow at his brother.

Ben shrugged nonchalantly. "He said he'd be back."

CHAPTER 11

LOTHLORIEN

The two brothers finished the patrol without incident and arrived at the camp just as the sun was sinking over the western range of hills.

Danna was leaning against the back of a tree holding her rifle and the Stranger was whittling a stick.

"See anything?" Danna asked.

Cameron glanced at Ben. "Nope," he said. "Not a thing."

The Stranger stood up and handed Cameron the stick, which was actually a thick, two-foot long branch that he'd sharpened into a lethal spear.

"Heard you talk about setting a boar trap; thought I'd help."

"Except we ain't trapping boar," Cameron said as he examined the spear admiringly. "This'll work perfectly. Now all I need are a couple of green tree limbs."

"You mean these?" Danna asked, holding out two thin, new growth branches. Seeing the surprised look on Cameron's face, she added: "What? You think we've just been standing around the whole time?"

Cameron snatched the branches out of Danna's hands, but not before tousling her hair. She smacked his arm in protest.

"C'mon, grab your guns," Cameron said, smiling smugly. "You guys need to see where I set this up — unless you wanna get pinned to a tree during an ill-advised midnight stroll."

He led them to where they had passed between two giant, moss-covered fallen trees on their way to the campsite. He stood for a moment, examining the path, then picked a spot.

Pulling out some thin rope, he tied the green limb to one of the fallen branches closest to the path. Next, he took one of two thick sticks that he'd found earlier in the woods and drove it into the ground. He then tied the spear to the green limb.

"Step back, guys," Cameron said. "This is where things get tricky." He unwound more rope and tied it from the thick stick across the path and onto a branch on the other side.

"The trip rope," the Stranger observed.

Cameron nodded and took out of his pack a small wooden dowel and fastened it at the other end of the line. Then he took a small slip ring out of his trapping kit; and pulling the spear back, he asked the Stranger to attach the ring to the trip wire on the far side to hold the spear back in tension. After that, the Stranger drove the second stick into the ring. The trap was set.

Cameron stepped back and examined his contraption. "So, bad guy or hungry animal will trip the line, which'll cause the ring to slip, the stick springs out of the way, and that spear plunges into a warm bloody heart—" He suddenly frowned.

"What?" Danna asked.

"Should've attached metal or some other kind of noisemaker to the trip line."

"No need," the Stranger said, patting him on the shoulder. "I think we'd hear the screaming."

* * *

Setting up camp took over an hour, and they finished just as the last light of day gave way to a starry night. Fortunately, there was no need to sleep in the open air: they had plentiful options for shelter.

Their campsite was next to a large fallen tree trunk, and the ground in front of it was dry and free of fungus and insects. That being so, they dug a hollow along the length of the trunk, which turned out to be roomy enough to fit at least four people with several feet of space in between.

Next, they gathered several armfuls each of long straight branches and laid them across the hollow and against the tree trunk. They then covered the sticks with moss and pine boughs, and the result was a fine lean-to.

Ben and Danna crawled in hastily and laid down their sleeping bags, five feet from each other, each dryly commenting on their palatial accommodations for the evening.

Cameron preferred his own sleeping arrangement: he took to a large pine tree that had snapped in half; and after weaving in other boughs for denser cover, he made for himself a crawl-in shelter.

Once camp was set up, they gathered together for dinner. Ben sat on the leaf-covered ground, and the first chill of the night blew on his face. He rubbed his hands together and looked over at Danna, who was sitting a few feet away from him on a small log, tapping her knees with her fingers as if to the beat of her own tune.

"How about I get a fire started," she said.

Ben noticed a hint of timidity in her voice. He knew her well enough to guess that she wanted to show off her fire-starting skills.

"I'm not that cold, actually," he said with a smirk.

Danna pursed her lips and stopped tapping her fingers.

"Yeah, not tonight," the Stranger said. "We can't risk getting seen."

"Not if we build a Dakota fire pit," Cameron said. "Danna, get my trench shovel from my pack, and I'll show you."

"I know what a Dakota fire pit is," Danna said hotly. She grabbed Cameron's shovel, unfolded it, and strode over to the base of the pine tree. After scraping away the surface soil, she began to dig.

"You shouldn't make a fire under a tree," Ben said teasingly. He shook his head in mock disappointment. "Amateur."

"It helps to disperse the smoke," Danna replied with a grunt. "Ask your brother."

Cameron nodded, visibly impressed.

"How does this work?" the Stranger asked, crouching next to Danna.

"If you don't want your fire to be seen (like us, right?), you wanna have green or damp wood. You dig two holes, twelve inches round and about a foot deep, about two feet apart from each other. Then, you connect them by digging a thin tunnel."

"Make sure to put the wood in the hole away from—"

"The downwind," Danna said, cutting him off. "Obviously. Maximizes airflow."

Two minutes later a healthy fire crackled in the pit. Cameron whittled some green saplings to use as grill plates and laid them across the fire hole. Reaching into his supply pack, he pulled out three "meals, ready to eat" — or MREs — and tossed one to each.

"Tonight's menu will be," he said, reading the package label, "vegetarian taco pasta with — quote, unquote — *flavored fruit drink*.'"

"And a piece of candy," Danna added, holding up something like a Tootsie Roll.

"Don't eat those," the Stranger said quickly. "Bad luck."

Ben shot the Stranger a quizzical look and shook his head in amusement. As the best cook in the group, it apparently fell upon him to make the food. He set the pot over the flame and added two tablespoons of water. Next, he added the packaged food and stirred.

Cameron leaned back and stretched. "My friends," he said ceremoniously, "tonight, we feast."

After dinner, they discussed the procedures for the night.

"Two people will be awake at all times while the other two sleep," the Stranger said. "We'll rotate every two hours." He glanced at Cameron. "We'll take the first shift."

Cameron nodded in agreement and looked at Ben and Danna. "Sound good?"

"Sure, but I don't think I'll be able to fall asleep," Danna said, getting up and stretching.

"You will," the Stranger replied, getting up. "You probably don't realize how tired you are yet."

"Oh, I realize it," Danna yawned. "I'm just nervous something will happen if I fall asleep."

"Don't be," Ben said lightly. "These guys got it taken care of. Besides, we need to be fresh for our shift."

Danna took two steps then stopped and turned around. "Oh! I forgot to mention. Every time my family went camping, we always named our campsite. For example, when we went up to the Redwoods National Forest, we called our campsite Ewok Village, because they filmed *Return of the Jedi* up there."

"Hmm," the Stranger said. "Interesting. Any suggestions, guys?"

"How about Lothlorien?" Cameron ventured. "The hidden forest in Middle-earth."

Ben perked up and gaped at his older brother. "You've read *The Lord of the Rings*? I thought you didn't even know how to read!"

"Shut up," Cameron replied, throwing a twig at his brother. "Yeah, my roommate at school gave me a bunch of his books before he was kicked out. Didn't have any more boxes to take them. Thought the book looked pretty cool, so I checked it out. Ended up reading all of them."

The Stranger nodded approvingly. "Lothlorien. I like it."

"Me too," Danna said.

Ben looked at his brother strangely and offered a bemused smile. "Lothlorien, it is!"

* * *

Ben sat near the fire, wide awake. Danna had already climbed into the shelter. He glanced at the Stranger; his bright eyes glittering in the light of the flickering flames. His brother was leaning his back against the tree and watching the campsite entrance, rifle in hand.

"What's her story?" the Stranger asked, nodding at the shelter.

"Pretty sad," Cameron said, shaking his head. He glanced at his brother. "You wanna tell him?"

Ben shrugged. "Our dads knew each other from their Navy days. Her parents were 'preppers.' They bought an old farmhouse ten miles from the retreat; right off the old highway."

"Why not somewhere more secluded?"

"The farm used to have vineyards," Cameron said, "and the house had this massive wine cellar."

The Stranger understood. "They converted it into a bunker. Got it."

"Right."

"Parents never made it, though," Ben continued. "Her dad worked at the naval base downtown; and when the Surge hit, he was supposed to meet Danna, Izzy, and their mom at their rendezvous point outside of the city. They waited till midnight, but then tons of people started coming. Things got crazy. People tried to steal their car. I guess their mom ran over an old lady trying to escape."

"Did they make it out?"

"Car accident twenty minutes later; some thugs had set a trap. Their mom started shooting and told Danna and Izzy to run for it. The two of them basically jumped down into a ravine."

"Two nights out there," Cameron said, shaking his head. "Danna and her seven-year-old sister. No guns. Nothing."

"They did have their bug-out bags," Ben said. "The food lasted till they got to the farmhouse. They hoped their dad was there. . . ."

"But it was just them," the Stranger said, shaking his head. "How did you come across them?"

"They stayed there for a week, holed up in the wine cellar. I guess Izzy was taking it pretty rough."

"I can imagine."

"Danna said one night she jolted awake and decided to head for our retreat. Packed everything they could carry and hiked over."

"I remember it plain as day," Cameron said. "She looked like she was gonna have a breakdown. Wouldn't blame her if she did. But she didn't say anything, just asked where their room was."

"Yeah, it took her a couple of days," Ben said somberly. "But she pulled herself together and started to pitch in." He chuckled. "As you probably can tell, she's bossy, so pretty soon she was telling everybody what to do. It was pretty funny."

"Tough kid," Cameron added.

"Don't have to tell me," the Stranger said. "Saw that right away."

"Anyway, we figured she wasn't going back to the farmhouse, so Cam got together a bunch of us, and we hauled back most of their supplies."

"Left a little bit there to keep it as an outpost."

"And your getaway house," Ben said sarcastically.

"What do you mean?" the Stranger asked.

"Cam gets sick of everyone pretty quickly, so he spends a lot of nights at the farmhouse."

"Too many whiny teenagers," Cameron said. "Drama."

Ben rolled his eyes. "Dude, you're still a teen — in case you forgot how to count."

"Yeah, but I don't act like one."

The Stranger took a swig from his canteen, trying not to smile. "And what about Izzy? Something didn't seem right with her."

"She's messed up," Cameron said, shaking his head.

"Dude, why do you keep saying that?" Ben asked, bristling. "She's doing a lot better." He turned to the Stranger. "I mean, you can just imagine . . . her seeing all that, you know?"

"She's pretty much sat in that room for the past year," Cameron said. "Holding on to that stinking penguin."

"Ah yes," the Stranger said. "Penny."

"How did you know that?" Cameron asked with a raised eyebrow.

"Long story."

"We've all seen so much," Ben said. "But, man, six, seven-years-old. In kindergarten." He looked up. "Once, Izzy told Danna that she slept all the time because she tried to escape the nightmares, but then her dreams were even worse."

"But she seemed happy in the garden room," the Stranger said.

"I gotta admit, she's got a green thumb," Cameron added. "You should've seen the vegetable plants before she started working on them. Pretty sorry looking, thanks to my little brother."

"Hey, I tried my best," Ben shot back. "Mom was supposed to do the gardening, not me."

"Danna said Izzy talked to you?" Cameron asked the Stranger.

"Yeah."

"Man, I've never seen her talk to anyone except her sister before. And usually, it's just in whispers."

"Perhaps I just have a way with people," the Stranger said with a small grin.

"Yeah, perhaps."

They were silent for a moment, lost in their private thoughts.

Ben cleared his throat and glanced at Cameron. "Back at the retreat, you said the first EMP was a solar flare. How did you know that?"

"Dad told me," Cameron replied slowly; "on the day of the Surge. He'd just found out. The government had known about it, and they'd kept it a secret."

"From the *entire world?*"

"They didn't want people panicking."

"Did Mom know?" Ben asked. His heart skipped a beat. "I mean, do you think Dad told her too?"

"I have no idea; he didn't say." Cameron looked at the Stranger, who was watching them dolefully. "Our mom was at work when it hit," he explained.

"She was a doctor, right?" the Stranger asked. "A surgeon, if I'm not mistaken."

The brothers nodded.

"I'm very sorry," the Stranger said emphatically. "From what I gathered, the hospitals were the first to get hit hard."

"Why is that?" Ben asked, uneasily. He immediately wished he didn't ask.

"Because most of the hospital patients in the last five years were the AR addicts," Cameron replied. "The ones that really got sucked in."

The Stranger nodded. "When those types of patients were admitted, the hospitals couldn't simply unplug them when they got there. They were all addicted. When the EMP hit and all those people came to, the hospitals couldn't ever have anticipated what was about to happen."

"She was doing a big surgery that day," Ben said bitterly. "Of all days." He shook his head and snorted in disgust.

Cameron fidgeted uncomfortably. "Dad told me to go straight to the retreat," he said, looking to the Stranger as if he were pleading his innocence before a judge. "He told me not to worry about her." His voice trailed off.

Ben looked up and furrowed his brow. For a moment, Cameron's eyes were filled with regret, then with anger. He'd never seen his brother look that way before.

"You've probably been told this many times already, but you can't beat yourself up about it," the Stranger said, leaning forward.

"No," Cameron replied sharply, locking eyes with the Stranger. "Nobody's told me that once."

Ben was silent for a moment, then said: "I've never blamed you for it. You did what Dad told you to do, and you saved all of us."

"No, not all of us." Cameron lowered his eyes and started drawing in the dirt with his finger. "You know, after we got to the retreat, I went back and searched for her. It was overrun. The whole city was overrun."

"That was when you were gone that whole week?" Ben asked, his eyes narrowing. "Why didn't you tell me? We all thought you were dead."

Cameron looked away, then muttered: "I probably should've told you. I just thought it was better if you didn't know. Didn't want you to be hurt."

"Yeah, but you still had to find out for yourself, didn't you? I could've gone with you."

"I barely made it back," Cameron replied, chuckling. "Like I said, it was overrun. And you would've slowed me down — no offense."

Ben clenched his jaw and heat coursed through his tensing muscles; he wanted to punch his brother in the face. "You gotta stop trying to protect me," he said crossly. "Am I slowing you down now?"

"You don't know what's out here yet, bro," Cameron said. "What I've seen." He nodded at the Stranger. "What we've both seen."

"I'm finding out now, aren't I? I can imagine how it is in the city. The deadheads must be starved to death by now — it's been over a year."

The Stranger shook his head. "No, millions are still alive. *Millions.*

"And those vagabonds you've met?" Cameron added in a condescending tone. "Yeah, they're the nice ones."

"Well, I can't wait to meet the nasty ones."

"Bad idea," Cameron said quietly. "They're the masters of the world now. You'll see."

Ben rolled his eyes and tossed a twig into the fire and stood up. He was getting sick of his brother talking down to him. They're equals now. There's nothing

Cameron could do that he couldn't. In fact, he knows more about these robots than anybody. And that's an advantage these days. He hoped he could prove him wrong soon.

His face soured, and he stood up. "Bedtime. Sweet dreams, fellas."

The Stranger looked up and furrowed his brow; Cameron just gazed into the darkness.

* * *

Cameron and the Stranger never woke up Ben and Danna, preferring to let them get their rest.

The night passed without any disturbances, save for a distant crack of a twig that Cameron said was just an animal.

Ben woke up just before dawn, stirred by the gentle wind rustling the leaves of their shelter. He was surprisingly warm, and as he stretched he felt no tightness from sleeping on the hard ground.

He looked over where Danna slept to find her sleeping bag already rolled up and attached to her pack.

He felt a pang of embarrassment for sleeping in past everyone, but he felt refreshed, and he knew that he was going to have a strong day.

He crawled out of the shelter. Danna sat on a log, cupping a steaming tin mug with both hands, while a small fire crackled in the fire pit. A tin pot filled with hot water hung over it.

"Good morning, sleepyhead," Danna said brightly. She tossed him a mug and a packet of instant cocoa. "You better make yourself some before they get back. Cameron's checking things out while the Stranger is washing up at the spring."

Ben ripped open the packet and dumped the powdered chocolate into the mug, then he carefully poured the hot water and watched it swirl around as powder rose to the top in clumps. He had nothing to stir it with. He unsheathed his knife, but then he felt a slight poke in his arm.

"Gotcha covered," Danna said, handing Ben a small, whittled twig.

He nodded in thanks and stirred his hot cocoa briskly then tossed the empty packet into the fire.

"Don't let Cameron see you do that," Danna remarked, nodding at the packet now folding in on itself in flames. "He doesn't wanna leave any trace behind."

Ben scoffed and took a sip. He looked up and saw the first paint strokes of daylight smear gray bleakness across the sky.

A chill mist sloughed through the treetops, giving life to the scraps of dark green moss that draped the sprawling branches. It was chilly, and he could tell by the weather pattern it wasn't going to get much warmer.

"Today's gonna be a long day," Cameron said roughly, coming up the path with the dismantled spear trap in his hand.

"How far do you think we'll go today?" Danna asked.

"I'm hoping we can be halfway to the Pass by tomorrow," he replied, tossing the spear in the fire pit. "Another day's march and we could be looking down on the city."

Ben rubbed his face. "I'm gonna start packing up."

"And wash up, too," Cameron said. "Everybody has to stay clean — teeth brushed, fresh socks, etcetera. It's mandatory."

Ben grinned. "If that's the case, I lost my toothbrush, so I'll have to use yours."

"Use your finger."

Danna gave Ben a playful pinch. "Did you actually try to say something funny? I had no idea you had a sense of humor!"

CHAPTER 12

THE ROAD

Ben was the last to climb down from their hidden forest, and as soon as his foot stepped on the rocky floor of the ravine, it began to rain. At first, a few raindrops splattered on his hat, but a steady downpour quickly followed. The rocks along the stream at once became slick, and a foggy murk filled the ravine.

At first, he didn't worry about getting wet because he trusted the quality of his waterproof gear; but the thick humidity would not be outdone, and soon he had water dripping down his face. *Today's going to be a great day*, he thought.

After an hour of picking their way down the ravine, they came upon an old concrete bridge. At the base of the bridge the bank wasn't as steep, so helping one another, they scrambled to the top and pressed themselves flat on the ground. Cameron scanned the road.

The rain was falling hard, and Ben half-expected to hear distant thunder. After much discussion, they decided that they would walk along the road for a while until the rain let up. The downpour would affect their visibility, and it'd be much harder to maintain a patrolling formation.

And so they plodded along the road for several hours, talking every now and then, whether it was pointing out obstacles or rehashing the attack on the retreat. Ben was happy to have the company. He figured they all were, for their spirits weren't as low as before despite the rain. But the Stranger was uncharacteristically grim, and he rarely spoke unless it was to warn them to stay sharp.

Shortly before noon, after a long, tiring uphill march, they arrived at the outskirts of Wynola Springs. After passing the welcome sign, they left the road and veered into the woods.

As they crossed the backyards of empty homes, Danna, ever the scavenger, peeked here and there into tool sheds and detached garages, hoping to find who knows what.

Dozens of homes were severely damaged or burned down. Apparently, a large fire had swept through town. Some homes seemed to have been hastily fortified:

planks were nailed over windows and blocks of concrete were stacked unevenly on front porches. But when they passed them they would see a large hole blown into the side of one house or ladders leaning up against shattered windows of another.

One particular home, however, seemed relatively intact; and as they slipped through the backyard, Ben thought he saw a shadow move behind an upstairs window. He didn't believe in ghosts, but to him, that could've been the only possible explanation.

"What?" Danna asked, her brows furrowing.

"Oh, nothing. Thought I saw something. It was nothing."

He was about to ask Danna to look, but they were already across the yard, and he didn't care anymore.

All was quiet except for the raindrops splattering on gutters and the occasional whisper of wind blowing through the tall pines. After twenty minutes, they reached the second county road, Highway 79, crossed over to the other side, and headed north to the junction.

As they crossed the highway, Ben saw a road sign indicating they were at an altitude of 3,900 feet. He remembered when his family would drive up here every year for apple picking, and how the southbound road zig-zagged down for several miles before leveling off into a plain.

He wished they could take that route, but they'd be forced to traverse the entire plain and along Lake

Helsingor, where there's bound to be at least some people. *Better down than going up*, he thought. *But better alive than dead.*

Ben snapped to alertness.

Vroom!

The grating rumble of a terribly loud engine ripped through the air, and the earth shook underneath him as the machine grew closer.

"Get down!" the Stranger yelled, and he ducked into a roadside ditch.

The others did the same; and thirty seconds later an enormous monster truck barreled up the road, blasting scathing music that was a mix between heavy death metal and a chorus of livestock at the moment of their decapitation.

The truck was painted black except for bright red hazard symbols plastered on the hood and the front doors. Jutting out of the hubcaps of its six-foot-tall tires were twisted black spikes stained with what Ben assumed was rotting flesh.

The monster truck charged past them and swung a screeching left down the road that they had planned to take. Ben's heart sank. He knew they couldn't go that way anymore.

They were trapped. *In Wynola Springs*, he thought. *Go figure.*

Then he heard another engine. This one was different: it sounded cleaner, more fine-tuned. Within ten seconds an all-black Ferrari convertible flew past them. Four men clad in black samurai-style armor rode in it; two sat on the edge, clutching enormous machine guns. *A Ferrari convertible in the open rain*. Ben laughed. *What next?*

He felt a hard elbow; Danna was giving him a stern glare. He threw his hands up and mouthed, *What?*

She shot him a black look and put a finger to her lips.

For five long minutes, they lay in that muddy ditch. Ben felt his socks sop up moisture, and his nostrils flinched at the smell of earthworms and decomposing plants. He looked at his dirt-caked fingernails, and he squirmed as a slop of mud trickled down the back of his neck.

Sensing that there'd be no further traffic, the Stranger motioned them all to get closer, so Ben elbowed his way through the slop to get within earshot.

"Our options are getting rather limited," the Stranger said in a normal tone.

"We've got to head down and take the valley road," Ben said. "It's that, or we go home."

Cameron scoffed, but then he said: "Ben's right. We should wait until dark before we move out, though."

"Lay here, in the mud, until dark?" Danna asked. "You're kidding, right?"

"Or we can hole up in one of these houses," Cameron offered.

"Bad idea," Ben said quickly, remembering that shadow he thought he saw in the window. "I think we should head down now. It's raining; those thugs aren't gonna be as watchful. You know, the whole visibility thing?"

"Go on," the Stranger said, scraping a clump of mud out of his ear.

"If we wait until dark, who knows what scouts these scumbags have around here?"

"How would you know there'd be scouts?" Cameron asked. "Their base could be miles from here."

"I don't think so," Danna said. "I don't think they'd ride out in a convertible in the pouring rain unless it was just a short trip from their lair."

"Good point," Ben said. "Yeah, it could be up near the orchards. Lots of places for a secure location."

"It's not worth taking any chances," Danna added. "I think we should get as far away from here as possible."

"Down we go then," Cameron said.

Ben slowly got to his feet and wiped the oily muck that coated his rifle. They'd need to clean their weapons as soon as possible.

Climbing out of the ditch, he slipped and fell one last time as a final remembrance of Wynola Springs. He gave a mock salute toward the town and stomped after his brother.

* * *

The rain had begun to move further into the mountains and over to the deserts beyond, and the pale orb of the sun radiated through the clouds. If it were possible, the humidity became even more unbearable, almost suffocating, like trying to breathe through a wet plastic bag.

Drenched in sweat, Ben and the others let gravity quicken their pace as they descended the mountain, sometimes following along the road but most of the time hiking above or below it.

About mid-afternoon, the descent leveled off for a half-mile, and the terrain changed from scrubby pines to the chaparral of tangled shrubs and stunted trees. The sky was overcast, and the air still smelled of rain.

Before them was a vast plain of low-lying hills and grazing pastures. Ben followed the road as it snaked down into the valley and met Highway 77 at a three-way stop cornered by a gas station and an antique store. Next to the gas station was a sandwich shop that his family used to visit during their yearly apple-picking trip to Wynola Springs.

He traced Highway 77 until it went alongside a glinting mass of dark gray water: Lake Helsingor. It was broad and oblong, and the southern shore was manmade to be geometrically straight (Ben couldn't remember why). The northern end was hedged in by a golf course and an enormous, desolated RV park, now obscured by a dense fog that settled over that half of the lake. A dozen single home lots dotted the western shore; but the other side was barren except for an ancient grove of gnarled oaks and a large, reeking marsh.

The highway continued beyond the lake for several dozen miles through Indian reservation land and then turned into switchbacks until it met the city highway five miles east of the San Jacinto Pass.

"As soon as we make it down," Cameron said as he glassed the valley with his binoculars, "we'll hike along the east shore and then stay close to the ridge lines until we get to where the old highway starts to climb up to the Pass."

"Boy, I am not looking forward to that incline," Danna said, looking off as Highway 77 disappeared on the northern horizon.

"You know what I keep thinking?" Ben asked, taking a sip from his canteen. "Why haven't we looked for bicycles? It'd make it so much easier."

"Yeah, and you can have the one with the squeaky wheel that'll attract the vagabonds," Danna replied. "But don't get me wrong: I've thought of that too."

"Easy often ends up being the hardest," the Stranger said didactically. "Plus," he added with a smile, "riding a bike would be too much fun. We're not allowed to have fun on this trip."

Ben snorted. "*Trip*? You sound as if this is nothing more than a pleasure hike."

"It is for *me*," Cameron said with a grin. "I'm lovin' it."

"Yeah, you can keep saying that until one of us gets knocked off," Ben said coldly. "It's only a matter of time, right?"

"Hey," Danna said sharply, smacking his shoulder. "Lighten up. You're getting to be unbearable."

Ben gave Danna a sidelong glance. Her face was full of concern, frustration, and annoyance — all at once. A flush crept across his cheeks. *Why can't you keep your mouth shut?* he asked himself. The last thing he wanted was to push Danna away.

"I'm sorry," he muttered, looking down. "I'll try not to be such a jerk."

Danna looked him steadily in the eyes and said emphatically: "*Thank you.*"

Reverting to patrol formation, they now left the road and descended a rocky slope toward the lake. After a while, the downslope became grassier, and the going was easier; they had now entered the empty grazing lands.

Within weeks after the Surge, all the livestock in the region had been slaughtered for food, often eaten on the spot with or without fire. Ben's dad thought about raising goats at the retreat, but he worried their roaming around would attract unwanted attention.

Ben was relieved; goats weirded him out.

They passed an old farm tractor half-buried in the withered grasses and followed along a barbed wire fence that paralleled a string of scraggly birch trees until they reached an old irrigation canal that cut a straight line across the pasture. It was about six-feet wide; they had no choice but to cross it.

The canal was deeper than expected. Ben lost half a breath as he slithered down into the stagnant water, which rose to his waist. Holding his rifle high over his head, he quickly trawled through the muck until he made it to the other side and up the bank, not without slipping once back into the water.

Fortunately, they could toss their packs to the other side before crossing, and his goods would stay dry. But he was now covered in mud and downright miserable. But he had a promise to keep to Danna, and with a forced smile he broke the gloomy silence and told her he didn't see any minnows when he'd waded across the canal.

* * *

Dusk was fast approaching, which stirred up a biting wind. Ben shivered; his clothes were still sopping wet. There'd be no fire tonight, too. Not with the killer crazies marauding the countryside.

They hiked along the ridge of the knoll until their path gave way to a low-lying flatland. A few farmhouses were checkered along a two-lane road that cut through the middle of the valley. And about a quarter of a mile away a dense cluster of trees surrounded an old building set off a hundred yards from the road.

"That's the old mission, right?" Ben asked.

"Yup," Cameron replied. "It'll also be our hotel for the night. Stranger's orders."

"We're spending the night in a church?" Ben asked skeptically.

"Why not? Homeless people do it all the time."

"*And* technically we're homeless at the moment," Danna added.

"Maybe *you* are," Ben said. He pulled out his binoculars. The lenses were caked with dried dirty water. He tried wiping them with his finger, but that only made the smudge marks worse.

"A little trust won't hurt you," the Stranger quipped.

Ben shrugged. "Well, let's at least give it another fifteen minutes till it gets darker. I don't wanna get picked off crossing that open space."

He sat with his back against the rocky ledge and watched the darkness hasten the fading canvas of light to the other side of the desolated world. Since they'd started out, he'd been wondering more about what the rest of the world was like. Whether the entire planet was a barren apocalyptic wasteland. The farther away from the retreat, the more skeptical he'd become. Besides, if the world hadn't collapsed, then there'd for sure be some help. But then again, the robots aren't going away easily. His dad had said that a million times. Of course, nobody listened to him. *And here we are....*

Danna slid down next to him and took a swig from her canteen.

Beyond the western horizon, bright bursts of light lit up the sky. Deep, resonating booms followed. Three, four at a time.

"That's definitely not a storm," Danna said quietly. "Coming from the city?"

Ben nodded. "Yup, our final destination."

"Our final destination is the retreat," Danna said. "The city is just a pit stop."

Ben watched the horizon intently. A cosmic blast of pure white light lit up the entire sky, followed by a thunderous boom. Ben felt the reverberation.

"That's some heavy artillery," Cameron said, jumping down from the ledge. "Looks like mankind is putting up a fight after all."

"Could be the robots putting up the fight," the Stranger said. "After all, they know how to press buttons."

"Not for long," Cameron grunted as he slung his rifle over his shoulder. "Let's head down."

With Cameron at the front, they crept slowly down the hill, fifteen paces apart. As they squeezed through a pasture gate, Ben spotted the remains of a cow half buried in the grass. The body cavity was sunken; its insides were ripped out; and the skinned head was four feet away from the rest of it. The eyes were plucked out, and its front teeth seemed to gnash at him with a delirious grin.

He blinked hard and shook his head. The darkness was messing with him. Or he was coming down with a cold.

The ground sloped downward until they came within a hundred feet of the mission. The light and boom show from over the hills had died down except for a final flash that illuminated the stained-glass window in the church's bell tower.

Ben remembered learning about the missions back in seventh grade. This one, Mission Santa Clarita, if he remembered correctly, was almost three hundred years old, built when the first padres came over the sundering seas to show the local Native American tribes the pathway to salvation.

The church was built in the adobe style: long, narrow . . . and just old. Gnarled olive trees grew around the brick paved churchyard, and a cracked fountain filled with a half-inch of dirty rainwater stood in an uneven pathway that led to thick double doors. In the opposite direction, the path led to an empty parking lot by the road.

The Stranger signaled to move forward.

Finger on the safety of his rifle, Ben darted across the yard and met the others at the front doors.

"You ever get the feeling like we're being watched?" Cameron whispered, just a hair too loud for Ben's comfort.

Danna rolled her eyes.

"Well," Cameron carried on with a smirk; "I don't feel like that now, so this place is heavenly — no pun intended."

"I'm so glad," Ben muttered. "Your intuitions truly have kept us alive."

"Someday you'll thank me for it, little brother," Cameron replied.

Then they each grabbed a handle and pulled.

Unlocked.

Strange, Ben thought. He stepped in, and his footsteps gently echoed across the expanse. The air was stuffy, yet clean, with scents of sticky wood polish and incense. It was dark inside but for a single red candle set on a fancy table at the far side of the church. *Looks like a banquet for one*, he thought. The candle cast a flickering crimson glow around it, reflecting especially upon a golden box in the center of the table.

Ben turned around. "Someone's here."

The Stranger nodded his head gravely and unslung his rifle. "Yes. But we'll be safer here than at any other place during our mission."

"I don't get it," Ben said, furrowing his brow. He glanced at Cameron, who shrugged. "Danna?"

"It'll be okay," she said. She, like Ben before, was shivering.

"Okay, then."

Once they were inside, Cameron shut the doors and slid his hiking pole through the handles.

"This stairway leads up to the choir loft," the Stranger said in a low voice. "Us guys can set up there for the night. Danna, you can have the sacristy if you'd like some privacy."

"The what?" Ben asked.

"It's the room in the back where the priest gets ready to say Mass," Danna explained. "Like putting on the vestments and such."

"Oh."

Ben didn't know what a vestment was either. His family hadn't been to church in a long time. Heck, he didn't even know if he believed in God anymore. Not since Faith. Especially not since Mom and Dad.

He'd given it more thought, however. He'd tried to pray. Many times, in fact, since it all happened. Nothing but silence.

The most deafening silence he could imagine.

Who knows? Maybe he wasn't praying right. Or maybe he didn't deserve to have God talk back to him. *Just a few words of assurance would be all I need*, he thought. Just *something*.

"I'll check out the choir loft," he announced. He was tired. Maybe more tired than everyone else. But he'll be darned if he showed it. Especially to Cameron.

He tip-toed up the stairs, clearing the cobwebs and taking care not to knock over the piles of old hymnals stacked on the stairway. The choir loft was larger than he'd expected. The front half was lined with two rows of chairs with the fearsome organ on the far side. Behind the chairs were a half dozen cots folded and stacked against a piano.

What a coincidence, Mr. Stranger, he thought.

He leaned over the balcony and eyed the Stranger. The man cracked a smile. Ben rolled his eyes and waved them up.

"Any weak floorboards?" Danna called up. "The last thing I wanna do is die in a church."

Ben looked down at her with a teasing smile and said: "C'mon, Danna, *you're being unbearable.* Lighten up."

Once they'd all made it up, they dropped their packs in a chorus of weary thuds.

Cameron picked up an old apple core. "Looks like someone's been here recently."

"It looks pretty old," the Stranger said, examining it. He lifted his arm to toss it away.

"Hey!" Cameron exclaimed. "I'll eat what's left of it."

"That's disgusting," Danna said.

"What, you've never heard of apple crisps?"

* * *

They spent the next half hour setting up for the night. After sleeping on the cold hard ground for the past few nights, Ben felt like they'd booked a room at a Hilton. He wanted to dive right onto his cot and check out until dawn, but he knew he'd better eat something first.

They split a bag of jerky and three protein bars. Afterward, they drew lots for the first watch.

It fell to him and the Stranger. Sleep would have to wait.

Ben lifted two chairs and set them next to a small window overlooking the churchyard. Placing his rifle across his lap, he peered outside.

It was a black night. The clouds hung low, which stifled the moonlight and blended the rolling hills into an endless sea of darkness. It'd be hard to spot someone—or something.

He thought about pulling out his night vision goggles; but the batteries barely last fifteen minutes, and he didn't want to use them unless absolutely necessary.

The Stranger sat down on the other stool and draped a knit blanket over his shoulders.

"How are you holding up?" he asked.

"Doesn't that thing stink?"

The Stranger smiled. "It hasn't been on an old organ lady for a long time. The mothball smell is pretty much gone."

Ben wrinkled his nose then glanced over at Cameron, then at Danna. Both were fast asleep.

"So?" the Stranger asked.

"So what?"

"I asked how you were doing."

"I'm all right," Ben answered, perhaps too sharply. "Why?"

"Just wondering. This isn't all exactly easy, you know."

Ben shrugged. "Still alive, right?"

The Stranger pulled the blanket tighter over his shoulders. Ben could tell he had more to say.

"Just say it."

"I was just thinking. . . ." the Stranger said slowly. "You know that military officer—the one who told your father about the government giving his research to the UN?"

"Yeah?"

"He was *my* dad."

Ben leaned forward. That made sense. "So, he ruined his career too?"

"I think my dad would say he was just doing his duty. God first; family second; America third — that was his motto."

"Yeah, definitely not *our* dad's motto," Ben replied. "Work first; prepare for the doomsday second; third, who knows." He lowered his head. "I guess I shouldn't be saying that, him being gone."

"It's all right."

Ben picked at a chunk of dried mud on his boot. "Sometimes I forget about them. My parents, you know? For two, three days. But then I remember them at some random moment. And then I feel so guilty."

"Like you betrayed them?"

"Kind of. But then again, when I do think about them. . . ."

"It hurts."

Ben nodded. "It's kinda like a vicious cycle. Whether to think about them all the time and all the bad things that happened, or just accept that they're dead . . . and maybe the pain will go away."

"Pain will never go away as long as there's evil in this world," the Stranger said, looking out the window. "It's unavoidable. I think when we experience pain, when we face it head on, it changes us. For better or for worse. For me, I always hope for the better."

"So you're saying I shouldn't try to move on?"

The Stranger brushed a piece of grass off his pants. "Just keep them close to you," he replied; "no matter how much you think about them. I think it was Cicero who said the life of the dead is placed in the memory of the living."

"And photo albums."

"Didn't know those still existed," the Stranger said with a smile.

"Dad always kept photos around the house. He was old school."

"You were close with him, weren't you?"

Ben gave a half-hearted shrug. "I liked tech stuff; he did too. Apparently, that made us 'close.' People made a bigger deal about it than it was. 'Two peas-in-a-pod,' they'd say. The truth is, he wasn't around much; and when he was, he was just *tired.* Just checked out, you know? By the time I got to middle school, I didn't even bother showing him things that I'd built or my cool science projects."

The Stranger nodded.

"With—" Ben swallowed. "Well, when Cameron started to get into trouble, things just kind of fell apart. Dad was gone all the time. And Mom, you know, was at the hospital. People changed. Then everything happened so fast."

"He'd be proud of you for what you and Cameron did. Saving all those kids."

Ben scoffed. "Not if he knew the other things I've had to do," he said, patting his rifle. "Fourteen-year-olds who kill people go to prison. Not even to juvie. I mean, I've never even kept count."

The Stranger leaned his back against the wall and nodded solemnly. "You did what you had to do, as terrible as that sounds."

Ben paused. "I got kicked out of school, did you know that? The year before it happened."

The Stranger shook his head.

"Yeah, I got into a fight during the middle of class. Just some random kid."

"Yeah?"

"I hurt him. Pretty bad."

"How bad?"

Ben swallowed. "Broken nose. Concussion."

"I'm sure you're sorry."

"It's not that. It's just crazy, you know? I beat up that kid; really hurt him bad. And like a month later, I'm shooting people like it's nothing."

"It's not nothing."

"Funny thing is, I can't even remember what the fight was about. After I got kicked out, my mom put me in Sierra Madre. She thought it'd be a good influence on me. Religion and all that."

"Religion and all that, huh," the Stranger said. "Smart lady."

Ben scoffed. "Well, apparently I didn't know what a sacristy was."

"So, freshman year, the new kid at a new school."

"Yeah, it stunk. Most of the kids in my class went to middle school together, so everybody already knew each other."

"But you knew Tomás, so that helped."

"He's not exactly that cool if you didn't notice." Ben chuckled. "So many things were stupid, though. We had to wear uniforms. Sure, you didn't have to worry about wearing cool clothes, but everyone was into making their hair look good. I spent forever every morning trying to get my hair right."

"I remember those days," the Stranger said with a smile. "If you didn't get your hair right, your day was ruined. Now your hair doesn't really matter anymore." He tousled his matted mane.

"Yeah," Ben replied with a grim smile.

The Stranger watched him, waiting for him to continue.

Ben pursed his lips and looked out the window again. "Do you remember the *first* person you killed?" he asked quietly. "*I* do. Day after the Surge. We stopped at a small gas station to siphon anything left into the van. Two men jumped us. Thought Cameron and I were just two scared kids. We put a bullet each in their hearts."

The Stranger leaned forward.

"Not one kid spoke the rest of the way to the retreat," Ben added. "And I shot another man by the time we got there."

The Stranger was silent.

Ben thought he was giving him that look that older people give when they think that look will make a kid feel better. He rolled his eyes. "You probably wanna say that I don't deserve all this, etcetera."

"You don't."

Ben stiffened. Pointing his finger out the window, he said: "Those kids back at the retreat? They don't deserve any of this. I mean, they're all alone! Their parents are dead; their families are gone. How messed up is that?"

"They're your responsibility, and you're feeling the weight of that."

Ben snorted. "To say the least. They all need therapy or something."

He thought about Ron. He thought about Tabitha, three weeks before. And on and on. He even thought about the kid he'd beaten up. What was his name? Frank?

"You don't think it's hopeless? All of this?"

The Stranger shook his head. "As long as there's still good in this world, then no."

Ben clicked his tongue. "Good? In this world? I don't know, man. Look all around you. There's not too much of a difference between good and bad these days."

The Stranger rubbed his chin and looked out the window. "Goodness still exists, even in the shadows and the pain. Friendship, courage, sacrifice; these have to come from somewhere. And it's usually when we're faced with evil or terrible difficulties that we prove our true friendship, find our courage." His voice grew quiet, then he added, "And be willing to make those sacrifices."

"But that doesn't mean it's okay for people to do evil things just so good can come out of it. That's messed up."

"No, it doesn't make it okay. But perhaps our goodness, no matter where it comes from, won't only save our friends, but also the people *out there*. Even the bad ones. Heck, it could even save the world."

"I'll see it before I believe it," Ben said, looking outside.

"I think you will before this is all over," the Stranger said with a soft smile. "Just remember: life is a gift. Sure, we have death, violence, vagabonds, sickness, you name it—"

"Cannibals."

"Yes, and cannibals. But these things are all just a part of life. And even though they can overwhelm us, like a never-ending nightmare, it doesn't mean that's all there is. That's not life. *You are*. I am. Cameron. Danna. Izzy. All of us. And as long as there's life, there's goodness."

Ben closed his eyes and rubbed the crown of his nose. "So, what you're saying is just because the world is over and everything has gone to pot doesn't mean that we're — I mean, humanity — done for? It's just more like—"

"Consider it a change of scenery," the Stranger said with a small grin.

Ben shook his head and smiled. *Maybe this guy isn't so bad after all*, he thought. *Kind of like a warrior monk slash guidance counselor.*

* * *

Late in the night, Ben awoke. He'd had a strange dream, the type one remembered what happened in it for only a moment, then it was lost forever. He rubbed his eyes and glanced over at his brother and the Stranger. Both were asleep.

He turned over to his other side. Danna's cot was empty. She must be on watch.

But she wasn't sitting at the window.

A beam of pale moonlight passed through the window, past the choir loft and toward the far side of the church.

Wood creaked down below.

He pulled out his pistol, slowly rolled off the cot, and peered over the balcony rail.

Two pews back from the altar area knelt Danna. Illuminated by the moonlight, her hands were clasped together, and her head was fixated on the golden box.

Ben couldn't see her face, but he knew she must look beautiful in the flickering candlelight.

He was confused. But then a wave of peace washed over him. He felt happy for Danna. Almost grateful. But to Who, he didn't know.

He stepped back slowly, returned to his cot, and fell into a deep sleep.

CHAPTER 13

WHILE AWAY

The four arose early to a windless and gloomy morning. After a small snack, they packed their things and quietly slipped out of the church.

Ben felt refreshed and tired simultaneously. He wanted to push it to the back of his mind, but he couldn't stop thinking about the Stranger's hope that things could change. He wasn't ready to believe it just yet.

They hiked north along the eastern side of the lake until the shoreline disappeared into cattails and rotted, mossy mounds. Cameron waded into the sharp reeds and signaled for them to follow.

Suddenly, several distant gunshots pierced the air, followed by a roaring engine. The three crouched down and ran low into the bog to meet Cameron. There they hunkered down in the sawgrass and waited.

Ben could hear nothing except for a turtle plopping into the water and the dry reeds rubbing and scratching against each other.

After ten minutes, it began to rain. Again.

"What are we gonna do?" he asked sharply, wiping the water from his face with his fingers. "Those gunshots sounded pretty far away."

"I think we should work our way through this bog for as long as we can until we get to the other side," Cameron said.

Danna bent down and tightened her boot laces. "It reeks," she said, scrunching her nose.

"Yes, this is what marshes smell like," Cameron replied. His face softened, and he reached into a vest pocket. "Want my bandana to wrap around your nose?"

Danna, taken aback, smiled sheepishly and shook her head.

Ben snickered. "I bet that thing stinks worse than this swamp."

"How about I shove it down your throat, and you can find out?"

"Okay, lead the way, Cameron," the Stranger said quickly.

Ben wondered how this guy could put up with it.

The rain continued as they waded single file deeper into the bog. Towering cattails swallowed them, and

Ben felt like an ant picking its way across a waterlogged football field.

They jumped from mound to mound, and more than once Ben miscalculated a step found himself up to his knees in sludge.

It was eerily silent. Ben expected to hear the usual sounds of croaking frogs or buzzing insects, but all he heard was the *plop-plop-thump-plop* of the rain and the sucking sound of his boots as they squished through the mud.

They all heard it at once.

Music. Faint. But nearby. In the marsh.

They dropped to the ground in unison. Ben raised his rifle and squeezed his temples to hear better. He could barely make out a song:

> *I could while away the hours, conferrin' with the flowers*
> *Consultin' with the rain.*
> *And my head I'd be scratchin' while*
> *my thoughts were busy hatchin'*
> *If I only had a brain.*

It sounded like it was coming from an old, phonograph record player. *Impossible*, he thought. He looked behind him. Danna and the Stranger were stone-faced, listening to the music and trying to come up with their own guesses.

Stooping low, he hobbled over to his brother.

"Should we check it out?" Cameron whispered.

"Tsk. Music playing in the middle of a swamp? We're heavily armed. Heck, yeah."

Ben wasn't a natural risk taker, but he made exceptions when it involved technology and related mysteries.

Cameron turned around and motioned to Danna and the Stranger to stay put, despite their silent, gesticulating protests. Glancing at Ben, he nodded forward, and they stealthily waded into the soft mire and sharp reeds.

After a minute of slogging through the reek, they spotted a clearing up ahead in which Ben could make out the tops of scraggly trees. *Dry ground.*

Meanwhile, the music played on, softly and sweetly:

> *When a man's an empty kettle he should be on his mettle,*
> *And yet I'm torn apart.*
> *Just because I'm presumin' that I could be kind-a-human,*
> *If I only had heart.*

Suddenly Ben's eyes lit up and his heart skipped a beat. He should've told Cameron they needed to fall back, but he was overtaken by that natural curiosity for technical marvels that had served him well in the past. Or not.

He tugged on his brother's sleeve and whispered: "Get the rail gun."

* * *

Cameron slowly set his pack down on a patch of dead grass and pulled the electromagnetic rifle out of a large side holster. It was disassembled into two pieces. Aligning the electrode rails with the receivers and the stock, he inserted the rails into the other two parts and pushed gently until he heard a click and a soft beep.

"Let me see it," Ben said. Taking it from his brother, he examined it admiringly for the tenth time in the last four days. A plasma railgun had never been converted into a handheld weapon before. *They must've perfected the mitigation techniques of the coaxial accelerators—*

"What are you doing?" Cameron hissed.

Ben flinched. "Checking for the charge," he whispered. "Three colors — see? Red, orange, and green. It's a three-step process to charge it. Red means no charge, orange means it's charging, and green means it's fully charged. I charged it before we left, but we only have three shots; it takes sixty seconds to load each shot."

"I know how to use it, remember?"

"Yeah, but Dad must've charged it for you when he left it in the cache—"

"Stop talking, Ben," Cameron whispered sharply. "We doing this or not?"

"Lead the way, loser."

Ben's heart raced as they quietly pushed aside reed stalks and moved toward the clearing. As they drew closer, he saw large wooden spears thrust into the ground, and decapitated heads of dead fish were punctured through each spearhead. His stomach twisted in revulsion as he crawled past the reeking head of a large catfish.

He cast a sidelong glance at his brother: Cameron's face had paled, and he was staring straight ahead.

By this time, they had inched up to the edge of the clearing and hid behind a small mangled swamp tree.

A spike of adrenaline hit his stomach, but it quickly grew into a gnawing uneasiness. He rubbed his forehead. *Maybe we should turn back. . . .*

Ben heard a clinking sound above him. Ornate dream catchers of various shapes and sizes hung from the tree limbs; each was adorned with feathers from different birds along with shiny beads fastened to leather straps and shoelaces.

A wave of goosebumps washed over him. Something had moved in the clearing. He dropped to one knee for a clearer view. *Yeah, just what I thought.*

Two vagabonds were at the far side of the clearing.

Identical in design, they both wore long, multicolored trench coats, and soggy brown boots ripped at the toes. Their blazing neon eyes illuminated their upturned mouths, which were crudely painted red with strokes that swept up to form mischievous, clownish smiles.

One was comfortably reclining on a large, moss-covered rock scrawled with painted pictures of sickly stick figures. It wore a raggedy blonde wig with several dangling pheasant feathers, and on its face were several paint stripes like tribal markings.

A large black crow was perched on one of its fingers; the bird cocked and tilted its head sharply as if it were swaying to the music that played from the vagabond's mouth-speaker.

The other vagabond stood next to the rock, trying to attract the bird's attention. A mohawk of long feathers adorned its filthy and mangled black wig; and three sloppy, faded yellow stripes smeared the sides of its face.

Ben met his brother's wide-eyed gaze with wonderment.

Cameron gestured at the railgun and mouthed: "*Three shots.*"

Ben gave him a thumbs-up and crouched back down. He stood up slowly to get an open shot; and as he did so, his head struck one of the dangling dreamcatchers, sounding off a dull clang like a wooden wind chime.

The music stopped.

Cameron froze, and Ben yanked on his brother's rucksack, telling him to get back down.

At that moment, the crow launched into the air, and with a great fit of cawing, flew directly at them. The bird swooped down on them and landed on the branch above them. *Caw! Caw!*

Ben and Cameron flattened themselves against the soggy ground. Both vagabonds jerked up and fixed their eyes at their direction.

Ben didn't know if they had heat sensors; he assumed that they did.

Suddenly the crow lifted off and flew behind them, and Ben felt the *whoosh* of its flapping wings blow across the back of his neck. He grinned in relief, but his brother dug an elbow into his side.

Ben slowly turned around. Ten feet behind him, a monstrous vagabond stood on a fallen log. The crow was perched haughtily on its shoulder.

A foot taller than the other two, the vagabond was draped with a large Navajo blanket; and over its cranium was the skinned head of a massive wild boar. The tusks and snout lay on its metal forehead like a barbarous crown, and the rest of the carcass dangled down its back. Weaved into the boar's hide was a string of giant fish heads that formed ridge-like dragon spikes along its spine.

The vagabond raised a crude wooden spear in its hand, and its red eyes flashed in the morning murk. Then it charged.

For the first time in his life, Ben saw his brother freeze in shock. He snatched the railgun out of Cameron's hands, and without aiming, pulled the trigger.

The charger accelerated a toroid of plasma down the two rails; and with an unnerving hum and a sharp, fizzling pop, the weapon fired and hit the vagabond just as it was driving its spear into Cameron's heart.

The pulse hit the vagabond dead on. Its legs stiffened, and its arms shot straight out from each side. The boar's head slipped off and fell with a thud as the robot wobbled forward, stumbled a step backward, then finally collapsed in a pile of twitching metal limbs.

Ben dropped the gun and grabbed his brother, holding him up. "You all right?" he cried.

Cameron stuck his finger in the hole in his shirt that was pierced by the spear. "Yeah, man," he replied shakily. "The body armor stopped the blow. Good thing it didn't go for my neck."

Ben let out a deep, ragged sigh of relief. Then he remembered the other two vagabonds. He picked up the railgun and aimed toward the clearing.

They were gone.

At that moment, the railgun beeped. A blue light flashed. *What the—?* Ben flipped a small switch next to the safety. Disabled. *Stupid thing's not waterproofed!*

"What's wrong with it?"

"Technical difficulty," Ben replied shortly. He looked into his brother's eyes. "We need to run."

Jumping to their feet, they turned eastward to get out of the marsh. Within two running steps, the other two vagabonds stepped in their way, spears in hand.

"Quick! Grab some mud!" Ben knelt and scooped up a heaping pile of muck. "Go for the eyes!"

The vagabonds charged them; and just as they were within skewering distance, Ben and Cameron flung the mud in the robots' faces.

The vagabonds staggered and stepped backward, clutching their faces.

"Run!"

They leaped past the robots and dove and ran — and stumbled — toward the mountains. Within thirty seconds, Danna and the Stranger were at their side.

"You two are idiots; you know that?" Danna barked.

"No time to argue," Cameron said quickly. "But for the first time, I agree with you."

Suddenly a spear flew from behind them, and with unnatural precision and force, it struck Danna in the back — her rucksack, fortunately — and propelled her face first into the muck.

In one smooth movement, she jumped to her feet, unclipped a smoke grenade from her belt, and threw it in the vagabond's direction.

Ben grimaced as the grenade plopped into a puddle of slime and fizzled out. "Good idea though," he said, panting.

"Faster, guys," the Stranger said calmly.

Ben glanced over his shoulder. The vagabonds were twenty feet behind, struggling through the muck. Up ahead was a dense bracket of tall grass.

"There!" he said, pointing. "Follow me!"

He led them into the grass, which grew in dense clusters on mounds surrounded by mud flats.

"These robots definitely have thermal imaging trackers," Ben said, dropping to his knees. "We need to mask out heat."

Taking off his pack, he plopped into the mud and rolled around, smearing a heaping scoop of sludge across his face. "Do it, now!"

Danna, Cameron, and the Stranger fell to the ground and covered themselves with muck. They forced themselves as deep as they could into the mud until only the whites of their eyes could be seen.

"Don't move," Ben gagged as mud seeped into his mouth. "The slightest motion of warm skin will give you away."

The sloshing suck of the vagabonds' boots grew louder as they hunted their prey.

A cloud of gnats buzzed around Ben's face and tickled and tormented his nose. Trying not to sneeze, he concentrated on watching the little air bubbles float to the top of the mud and pop.

He could hear Cameron's rapid breathing next to him, and his heart was hammering in his chest like it wanted to betray him.

The vagabonds stopped. Ben guessed they were ten feet away.

Silence.

The sloshing steps began again and moved farther away until Ben could hear them no more.

They waited another ten minutes in the cold mud. Then he thought of leeches. He hated leeches more than anything on earth.

"I think we're good," he said, rising perhaps too swiftly. "But we need to get outta here — now. We actually might have a chance."

Cameron threw up his hands. "Might have a chance?"

"Complex environments swamp a robot's computations (no pun intended), which bogs (again, no pun intended) down their decision-making and increases their probability of error. This swamp? Complex environment. We need to keep them in here as long as possible."

"How are we going to do that?" the Stranger asked.

"Let's split up, stay within each other's eyesight, and zigzag as we all head east."

"It confuses their tracking," Danna said, nodding. "Got it."

They left in four directions, all facing east, and disappeared into the reek.

* * *

Danna was the first to spot a vagabond. Or Danna was the first that the vagabond spotted. It had crept up upon her left flank and was now within a stone's throw. She picked up her pace, but the muck fought her every step.

The vagabond was fewer than ten feet away when Ben crossed ten feet in front of it, heading in the opposite direction from Danna.

The robot stopped and shifted its head back and forth, eyes blinking twice, and lurched after Ben.

Danna pumped her fist and moved east again.

Ben was running out of breath. His pack was over seventy-five pounds, and his soaked clothing weighed him down even more. He could hear the robot struggling to pursue him.

Naturally, he had to glance behind him, and at once he was face-first in the mud. He later concluded that tripping over that slimy log was a stroke of luck.

As he stood back up, he grabbed another pile of muck and waited until the robot was within five feet — then hurled it at his face.

But this time the vagabond dodged it — *it adapted!* — and raised its spear to strike.

At that moment, the Stranger popped up from behind the vagabond with a handful of mud; and half-leaping on the robot's back, he smeared the muck into the robot's eye cavities.

The robot froze, and the Stranger used that split-second to take two steps back and charge into it shoulder-first.

Ben raised his hand to tell him to stop, but it was too late: The Stranger rammed into the robot and at once fell backward, wincing in pain and grabbing his shoulder. The vagabond barely moved from the impact and turned to face the Stranger. But then it froze again.

Ben had to act quickly. He ripped the wig off the robot's head, reached around the back of its skull, and curling his fingers upward, he felt around for a pressure button. The vagabond flinched. *C'mon, where is it!* He pulled his fingers out of the skull and wiped the mud off them, then he tried again. *There you are.* He pressed the button, and with a violent jerk, the robot slumped forward.

"*Now* you can try ramming into him," Ben said, letting out a deep breath.

"I'll pass," the Stranger replied dryly.

Ben double checked that he deactivated the robot correctly, then he joined the Stranger and together they stumbled their way through the marsh and out into the open.

Behind them, the vagabond's eyes blinked, and its fingers twitched.

When Ben and the Stranger cleared the marsh, Cameron was already out, but he was fifty feet north and waving frantically at them to hurry.

"Where's Danna?" Ben cried, his heart dropping.

Just then she burst through the reeds twenty feet south. Wiping mud-caked hair out of her face, she hobbled toward them with a dreadful limp.

Ben grabbed the Stranger's elbow. "Go meet up with my brother; I'll help Danna."

The Stranger nodded and trotted toward Cameron, who was anxiously jumping up and down.

Ben ran as fast as he could and met Danna halfway. "Let me take your bag," he said breathlessly.

"Thanks, I'm okay" she gasped, waving him off. "I hit my knee on a rock."

Ben lifted her arm around his shoulder, and together they limped to join the other two. When they were nearly caught up, Cameron waved them to move faster then ran northward out of their sight.

Ben and Danna picked up their pace; and rounding a large thicket of cattails, they saw Cameron and the Stranger standing next to a dirty old Jeep Wrangler.

Ben blinked twice. *What luck!*

"C'mon!" his brother yelled impatiently. "The keys were in the ignition!"

They lifted their packs into the back and scrambled in. Ben flung his head back on the seat, wheezing and gasping for air. His teeth ground against the dirt still caked in his molars.

Cameron shifted into drive, not before adjusting the mirrors.

"Hey, wait a minute!"

Ben spun around. A hulking, overweight man in hunter's camouflage tumbled out of the cattails with a large black garbage bag slung over his shoulder.

"That's my Jeep!" the man hollered.

"Go! Go!" Danna cried, slapping Cameron's shoulder.

Cameron let off the clutch and stepped on the accelerator.

"No, stop!" Ben shouted. "We can't leave him here!"

Cameron slammed on the brakes and slapped his hands on the steering wheel.

"We can't leave him here to die," Ben insisted. He made eye contact with the Stranger, who was gripping his pistol.

"Ben's right," the Stranger said, still trying to catch his wind. "That'd be wrong of us. In fact, I wouldn't be here right now if he hadn't picked *me* up."

Muttering under his breath, Cameron shifted the Jeep in neutral and pulled the parking brake.

"I'll handle this," the Stranger said. He hopped out of the car and walked toward the man, who was trying his best to catch up with them. He held up his pistol and barked: "Hands on your head! Keep walking. Move it!"

The man obeyed the Stranger's orders; and as he walked toward the Jeep, he closed his eyes and let out a ragged breath.

"Come closer," the Stranger ordered. Holding the gun up with his right hand, he approached the man and patted him down for weapons, only finding a large Bowie knife.

He was a heavyset man, pasty yet sunburned, with a shiny, round, and flabby face. His nervous, eager eyes were small and blue, his brows thin and arched, which accentuated his rotund features. He had large ears and a small mouth set above a clean-shaven double chin.

"What's in the bag?" the Stranger asked.

"Cattail shoots, sir," the man answered nervously but plainly. "For cattail soup."

"Who are you making soup for?"

"Just me, sir," the man said, trying to keep a blank face.

The Stranger cocked his pistol and aimed it at his head. "Who's the soup for?"

"I've got people, sir. They're countin' on me."

"What people? How many?"

The man paused. He straightened up, suddenly stouthearted. "You'll have to kill me then, sir. I ain't givin' 'em up."

The Stranger motioned at the man with his pistol. "Get in."

"I ain't takin' you to 'em, sir," the man said, his tone a mix of fear and indignation. "Like I said, you're gonna have to kill me."

"Look, *sir*," the Stranger said, dropping the gun to his side; "we're not going to kill you. If we were, you'd already be on the ground."

Danna leaned out of the Jeep and said: "Sir, there are bad things in that swamp. Either you trust us and get in, or you're gonna have to pull a spear out of your back."

The man looked hesitatingly at the Stranger, who nodded affirmatively. He clutched the black garbage bag and moped over to the Jeep. The Stranger ordered him into the front seat, where a smiling Cameron, cradling a twelve-gauge shotgun, greeted him.

"You left your gun in your truck?" Cameron asked with a smirk. "C'mon, dude. How come you're still alive?"

The man sat there stone-faced as the Stranger climbed into the backseat and stuck his gun into the back of the man's neck. "Feel that?"

The man nodded slowly.

The Stranger lowered his gun and leaned back in the seat. "Good," he said, shooting Ben and Danna a quick wink.

Cameron laughed and slapped the man on his shoulder. "C'mon, man, we're not gonna hurt you. What's your name?"

"Oswald," he replied firmly, regaining his composure.

"I'm Cameron; this here's my brother, Ben; the one-and-only Danna; and this dude forgot his name, so we just call him the 'Stranger.'"

Oswald turned around to greet them, and he looked past them. "And what do you call them things?" he said, pointing over Ben's shoulder.

Ben spun around again. Two vagabonds were rushing at them, each armed with two spears. And one of them was the robot that he'd deactivated.

"Hit it, Cam!"

Cameron shifted into first gear and let off the clutch. The Jeep lurched, then it stalled. He looked up sheepishly. "It's been awhile since I drove a stick!" Putting the Jeep back into neutral, he restarted the truck and gunned it.

"Head for that gravel road," Oswald exclaimed. "I trust y'all!"

Cameron nodded and elbowed the man. "I think you're gonna be all right, Ozzy."

"The name's Oswald!"

Meanwhile, Ben had taken apart the railgun and pulled a pinch of stringy plant matter out of the capacitors. He rubbed the terminals with a dry rag from his pack and was blew on them to dry them out. As the Jeep got moving, he snapped the gun together. Red light. He grinned as he primed the charger — sixty seconds.

By this time the vagabonds had picked up speed and were gaining on them. Ben looked at the speedometer: 45 mph.

"Faster!"

"This thing's a dog," Cameron shouted. "I'm trying!" He passed the shotgun back to Danna. "Here, make yourself useful!"

Danna cocked the shotgun and turned around and rested the barrel on the backseat. She squeezed her left eye shut and sighted on the black-haired vagabond fewer than ten feet away. She pulled the trigger and —

boom! — a lick of flame then the pattering sound of a thousand lead shots hitting solid metal.

The force of the shot tripped up the vagabond, and it lost balance and stumbled to the ground. Getting back up, it ran after them as if nothing had happened.

Ben watched the railgun shift from red to orange to green. The blonde-wigged vagabond picked up speed and was soon within leaping distance.

He raised the railgun to fire, but at that moment a spear whizzed past his head and smashed through the Jeep's front windshield, but not without grazing Oswald's shoulder first.

Ben blinked and set his sights on the robot. It wasn't there. Suddenly there was a smash as the robot landed on the back end of the Jeep.

For a split-second, Ben thought the leering vagabond made eye contact with him, which made it even more enjoyable for him as he pulled the trigger and watched the robot get plastered with an invisible mass of plasmodic energy.

"I win," he said triumphantly.

Without a sound, the robot toppled backward and fell into a tangled heap in the middle of the road.

Oswald turned back around to face them. "Nice to meet y'all!" he said enthusiastically. He then winced in pain and clutched his shoulder.

CHAPTER 14

THE ARX

It was midday now, and the clouds hung low over the land and covered the hills with a pale haze. Ben leaned back, closed his eyes, the wind blowing in his mud-caked face, enjoying the comfort of the ride after so many miles of hiking on foot.

They were on Indian reservation land, and the road passed into a small valley surrounded by low-lying hills. He didn't care where they were going; he just hoped wherever it was would be as comfortable as this limousine ride.

"Look!" Danna exclaimed, elbowing him.

Ben opened his tired eyes and saw a tall tower looming in the middle of the valley a quarter-of-a-mile ahead. Rubbing his face, he sat up straight and leaned forward. *What the—*

It wasn't a tower but an engineering marvel. The entire structure, about one hundred feet high, was a mishmash of mobile home trailers stacked haphazardly on top of each other. Each trailer was a different color — some blue, others white, one yellow — and was connected to the others by winding staircases and metal mesh balconies. And all of it was supported by an intricate system of rusted steel scaffolding and massive hanging wires latched to iron supports in the ground.

Attached to the northern side of the tower were two leaning grain silos and several forest green railroad boxcars. At the top of the tower, hanging from the balcony of the highest trailer, an enormous American flag draped over an entire side of the trailer underneath.

Several mobile homes and RVs were parked at the base of the tower, and the entire compound was surrounded by a chain-link fence topped with barbed wire.

As they neared, the Stranger held up his pistol and poked the back of Oswald's flabby neck as a reminder.

"I know, I know," the man replied. "Just pay attention here, Cameron. We're gonna come on in real close, so you better slow down."

"What are you talking about?" Cameron snapped.

"The way in," Oswald replied, peering and squinting over the dashboard. He held up his hand. "Here, hold up."

Cameron came to a stop and glared at Oswald.

"Now pull off the road at this rock, nice and steady. Now take a sharp left. Slower! Now you're gonna come up on this log; drive right up past it and then hang a right and stay straight. Yep, that's it. Good. Now you can get back on up the road."

"What was all that for?" Danna asked.

"Minefield," Ben answered. He felt beads of sweat on his forehead.

Cameron pulled up to the gate. Two armed guards clothed in hunter's camouflage stormed out of a small trailer and strode over.

"Nice and easy," the Stranger said quietly in Oswald's ear. He looked at the other three. "Everybody loaded? Keep an eye out for snipers up above."

As the men approached, Oswald held up his arms and, in a friendly voice, said: "It's all right, boys. Just got ourselves a little misunderstandin', is all."

The men stopped just inside the gate and held up their shotguns.

"Oswald's right," the Stranger called out. "We came upon his Jeep, thought it was abandoned, got attacked by androids, and we picked him up. We don't want any trouble." He paused, then added: "But we're all armed."

The men didn't reply, and one of them looked up at the tower. Ten seconds later, a heavy door swung down from underneath the bottom trailer with a steely clang. A metal ladder slid to the ground, and an elderly man climbed down slowly. As he made his way toward them, Ben saw he had only one arm.

"What's going on here?" the old man demanded, coming up to the gate.

He was tall and lean, with a hard face lined with wrinkles of one who has done much and seen much. His eagle eyes were a bright, sharp blue, his nose long and angular, his mustached mouth tight-lipped and grim above a trimmed gray beard. He was bald except for a crowning tuft of white hair that wrapped around his head above his ears He wore a flannel shirt with a dangling sleeve and dirty jean overalls.

Oswald repeated what he'd told the two men.

After hearing what happened, the old man stood there and stroked his beard. "Where are you folks heading?" he finally asked with authority.

"To the city," the Stranger replied.

"What in heaven's name for?"

"We're delivering aid," the Stranger said coolly. "That's all you need to know for now."

Ben chuckled inside.

The old man scratched his head. "Entire city is a hell-hole," he mumbled under his breath. "Anyway, my name's Whittaker — friends call me Whit." He glanced at the passengers in the Jeep. "Looks like we got ourselves a little situation with you."

"Indeed. So, what now?" the Stranger asked, shifting from one foot to the other. "Oswald has a wound that needs tending to."

Whit stroked his beard. "Well, you brought the old dufus back to us, and I see you've got kids riding along with you, so I'm gonna take a chance here and welcome you in for the night."

Ben and Danna rolled their eyes. *Kids? We're holding semi-automatic rifles!*

Cameron glanced at the Stranger. "You sure about this?"

The Stranger furrowed his brow; then he nodded. "Yeah. We'll be okay. They're good people."

"We'd appreciate it," Cameron called out to Whit. "But one condition: we keep our weapons."

"Oswald?" Whit asked, turning toward him.

"I'll vouch for them," Oswald said calmly.

Whit nodded, and the two men swung open the chain gate. Cameron drove in and parked next to a battered light blue '57 Chevy pickup. He turned off the Jeep, and glancing at the keys, he reluctantly handed them to Oswald. "Thanks for the ride," he said sheepishly.

Oswald pursed his lips and swallowed. "Sure; anytime."

At that moment, a tremendous explosion erupted down the road, which sent a tremor through the valley and a high plume of dust in the distance. The four lifted their rifles and assumed firing position.

"What the heck was that, Oswald?" Cameron demanded, calling over his shoulder.

Oswald grinned wryly. "That, my friends, was that other darned robot — stepped on a mine." He made a wide sweeping motion with his arms toward the tower. "Brothers and sisters, welcome to the Arx."

* * *

As soon as they climbed out of the Jeep, the tower came to life; people moved in and out of trailers and down gangplanks and stairways. Voices of all ages floated out of the windows and from the balconies.

Whit led them to the far side of the tower, and coming underneath a large corrugated metal panel, he tugged on a thin chain. The panel opened, and a ramshackle, grating elevator descended and came to a squeaking halt.

Ben glanced at Danna, and she raised her eyebrows and shrugged.

The four stepped into the elevator, joined by Oswald and Whit, who gave another tug on the chain. With a jerk, they ascended.

"Who built this?" the Stranger asked.

"We all did," Whit replied, "but I am — or *I was* — an engineer, retired ten years before it happened. Took us some time. Plus, we had more people in the beginning." His voice trailed off.

As the elevator ascended the tower, Ben could hear the sounds of life: knives chopping vegetables, chairs sliding, hammers pounding, people arguing, babies crying. Ben craned his neck. He hadn't heard a baby cry in ages. In fact, he didn't even know there were babies anymore.

He shot a darting glance at the others; they were smiling too.

They reached the second-highest level, and the elevator came to a rattling stop. Whit pushed aside the makeshift gate and led them into a large, vinyl-sided trailer. The trailer was one large room, and scattered around it were mismatched furniture, two cots, and a stack of PVC pipes piled neatly in a corner. Though it was musty and smelled of mildew, overall it seemed clean and hospitable.

"Pardon the mess in the corner," Whit said, putting his hands on his hips. "We just finished installing the bathroom two days ago. You'll have running water, but there's no heat, so if you're planning on taking a shower then know it'll be a cold one."

"So, you're really fine with us staying here?" Cameron asked, cocking an eyebrow. "You barely even know us."

"Heck, we've let worse people pass through our gates," Whit replied with a laugh. "Truth be told, I can tell by your fearsome looks that you're good people to have on our side."

With a bemused smile, Cameron set his pack down. "I can agree with that."

Whit continued: "We eat dinner down in the mess trailer on the ground; Angelica will ring the bell. So, rest up, and we'll talk more after dinner."

After Whit had left, everybody was silent. Danna checked out the bathroom, the Stranger reorganized his pack, and Cameron sat on a sagging sofa, wiping the grime off the muzzle of his M16 rifle. Ben fiddled with the railgun for a bit, but after a while, he grew restless and stepped out onto the balcony.

The sun had come out and burned away the fog. For some time he stared out on the narrow valley and the nearby hills, at first appreciating the unique view but then looking for any slight glint of sunlight reflecting off a vagabond.

On the ground below, several people were tending to vegetable garden beds; and he noticed that a large chicken coop stood next to a sheep pen. *Pretty sure they don't let the sheep graze outside the fence*, he thought with a smile.

He walked around the corner of the balcony and gazed down. At the foot of the tower, Oswald and a man and a woman were engaged in a heated argument. He leaned closer to make out any words. The woman gestured with her hands and looked up sharply in his direction.

Ben yanked himself back and out of sight. He waited a minute, then ventured another peek. The man and the woman were gone; only Oswald was standing there, looking forlornly down the gravel road.

Two hours later a loud bell clanged for dinner. Inside the mess trailer, about thirty people young and old were eating at two long rows of tables. On the far side was a small kitchen with two large steaming pots supervised by a big-boned woman with golden hair wrapped tightly into a bun.

As soon as they walked in, the room became quiet, then a few murmurings broke out before it fell silent again.

Whit was eating at the far side of the trailer; he wiped his mouth and pushed his chair back to stand. He cleared his throat, and raising his voice, he said: "As y'all know, these are the folks that rescued Oswald this morning."

Ben glanced at his brother.

"They'll be staying with us for the night," Whit continued, "then they're carrying on their business tomorrow." He turned to the large woman in the kitchen. "Angelica, fix them each a plate, will ya?"

"All right, c'mon down, folks," Angelica called out to them in a booming nasally voice. "We've got cattail soup and potatoes. Don't mind these grumpy faces. Some of 'em like ol' Bill Fierney thinks y'all cost everyone an extra potato."

"Well, for heaven's sake, Angelica," an old man, presumably ol' Bill, wheezed. "That's a lie if I ever heard one."

The quiet chattering resumed. The four guests sat down next to ol' Bill with hot bowls of Oswald's cattail soup and listened to the chatter of the latest news and gossip at the Arx. But every time Ben looked up, he saw a dozen eyes staring at him that quickly darted away.

An unusual amount of tension moved throughout the room as if everyone was in on a big secret. He and Danna exchanged glances.

* * *

Later that evening, Whit led them up to a small patio on the third level that overlooked the vegetable gardens. Several wicker chairs were placed in a circle, and two kerosene lanterns were hung from shepherd hooks drilled into the flooring. The smell of citronella candles was heavy in the air.

Awaiting them was the Arx's doctor, a British man named Roylott. He was a pleasant-faced fellow, early forties, and short, built like a rugby player, with a mop of curly red hair and pale skin that pinked at the tips of his nose and ears. He had large, thick-lidded eyes, thin lips, and his cleft jaw jutted out, forming a small knob.

Ben later learned that Roylott was attending a medical conference at a mountain resort when the Surge hit. He spent a month holed up with their other attendees, but soon the meager food supplies ran out, and people lost it. Trying to get back to the city, the doctor eventually found his way to the Arx.

Whit sat down in the chair with a pained groan and eased back into the cushions. He took out an old corn cob pipe and lit it. "Running low on tobacco, so I've been trying to conserve," he mumbled with the pipe on his lips. "Figured tonight's a good night for a puff, though."

Ben cringed at the smoke, resisting the urge to fan it away. He leaned forward in his chair with his elbow on his knee and his chin resting in his palm. A black and white cat appeared from the shadows and jumped onto Danna's lap, purring.

"That's Trixie," Whit said. "Our resident rodent killer. Although not a good one." The old man took two puffs from the pipe, then said: "Well, I'm not gonna inquire about your business in the city, but I wanted to give you my final piece."

"And what's that?" Cameron asked in a tone that assumed he already knew the answer.

"It's been a year since it all began," Whit replied; "and we've managed to stay out of trouble. We've been taking in people who made it out alive." He took another deep puff. "One thing's for sure, though, is that each one of us

seen it, in one form or another: the panic, the killings. . .
."

"The very worst of human nature," the Stranger added.

"More like a monstrous apparition of evil," Doctor Roylott said gravely. "Retching itself out to participate in the devilry of a world gone mad."

"Please pardon the good doctor, folks," Whit said, nodding at Roylott. "He waxes poetic from time to time, especially when he has an audience."

"All the world's a stage, Whitty," Roylott replied.

Ben shifted restlessly in his chair. He thought about the bed waiting for him upstairs. He glanced at Danna, who was absently playing with her hair.

"I think we've been lucky so far," Whit continued, looking out past Ben to the moonlit plain. "Sure, we've lost people, especially before we laid the minefield."

"We've only recently been venturing out," Roylott added. "Trying to gather more information."

"And what have you found?" the Stranger asked.

"Prison gates cast down, armories of military bases and police stations cleaned out; and the new law of the land is that anything and everything possessed by another person will be taken by force."

"We've seen plenty of that," Danna said. She lifted the cat to the ground and sniffled. "Sorry, Trixie, but I'm allergic to you."

"We've come across cannibals too," Ben said.

"You mean the revenants?" Roylott asked, raising an eyebrow.

Cameron shook his head. "We call them deadheads," he said, cracking his knuckles. "They haven't been up to our area. Nah, the ones that attacked us were just crazies."

"Deadheads," Dr. Roylott repeated in a quiet voice. "Interesting." He paused for a moment, forming a steeple with his fingers. "They're still out there, ever languishing for dead worlds of happiness, and always hungering for anything — or anyone."

A shiver ran down Ben's spine. *The deadheads.* We haven't talked about them a lot in the past year. *Cannibals, too?*

Roylott continued: "Ordinary people living in their virtual reality worlds; the long-expected technological apocalypse arrives, and they're ripped away and cast back into the world of flesh and blood with their souls and sanity warped and wrapped into nothingness."

"A curse on humanity is what they are," Whit said.

"I disagree," the Stranger muttered under his breath.

Life is precious, Ben thought. *That's what the Stranger had meant.*

But at that moment, a hatch opened, and Oswald climbed through, barely avoiding the bulkhead. He sat down quickly in an empty chair and rubbed his hands along his pants.

Ben gave Oswald an odd look when the man started chewing on his fingernails.

"And what about the robots?" Danna asked. "Have you come across many?"

"We know a little bit," Whit replied. "Seen some new ones though lately. Nasty fellas. Last week alone the minefield got four of 'em trying to attack us. But the city is still crawling with 'em."

Ben perked up. "What do you mean by nasty?" he asked, leaning forward.

"Aggressive," Roylott replied. "Extremely violent. Some of them even carry weapons. Frankly, I didn't know that was possible. And they've gotten worse."

"Since the Surge?" Ben asked.

"I'm assuming you mean the EMP," Whit said. "The first one, that is."

Danna twitched. "Wait, the *first* EMP?" she asked, gazing sharply at the old man.

"A second EMP hit nearly two months after the first."

"What do you think it was?" the Stranger asked as he reached down to pet the cat.

"Wasn't a solar flare, that's for sure," Roylott said. "Our hunch is that it was a bomb."

"We nuked 'em in retaliation," Oswald added.

"Retaliation for what?" Danna asked. "Against who?"

Whit took a long puff of his pipe. "Invasion."

Cameron's eyes lit up, and he turned to Ben. "Back at the retreat, you remember what those vagabonds had on, right? The ones we took down?"

Ben rubbed his forehead. So much of it was a blur. Starting slowly, he said: "They wore blue and gray camouflage; and ripped too as if they took the clothes from somebody. And one of them, a bright blue cap." He paused — it was coming back to him. "Another one had a badge on its camo jacket that said, 'Global Federation.' I remember thinking that was strange."

"Global Federation, I've seen them," Whit said. He nodded at Oswald. "Him too."

"I don't understand," Ben said, running his hands through his hair.

"My guess is that America collapsed," Cameron said, "and the entire world went haywire."

"Collapsed?"

"Most likely," the Stranger said. "The United Nations came in and tried to put some form of government together."

"Wait," Ben said, looking at the Stranger. "You know about this too?"

"Not everything. Whit is certainly filling in some gaps. And I've had my theories."

Ben wondered why the Stranger had never shared this with him. He furrowed his brow and dimly recalled what he learned in Civics class about the UN, a lifetime ago. "So, they're here? Restoring order?"

"Truth be told, Ben," the Stranger said. "You and your friends — fortunately — have been holed up pretty good at your retreat. So much has happened in the last year. A lifetime's worth of history."

"What's your theory?" Roylott asked the Stranger.

"For the first few months, the military and police were completely powerless to stop AR violence and the robot uprising, with the electricity being gone. And that's not including the general mass panic that naturally occurs with catastrophes of that magnitude. So, it's likely this Global Federation put together a massive peacekeeping force and deployed to America."

"But this wasn't a peacekeeping force," Whit said. "It was an invading army."

"Why do you think that?" Danna asked.

She had been silent for some time, looking like she was out of her comfort zone. Or maybe she's shy around adults, Ben wondered.

Oswald cleared his throat and said: "Cause there's thousands of killer robots wanderin' the city killin' everything in sight. Robot *soldiers*."

Ben blinked and his pulse quickened. Suddenly, it all made sense. He turned to the Stranger, then to Cameron, and exclaimed: "Dad's plans! This Global Federation must've used his stuff that the government gave the UN." He tapped his legs excitedly. "And they did it. They built—"

Danna and Cameron glared at him. Roylott cocked an eyebrow up.

Ben's stomach dropped. *Idiot!* He wanted to bang his head against the lantern.

"What's that?" Whit asked as if he didn't hear correctly.

"An army of artificially intelligent soldiers," Cameron said quickly, finishing Ben's sentence and ending it right there. "Our dad used to do some government work."

"After this army landed, the second EMP hit," the Stranger said. "And apparently these androids were affected — but not disabled. Same thing with the other robots." He glanced at Ben.

"It's insane out there, bro," Cameron said earnestly. "I don't think the kids at the retreat realize how lucky we've all been."

"So, America is gone?" Ben asked.

"I guess the America as *we* knew it," Danna said.

"My hope is that there are still *Americans* alive," Whit said. "That's why we got the flag up there. But the government and the military. . . ."

"Gone," Cameron said. He whistled.

A heavy silence fell upon the group. Ben gazed fixedly at the cat, which was rubbing its head against the Stranger's legs. He thought about America's history: the Declaration of Independence, the Civil War, World War II, 9/11, the Sino-Korean Naval War. Space colonization.

All of that gone, he thought. *All that for nothing? So it could come to this?*

How could anyone possibly have any hope left?

CHAPTER 15

SAVING THE WORLD

Ben was awakened by a cold steel muzzle pressed into his temple. His eyes snapped open to Oswald's sweaty face inches away and a trembling finger to his lips.

Out of the corner of his eye, Ben saw a man and a woman, both armed, holding Danna at gunpoint.

Cameron and the Stranger were inexplicably still asleep on the floor.

Then he remembered: he had watch duty. He'd fallen asleep. *They trusted me.*

Bolts of guilt and helplessness surged through his body and his fists clenched and his heart wanted to explode.

His eyes flashed in anger and his stare tore two holes in Oswald's face. *You're going to pay for this.* For a moment he closed his eyes, forced away the grogginess, and yanked his mind into alertness.

Noticing Ben's wrathful eyes, Oswald twitched. "We just want your guns, is all," Oswald whispered weakly. "Ain't nobody gotta get hurt now. Just promise me you'll be quiet."

Ben knew he had to decide. He lunged forward and head-butted Oswald on the crown of his nose. Oswald dropped his gun and reeled backward, clutching his face while letting out a pained yowl.

As soon as Ben had made his move, Danna fell to her knees and sprung free from her two captors and bounded down the stairs. The man and the woman stood there stunned, their mouths agape.

Cameron shot up straight from his sleeping bag, and seeing Oswald standing over his brother, he dove for his legs, knocking the portly man over with a loud crash.

Ben grabbed the gun and pressed it to Oswald's temple, returning the favor. His head hurt and he could see stars and his forehead was swelling up.

Before the other two intruders even raised their handguns to shoot, the Stranger disarmed the woman, held her arm upwards behind her back, and pointed her gun at the man's frightened face.

"Drop it," he snapped in a menacingly cool tone.

The man paled. He slowly knelt and placed the handgun on the floor. The Stranger reached down and picked it up and tucked it in his pants behind his back.

The Stranger motioned with the gun and said, "Now take two steps backward and sit against the wall with your hands on your head." He moved the woman forward. "You too. Sit."

"Same for you, Ozzy," Cameron said harshly, pushing him toward the other two.

Oswald had a small gash on his nose. Ben, not before grumbling, pulled a handkerchief out of his back pocket and tossed it to him.

At that moment, an out-of-breath Danna returned with a fire pick. Despite the gravity of the situation, both Ben and Cameron laughed.

"Danna, keep watch," the Stranger said, handing her the gun. He turned to the three assailants, and his eyes narrowed. "You know I could've shot you both the moment I opened my eyes. Now tell us what in the world were you thinking."

"Oswald told me he wanted our guns," Ben said, rubbing his forehead.

The Stranger glared at the cowering man. "For what?"

Oswald was drenched with sweat, and his hands trembled. "Not just your guns," he said hoarsely. "We especially wanted your grenades." He swallowed hard. "*And* . . . all your other supplies too."

The other man gave Oswald a black look.

"What?" Oswald said, throwing up his hands. "Ain't no reason not to tell the truth."

"We didn't mean you any harm, I swear!" the woman cried. She was in her early forties, frail, with a hollow-cheeked face and crispy red hair streaked with gray.

"Shut up, lady," Cameron snapped. He crouched in front of Oswald and looked him fiercely in the eyes. "You're gonna stick a gun to my brother's head, scumbag?"

Ben stepped forward. "Knock it off, Cameron," he said softly. "It's over."

"Please, we only needed help," the woman squeaked. "Please, don't hurt us." Her voice trailed off.

"I told you to shove it," Cameron growled.

"Cam, it's okay," the Stranger said, touching his shoulder. He studied the woman. "What do you mean *help*?"

Ben furrowed his brow and a knot twisted in his stomach.

"They've got my baby girl!" the woman sobbed into her hands. "And Sammy."

Danna knelt next to the woman and touched her shoulder. "Who has them?" she asked gently but firmly. "Who has your daughter?"

Oswald, holding the handkerchief to his nose, cleared his throat and spoke up. "They call themselves the Witchers," he said quietly. "Two days ago, Sammy — that's my boy — and Ramona's daughter, Claire Marie, was out gathering firewood with two of our folk. Then them Witchers, they come outta nowhere in a big ol' van, shoot Mr. Hines in the head and take off with my boy — and Claire Marie. They shot Mrs. Hines, and she only lived long enough to tell what happened."

"So, these Witchers kidnapped your two children?" the Stranger asked.

Oswald and Ramona both nodded slowly.

Ben fidgeted. He didn't like where this was going, and he suddenly had the urge to pack up and bolt and forget about these miserable people.

"We were gonna make a run for 'em," the other man said quietly. "Once we got your weapons we were gonna work up a plan."

"You mean rescue your kids?" Cameron asked. "From these so-called 'Witchers'?"

"We know where their base is," Oswald said. "Johnson's Quarry, six miles up Route 77. Big old place."

"A *base*? How many guys do they have?"

"At least a dozen," the other man replied roughly. "But there could be thirty of 'em."

"And all of them armed?" the Stranger asked plainly.

"Yes, sir," Oswald said earnestly. "They've been ruling this area pretty much since the day everything went down. Only reason we're still here is that we've put down them mines throughout these fields. Mr. Hines had this old army booby-trap manual—"

"So, let's be clear," the Stranger said matter-of-factly. "Your two children are being held hostage by twenty-something men armed to the teeth in a fortified base?"

"Yes, sir, we believe so. But they're more than just men; they're into black magic. Some say demonic."

Cameron scoffed and shook his head. "And you think you're gonna rescue them by taking our stash? Hah!"

The woman burst into a fresh round of sobs.

"We weren't gonna kill you, ya know," Oswald said, pleadingly. "We really weren't."

The Stranger waved him off and began rubbing his chin. Then he looked up. "I don't blame you for what you did here," he said. "If I were in your shoes, I would've done the same thing."

Ben doubted that. *They could've at least asked us first.* These people were sloppy. And weak. And after seeing the Stranger in action the past few days, he wouldn't have been surprised if *Mr. Theo* would've put bullets in their heads *before* taking their gear.

The Stranger cleared his throat. "But. . . ." His voice trailed off.

"We could've just asked you?" the woman said, finishing the Stranger's thought.

Uh, duh.

The woman snorted and said: "As if you'd actually be willing to put your lives on the line for two stupid kids who are probably gonna get killed by them cursed robots by next month anyhow?" She laughed bitterly.

"People don't do nothing for nobody anymore. It's all about *takin'* from other people."

"But you were kind enough to let us stay here," Danna said.

"Hey, what about Whit?" Cameron asked suspiciously. "That old—"

"He don't know nothin' about this," Oswald replied, putting a hand up.

"Well, if you go through with this, you're all going to get yourself killed," the Stranger said sharply. "*And* your two kids." He stood up. "I get what you're doing, but let's face it: you can't do this on your own."

"It's suicide," Cameron added.

Oswald lowered his head; the other two sat there with empty faces.

As the Stranger spoke, Ben's heart sunk. *I have a bad feeling about this.* He exchanged glances with Danna and let out an exaggerated sigh. *What is he going to get us into?*

After a moment, the woman said: "What, you're gonna help us now, after what we was gonna do to you?"

"Not help *you*," Cameron said. "Help those kids." Looking for affirmation, he glanced at the Stranger, who nodded solemnly.

Ben threw up his hands and let them fall at his side. His mind raced. *Well, this mission didn't last long,* he thought, *because it's all gonna end here. Ha! This wasn't even a mission — we just left home to put ourselves on death row.*

He gave a derisive laugh and stormed out of the room.

* * *

Ben stood outside on the top level that overlooked the vast minefield supposedly keeping them safe. *Safe from the outside*, he thought, *but not from the inside.* The moon hid behind a thin layer of clouds, bathing the quiet lands in a pale blue light and casting the blackest of shadows. Beneath him, he heard the stack of piled trailers creak and scrape and the muffled voices of the night watch.

"Hey," someone called softly behind him.

"Can you believe this?" Ben said, not turning around.

"I don't like this any more than you do," Danna said, coming alongside him. "But we can't just let them die there."

"So, we're gonna die instead?" He gave a spiteful laugh. "What happened to us and this mission to save the world? Doesn't the world need us alive right now?"

Danna picked at a fingernail. "What would you do if it were *one of us* who was caught?" she asked softly. "What if, instead of them, it was JB and . . . Izzy?"

Ben didn't respond. *Of course, we'd get them*, he thought to himself. *They're our family, but these people. . . .* He rubbed his swollen forehead.

"You know," Danna said, leaning against the steel railing and clasping her hands together; "you talk about us saving the world. Maybe it starts right here."

"What do you mean?" Ben asked, glancing at her attentively.

She turned and faced him. "Well, maybe these people needed *us*. Maybe we're *meant* to be here, and we're *meant* to save them."

"What does that have to do with saving the world?"

"I think the world is as big or as small as we make it. And right now, our world *is* small." She took hold of his elbow and smiled. "These people are a part of it whether we like it or not."

Ben studied Danna. *She's changed so much; the wisdom, the gentleness. Before, it was just about protecting Izzy; but she sees something more now. And I want to see it too. Am I missing something?*

Then he recalled last night's conversation with the Stranger.

"We save the world by saving them," he said slowly and solemnly.

Danna squeezed his wrist and smiled. "It's a start."

* * *

The following afternoon, Cameron and the Stranger gathered a small crowd around a patch of dirt next to the storage trailer. Oswald had given them a map to the Witchers' compound. Using a secret path through the minefield, they slipped out during the middle of the night to scout the area. They returned after breakfast, weary and grim.

Ben was the last one down, even though he'd barely slept. The wind had picked up during the night, and the tower creaked and groaned like it was about to fall over. *And that darned rooster. . . .* At any rate, he felt like a zombie, he was hungry, and the sun beat hotly on his neck, causing him to sweat.

He shouldered his way to the front of the crowd and saw that the Stranger had scraped out a map of the Witchers' stronghold on the ground using twigs and leaves as markers. Danna stood nearby, munching on a piece of toast.

"Where'd you get that?" Ben asked hungrily.

"At breakfast. You missed it about an hour ago. No leftovers either."

Ben pursed his lips. His stomach growled. He thought about going back upstairs to grab food out of his pack, but the Stranger cleared his throat to begin the meeting.

"Hate to break it to you, folks," the Stranger said after the conversations had died down, "but the rumors are true: these Witchers are as advertised."

Cameron added: "Black magic; insanely creepy rituals; you name it."

Murmuring broke out among the crowd. Many got up and left, but a small group edged in closer.

Lowering his voice, the Stranger continued: "The compound is protected by a tall chain-link fence topped with barbed wire. There are only two exits: one that leads down into the quarry pit; the other through a fortified chain gate to the road. The guard post at the top of the building has a three-hundred-and-sixty-degree view of the surrounding area for a quarter mile."

"How many men are there?" a sour-faced old man asked.

"We counted at least twenty, so—"

"*At least* twenty? There's no way—"

"No way *what?*" Cameron snapped.

Red-faced, the man slunk to the back of the crowd.

"Cameron will set up initial fire support as our sniper," the Stranger continued. "We'll attempt to enter the building through or near a utility door on the bottom level. Using stun grenades and firearms, we'll engage and disable every Witcher we meet."

Ben knew precisely what "disable" meant: *kill.*

"Working in two teams, we'll move room-to-room until we locate, identify, and secure Sammy and Claire Marie. Then we'll take them to the extraction site. Cameron already spotted a good place for an ORP, just out of sight and sound from the base."

"Can you speak English, please!" someone from the crowd called out.

"Objective Rally Point," the Stranger said quickly. "It's where we'll make our final preparations before the raid, and it'll be the rendezvous spot after extraction."

"Extraction means once we get the kids," Cameron explained.

"Do you know where they're keeping them?" Oswald asked.

"No, but I'm assuming they're being kept close to the sleeping quarters," the Stranger replied.

Oswald looked up and frowned.

"I'm sorry," the Stranger said quietly, putting his hand on Oswald's shoulder. "It's my best guess; we got as close as we could."

"Anything else?" someone asked.

"They've got at least three dogs, and we did get close enough to observe the guard rotation and how often they change shifts."

"They're lazy," Cameron said. "We're not gonna take chances, but we're sure those guys don't last more than fifteen minutes up there before they're sawing logs."

Danna cocked an eyebrow at him.

"He meant they fall asleep quickly," Ben explained. "The guards are loose watchers."

"I'm assuming you'll engage shortly before dawn," Whit said.

"Exactly," Cameron replied. "Most of those Witchers will be warm and snuggly when we come knocking."

"Not *you*," Ben reminded his brother. "You'll be nice and safe hiding in the bushes."

"Hey, there could be cougars out there," Cameron replied with a smirk.

Oswald cleared his throat. "What's next, Stranger?"

"Well, the objective is simple: we need to first establish blocking fire positions to suppress their fire, get in, find the kids, and get out."

A brief, somber silence fell over the crowd.

"You said you need two teams." A short, athletic woman had stepped through the crowd and now stood next to the Stranger. She was black, with round cheeks, crystal blue eyes, and a short, freckled nose. She wore olive-green cargo pants, a black cotton t-shirt, and a tan ball cap. "I'm assuming you need to get a squad together," she said, crossing her chiseled arms.

"This is our security guru, Kaela," Whit said. "She was a Marine."

"*Was?*" Kaela asked, putting her hand on her hip.

The Stranger smiled at Whit. "Once a Marine, always a Marine, Whit."

Kaela laughed and cocked a thumb at the Stranger. "I like this guy."

"Do you know OBUA?" the Stranger asked.

"You bet — *and* CQB."

Ben glanced at Danna and scrunched his eyebrows as if to say, "huh?"

"Perfect," the Stranger said, clasping his hands together. "You'll be lead on Assault Team One. Danna here will be your second."

Kaela smiled and fist-bumped Danna. "Girl power."

"You got that right," Danna replied with a grin.

"Who else?" Whit called out.

"Any other military here?" the Stranger asked, looking around.

"Right here." A thin man, early twenties, stepped through the crowd. He had a shaven head, dark eyes, and a tattoo of a snake on his lower neck. "Corporal. Army."

The Stranger shook his hand. "Glad to have you, Corporal. You'll lead Assault 2 on Delta Fire-Team. You got a name?"

"Patrick Robinson, but my friends call me Poncho."

"You got it, Poncho." The Stranger rubbed his forehead. "Anybody else military?"

Poncho cleared his throat and stuck his thumb behind him. "My man, Ivan, he's not military, but he took a lot of tactical classes before the Robopoc. He's a mean dude with a rifle, man."

The Stranger gave a thumbs-up. "Okay, Ivan, step up."

Poncho grinned sheepishly. "Uh, he's not here, man. He's out laying more mines. Loves that stuff."

Cameron smirked. "All right, sounds like our kind of guy."

The Stranger rubbed the back of his neck. "We still need Delta Fire-Support," he said to himself as if thinking out loud.

Kaela heard him, and raising her voice, she called out: "We need two people for long-distance fire support. Must be good shots and comfortable with assault rifles."

A man and a woman, both wearing hunter's camouflage, stepped up. "We'll go," the man said, his hand half raised.

It was Jasper, the man who assaulted them last night. The woman was his twin sister, Jade.

"Thank you," the Stranger said. He put his hands on his hips and nodded. "Looks like we've got ourselves a squad." He turned to Whit. "Does anyone besides Dr. Roylott have medical training?"

"Just Arlene," the old man replied, scratching his head. "She was a physician's assistant before everything happened. But there's no way—"

Dr. Roylott stepped forward. "I was planning to go," he said with a slight frown.

"I figured as much," the Stranger replied. "But it'd be unwise to risk the Arx not having a doctor." He turned to Cameron. "You'll keep the medipac."

"Just pile it on, dude," Cameron said flatly.

The Stranger grinned and clapped Cameron on the back. "Anything else I miss?"

Cameron scratched the back of his head. "Just that we're packing light: a rifle and pistol each and enough ammo to keep them off for twelve hours, if need be."

"We need grenades, too," Ben said.

"Good thinking."

The Stranger scuttled the dirt map with his boot and addressed the squad: "Take the next couple of hours off. Eat. Sleep. Clean your guns. Then we start drilling."

Everyone was quiet. A wind chime clanged above them, and Old Glory billowed and clapped in the wind.

The Stranger turned around and faced the crowd. "We're going to get them out of there. I promise you."

Some nodded, others scoffed, and many simply walked away.

"Thanks for the encouragement," Ben said flatly.

CHAPTER 16

THE WITCHERS

The sun had just set when the group left the Arx; they were heavily armed, steely and grim. As they marched, Ben waited for the moment when the adrenaline would kick in and his heart would beat like war drums. He never knew ahead of time when it'd happen — it'd be like getting stage fright two minutes after starting a speech.

It doesn't matter. I'm going to war. And the thought of *that* made his heart leap.

But what if I forget everything after shots break out?

He rehashed the mission details in his head: how to breach the building, who goes in first, fire-team names, code words, how to clear a room. He blinked hard and shook his head and smiled. *I got this.*

After a mile of trooping down the gravel road, they cut across a field and came upon a well-paved road that paralleled Highway 77. This they took, out in the open and under the stars, for five miles until they reached the edge of a large, rocky promontory.

The Stranger held up his hand. "Two-minute break," he said in a hushed voice. "We hike to the ORP from here. The quarry is a mile north and to the right."

Ben leaned against a boulder and glanced at Oswald, clearly struggling with the march.

He doubted whether bringing him along was a good idea. But the Stranger wanted him to come. *I guess I wouldn't want anyone to think the same about me*, he thought.

Shaking his head, he glanced at Oswald, who was taking big swigs of water from his canteen. Satisfied, he twisted the cap and fastened it to his pack.

"Dump it out."

Oswald, water dripping down his chin, looked up to see the Stranger staring at him. "Huh?"

"Dump it," the Stranger repeated.

Cameron leaned over and, in Oswald's ear, said: "If your canteen is sloshing around half-empty, it'd be the same as if we're stumbling through the woods like a herd of deadheads. A scout could hear us three hundred yards away."

Oswald frowned and looked at his canteen dolefully.

"I'll share," the Stranger said, patting him on the back.

The big fella took another swig and emptied the canteen on a patch of wildflowers, which were blooming everywhere because of all the rain.

And that was the last Ben smiled for a long time.

The squad picked their way among the crags until the ground sloped upward, halting briefly so Oswald could catch his breath then moving on again.

Cameron and the Stranger led the way, forging ahead in steely determination.

Every second counted now.

This is the last night these children sleep afraid, the Stranger had said.

Ben hoped more than anything that the kids would be there, still be alive — if only so he wouldn't have to see Oswald's face if they weren't.

He gazed up at the blurry stars. *So much pain. So much fear. When will it stop?* At that moment, a streaking meteor scraped the sky then vanished without a flash. His heart jumped, but he didn't know why.

Night deepened. They moved forward up the rocky slope, the Stranger leading the way. Although the moon shone brightly, Ben could hardly see the way before him. A blackness lay upon the barren landscape, like a wild graveyard with the boulders and rocks as tombstones. *Strangely dark*, Ben thought. Every now and then somebody would stumble, but there was always a hand to lift him up.

The Stranger led them through a few scattered groves of eucalyptus trees; then around a deep drop into a ravine; and finally, halfway up a steep, shrub-covered hill until they reached a small depression between a semi-circle of large boulders. He called for a halt. They'd reached the ORP. The quarry was on the other side of the hill.

Ben set down his pack and surveyed the land they had just hiked, and for a moment he thought he saw twinkling lights miles away. He figured vagabonds had found a couple of flashlights — maybe the cursed flashlights he and Danna had left at the Rite Aid.

"Okay, this is it, guys," the Stranger began. "Cameron sets up as a sniper on the eastern hill. His objective is to take out as many guards as he can before we initiate contact. When that happens, Jasper and Jade will provide fire support. That's when we make the breach."

He leaned in, his jaw set and his brows furrowed. In a steady, lower-pitched voice, he said: "Guys, we need to execute this mission *aggressively*. Violent. Chaotic fury. They'll get confused and think they're under a large-scale attack."

"Aggression and violence," Oswald said in a strained voice. "Got it."

Cameron cleared his throat. "Just remember: you'll probably be fighting in close combat, possibly room-to-room, in near-dark visibility. Be prepared for the worst."

"And some of these Witchers might have military training," Kaela added.

"It doesn't matter," Ivan said, tossing a pebble into the dirt. "If everyone follows the plan, then it's not gonna matter if that place is full of four-star generals." His eyes flashed as he spoke.

Ben listened absently as the Stranger continued on with the plan. They'd wait here for two hours before beginning the raid. In one hour, Jasper and Jade will move to the far side of the quarry to set up their fire support location. But for now, it was time to rest and get something to eat.

They snacked on food bars in stony silence and uncertainty. Ben observed his friends. Danna sat quietly on a rock next to Kaela, her hands folded in her lap; the Stranger stood ten feet away, facing the quarry, hands clasped loosely around his back and gazing down; and his brother Cameron was crouching on a boulder, unnaturally still, his eyes thoughtful and dark.

Abruptly, Cameron stood up and said he was going to do a quick scout patrol. Ben understood. His brother always preferred to be alone whenever he felt stressed.

Those two hours were the longest of Ben's life. He was about to close his eyes when the Stranger stepped into the center of the clearing. He was stone-faced and rigid. Everyone stirred to life and waited for him to speak.

"We're moving out," he said in a low voice. "Remember, you must be fast; you must surprise them; you must kill them."

"And stay down," Kaela added as she tightened her body armor straps. "If they see any one of us, it's over."

Ivan stood up and clutched his rifle. "Let's do this."

* * *

The squad moved quickly, the Stranger leading the way. At first, Oswald kept pace, but he slowly fell behind. Ben kept his eyes ahead and pushed it out of his mind.

He sensed the quarry getting closer. Thoughts raced through his mind. *Why is the Stranger going so fast? I wonder what Danna is thinking about. I wish I had HULC right now. The wind's picking up — I bet Cam is cussing under his breath.*

The terrain began to get less rocky, and they entered thickets of chaparral brush. It wasn't the best cover, but it was better than picking their way among the rocks. They slowly made their way around the hill, and after a short dip, they climbed up a steeper-than-expected ledge and stopped.

Before them, just five hundred yards away, loomed the quarry.

It was dark, quiet, and terrible.

Ben took out his binoculars and glassed the landscape. The quarry was a vast space of wasteland, cleared of any living thing. Near the middle was the giant pit itself, a menacing crater broad and deep. He could imagine the inky black water festering at the bottom, lifeless and cold. *That's where they throw all the bodies*, he thought.

He moved the binoculars to the right. Next to the pit was a massive corrugated metal facility with a towering smokestack and three large conveyor belts leading into the crater. The Witchers' fortress.

On the opposite side of the pit, the building featured a large delivery bay, where two dump trucks and several pick-up trucks were parked in rows.

The barbed wire fence was higher than he expected. He could only see one gate; and next to it was a small administrative trailer with a single light flickering in a window.

The Stranger signaled for them to crouch down. "Take your last drink," he said quietly, handing his canteen to Oswald.

With a clenched jaw, Oswald shook his head and waved it off. The Stranger took a deep draught and dumped out the rest.

Ben felt Danna next to him. Her face was pale, and her lower lip trembled. "You okay?" he asked softly.

"I'm scared, Ben," she replied, barely audible. "I'm really scared."

Ben wrapped his arm around her and squeezed. Gazing at the Witchers' fortress, he said: "Me too."

The squad waited another minute, then the Stranger motioned them forward. Up ahead, the brush thinned into sparse thickets and cactus bramble. Ben pursed his lips: they didn't tell him this part would be so exposed.

Crouching low, they began the slow descent, step-by-step. After fifty feet they came upon a large, flat-topped boulder that jutted out over the slope.

Cameron stopped. "Well, this is my stop," he said softly. "I'm setting up on top of that boulder." He paused for a moment, studying his brother's face. "You'll be all right," he said, squeezing Ben's shoulder. "Give 'em fire and brimstone."

Ben wanted to say something back, but his tongue was stuck to the roof of his mouth, so he just nodded and gave his brother a thumbs-up.

The Stranger signaled forward. They formed a patrol line and continued the descent.

The waxing moon cast a pale light on the Witcher's base, now less than five hundred feet away. The eerie sight must've caught Oswald's attention because at that moment he lost his footing and set off a crumbling slide of fist-sized rocks.

Ben's muscles tightened, and his ears rang. And that's when the adrenaline hit him. The rock slide must've triggered his adrenal glands.

His body coursed with a sharp fire. He resisted the urge to glare at Oswald, who was now officially a liability.

But nobody said anything; in fact, the Stranger ignored it.

As soon as they were down on level ground, they scampered to their first cover: a small trench in which they could hide. Here they waited, giving time for Cameron to set up his spot. Ben glanced up at his brother's location and hoped that he wouldn't see him, because if he did, then they could too. He exhaled quickly and turned to face the base again.

After two minutes, the Stranger waved his arm forward. The squad took ten steps when suddenly he whispered harshly: "Down!"

They all dropped.

Ben lay flat on his stomach, his eyes on the Stranger. In the cold earth, he felt the reverberations of his heart pumping as if he were lying on a cellar door and some monster was pounding to get out.

The Stranger moved forward, and Ben found himself doing the same. *Just don't lose sight of him*. They covered the open ground in what seemed like two breaths and then they were just fifty feet away from the chained fence. *You can do this*.

He hid behind a pile of hewn rocks. Closing his eyes for a moment, he rolled his head around his neck and scrunched his shoulders.

All was silent except for the living night. The soft wind. The chirping insects. The squeak of a rusted piece of gutter dangling from the side of a toppled shed.

He looked to his left. Danna's eyes were fixed in a frozen stare on the fence. She held a pistol in her right hand and a pair of wire cutters in her left.

Kaela patted Danna's shoulder and nodded once. Bracing herself, Danna darted forward, keeping low. Within seconds, she'd reached the fence.

Snap.

Ben leaned forward and grimaced: if he could hear it then so could they.

Snap.

He clenched his fists. *She's gonna get shot*, he thought. He wanted to stand up and yell at her to run back to them, where she'd be safe, and then they'd retreat, and nobody would have to die.

There was a pause. Ben looked over at the Stranger, who was animatedly waving him to move forward. Keeping low, he stepped out into the open space.

A deflating vulnerability swept over him as if his soul, expecting a bullet, took a head start and ripped itself away from him and fled to whatever lay beyond.

But he kept moving, one step at a time. *Just get to Danna*, he told himself. *Get to Danna.*

She and Kaela were holding up a three-square-foot strip of fence. The Stranger was already on the other side, his muzzle aimed at the dark windows of the building. Danna waved Ben forward. After passing his rifle to Danna, he squatted down and carefully crawled through the opening.

Oswald handed his rifle to Ben and bellied his way through the hole. He was almost through when his left heel clipped the top side of the hole, sending a rattling shockwave down the fence.

You might as well have climbed the fence, you big oaf.

They all fell flat on their faces and froze.

Ben dug his fingers into the earth, needing to grab on to something. The Stranger was in his line of sight, but he never took his eyes off the windows, not even to shoot Oswald a deathly glare for his carelessness.

At least that's what I would've done, Ben thought.

Suddenly a flashlight lit up from one window. It probed along the fencing.

It's over.

He waited for the alarm and the gunfire. Instead, he heard the light pattering of hoofs. The flashlight beam snapped up and tracked a large doe bounding in the opposite direction.

Then it shut off.

Ben glanced upward at the stars and let out a deep breath.

After Poncho and Ivan had made it through, the squad split into their teams and darted for separate cover. Ben and the Stranger ran to a stack of wood pallets and hunkered down behind them.

The Stranger elbowed him and nodded toward the building.

Thirty feet above, a Witcher was leaning casually against a makeshift railing on the roof. Behind him was a ramshackle, open-air guard shed. He wore a long leather trench coat with a dark black hood that covered his head. His face was obscured except for two giant bulbous red eyes that illuminated a metal gas mask wrapped around his face. He carried an AK-47.

"A vagabond?" the Stranger whispered.

Ben squinted, then shook his head. "It would've detected our heat signature by now. He's human."

"Or used to be."

The Stranger took out a laser pointer and flashed three times in Cameron's direction.

Thirty seconds later, Ben heard a soft pop and a commotion at the railing. Then a dull thump. He peeked around the pallets; the guard was laying on the ground, his limbs twisted in unnatural directions.

A lantern flickered on in the guard shack, and a Witcher rushed out onto the railing, looking for the other guard.

He took the .50 caliber bullet to the chest in a clean shot. But as he fell, his contracting finger pulled the trigger of his AK-47, sending several rounds into the sky until his hand hit the walkway and the rifle tumbled to the ground.

Dogs began barking, and a harsh, tinny alarm wailed across the quarry.

Showtime.

* * *

As soon as the shots were fired, the Stranger stood up and shouted: "Charlie, move! Delta, move!"

Both assault teams charged ahead to the building, fifty feet away. They reached the utility door and pressed themselves on both sides of it.

The Stranger tapped Ben on the back of his shoulder. "Now, Ben!"

Ben unclipped a grenade from his belt and threw it as far as he could in Jasper and Jon's sector. The grenade exploded ten feet from the side of the building, shaking the ground and letting the vermin that teemed inside know that they had serious company.

Ben heard a docking bay door roll up, and four cloaked men rushed out into the yard, guns blazing erratically. Hidden in the chaparral, Jasper and Jon answered with a salvo of machine gun fire, cutting them down in seconds.

The Stranger nodded once, and Ben unclipped a smoke grenade and tossed it in the same direction; it exploded with a bright flash, and soon half the yard was shrouded in a blue haze.

"Weapons up and lights on," the Stranger said.

Ben flicked on the light mounted on his rifle and clenched his jaw. Sweat was dripping down his face, and he was already out of breath.

The Stranger pulled a device out of his pack, turned two knobs, and stuck it to the metal door with a magnetic *thump*.

"Move away!"

Both teams stepped back ten feet and crouched and covered their ears. The bomb exploded with such force it ruptured the steel door in half and blew it twenty feet into the yard.

Unclipping a smoke grenade, the Stranger ran to the door and tossed it in. There was a loud pop, and smoke billowed out of the entryway.

"Charlie One, move in!"

Like a calm, methodical blur, Kaela and Danna disappeared into the building.

Ben waited tensely for Kaela to call out "clear."

Five seconds. Ten seconds.

Suddenly a torrent of gunfire ripped off inside. His stomach turned in on itself.

"Keep your head up, Ben," the Stranger said crisply, looking into his eyes. "Watch out for goons."

Ben blinked hard and wiped his left hand on the side of his pants. *You have to do this,* he told himself. *You WILL do this.*

The Stranger moved to the edge of the doorway and called out: "Status!"

There was a pause, then a faint, "Hallway clear!"

"Ben, let's move. Delta, cover us! Coming in!"

And then, as if in a dream, Ben was rushing down a smoke-filled hallway. Dim overhead lights crackled above, debris crunched under his boots, and his heart pounded in his ears — *or was that gunfire?* He glanced over his shoulder; Poncho and Ivan were right behind him, their faces set to kill.

They arrived at a T in the hallway; Danna and Kaela were planted against the walls on each side. Bodies were sprawled out at their feet. A foul haze haunted the passages, and the air reeked of gunpowder and rotting flesh mixed with sweat and leaking sewage pipes. The floors were strewn with shattered glass, cigarette butts, and broken pieces of drywall.

Ben looked up past the crude markings and bullet holes that decorated the walls and took a cautious step backward. Attached to metal dog chains and swinging from the bare, pipe-lined ceilings were dozens of dead animal carcasses — rats, opossums, and even a sheep.

No wonder these Witchers wear gas masks.

"What's the layout?" the Stranger asked, nonplussed about the hallway decorations.

Kaela covered her mouth and nose with one hand and pointed down the south-leading hallway. "That way goes out to the garage, so we need to split up."

"Got it. We move door-to-door. You all know the drill. Shoot anybody with guns." The Stranger turned to Ben. "You're the link man, so you're going to be talking back and forth with the squads. *Don't* get lost."

Ben rolled his eyes and muttered, "Got it."

"Okay, let's move," the Stranger said after checking his ammunition. "Charlie One take right side; Delta One, take left. Remember: dominate your position!"

Ben felt his head nodding at the Stranger's words, then everything flashed and tumbled and shook.

"Grenade!"

Boom!

"Move in!"

"Short room, Alpha, skip. Clear."

"Coming out."

"Status?"

"Delta clear!"

Rat-tat-tat-tat.

"Get down!"

Click. "Stoppage. Wait, ready!"

"Status?"

"Charlie, room clear!"

"Ben, you there?"

Blinding blurs, chaos, everything so fast.

"Ben!"

Ben shook his head, then yelled: "Go long!"

Obscured by shadows, Delta One quietly moved like specters farther down the opposite hallway and up the stairwell.

"Contact!"

Dogs barked.

Rat-tat-tat!

"Man down! Man down!"

Ben shook his head and blinked. He heard furniture crashing and people yelling. A violent struggle was going on in the next room. The door was shut.

A single shot. Then a loud smash.

Filling his lungs with air, Ben shouted, "Coming in!" Then he kicked in the door.

A monstrous man in a rusted gas mask stood there, huffing and puffing.

Ben whistled. "Wow, you're ugly!"

The man swung his brass-knuckled fist at Ben's face.

Ben ducked, then lunged forward; and right when the man was still off-balance from throwing the punch, he jammed the butt of his rifle into the back of the man's head with all his strength.

There was a loud crack, then a thump as the man hit the floor.

"I've gotten kicked out of two schools for fighting," Ben told the body; "including beating up the one jerk's older brother *and* his friend." He'd forgotten to tell the Stranger about the other fight.

He slid to his right then pressed his back against the wall, checking both sectors of the room, which was lined with bunks and overturned filthy cots. The room was clear, but a nasty fight left its evidence in broken furniture and shattered glass.

"Room clear!" he shouted hoarsely.

But nobody answered.

On the far side of the room, a large paneled window had been smashed through. Ben knew what had happened. Rushing to the window, but taking care not to be seen, he slowly peered down. The drop was about fifteen feet to a dirty alleyway enclosed on all sides. Distant gunfire was being exchanged, and the smell of sulfur was thick in the air.

At the bottom, a man lay sprawled out, surrounded by shards of glass.

Ben's heart leaped: it wasn't the Stranger. *But I better go find him*, he thought. *Otherwise, I'm not getting outta here alive.*

He checked his ammunition count then moved swiftly out of the room. Turning right, he came upon two armored Witchers barreling down the hallway with razor-sharp javelins the length of elephant tusks pointed straight at him.

Boot steps pounded behind him, and he spun around. Another two goons, but these ones had Uzis.

Ben fired two quick rounds at the gun-toting Witchers then dove over Mr. Ugly and back into the room as a hail of bullets swept over him.

Scrambling to his feet, he unhooked the last grenade from his assault pack and tossed it underhand into the hallway. Then with three running steps, he was through the window.

* * *

The grenade exploded as he hit the ground fifteen feet below. He'd landed on his pack to soften the blow, but the impact still knocked the wind out of him, and his lungs felt like they'd collapsed.

For a moment Ben lay there, his chest heaving, unable to move as if crushed by sandbags. But his wits forced him to get up, telling him he was an open target lying on the ground.

He struggled to his hands and knees, then slowly staggered to his feet. He felt numb — broken in half. His ankle sent a searing pain up his leg.

Shaking the fogginess out of his head, Ben noticed that just above the alley floor were windows to rooms on a lower level.

Still wheezing, he squinted into the one closest to him. Too dark. He moved to the second window five feet down and peered inside.

Suddenly a *pop-pop* of gunfire blistered the air, and two slugs hit his chest as if he'd stood in front of a cannon.

Ben stumbled backward, but he quickly gathered himself and planting his feet into the ground, he dove helmet first into the glass window just as another two rounds shredded the corner of his pack.

The room was pitch black except for the beam of dreary light from the window, and a nauseating smell of ammonia and sweat washed over him. He stood up and brushed the shards of glass off him, and he checked himself for broken bones. Maybe a sprained wrist, but nothing serious. He ignored his ankle; that was a given.

He blinked hard to adjust to the darkness. His chest was on fire, and after fingering the dents in his ceramic plated body armor, his throat tightened.

Something rustled in the corner. Ben flipped on the rifle-mounted light and shone it in that direction.

Two pale, sickly creatures were cowering in the corner of the room, cringing and blinking sharply, blinded by the light.

Kids.

Ben took two steps toward them, and more pieces of glass dropped from his body and splintered on the concrete floor. The children wedged themselves further into the corner.

"I'm not gonna hurt you," Ben said hoarsely. He cleared his throat and swallowed but his tongue still stuck to the roof of his mouth.

The one closest to him was a boy of about ten, with matted brown hair and a round, freckled faced. He wore a long black tunic, which he used to partially hide the other child, a sandy-haired girl of about eight. She wore a filthy white tunic with ghastly symbols stitched all over it.

"Sammy? Claire Marie?"

Neither child moved nor said a word.

I don't have time for this. Where's Danna? She's good with the kids. Well, maybe not. . . .

"Sammy, I'm with your dad," Ben said firmly.

"My dad's here?" called out a reedy voice.

Ben perked up. "Yeah, he sure is."

"He's here to rescue me?"

"Yes. And so am I."

The girl moved Sammy's cloak aside a little. "And my mommy? Is she here too?"

"No, but she's waiting for you back home. Do you wanna go home?"

The girl nodded but stopped abruptly. "Are you a bad guy?"

Ben paused. "No," he replied uneasily. *Food for thought.* "Nope, I'm here to rescue you."

"Is my dad waiting for me outside?" Sammy asked.

"Sure, maybe. Why don't we find out? Can you both walk?"

The children stood up, but they stayed huddled in the corner.

"Are you gonna come or not?" Ben asked impatiently.

Sammy hesitated, but then he nodded and grabbed Claire Marie's hand and stepped forward.

Now how am I going to get out of here? It was quiet. Too quiet. He hadn't heard gunfire in several minutes.

He tip-toed over to the window and peeked his head out. His heart skipped. *Those guys knew which room I jumped into.* He was wasting time.

"Quick!" he said, ushering them back into the corner.

"You're leaving us?" the girl squeaked.

"Shh! No, no, I'm not." He flashed the light around the room. It was bare except for a small bucket in a corner. "Just sit here and be *quiet*!"

Ben shut off the light, knelt in front, and faced the door. He felt four small hands latch on to his shoulders and squeeze like clamp-on vises.

After a silent minute, heavy footsteps thudded on the other side of the wall and shadows appeared in the thin crack under the door.

"Not a word," he whispered.

The doorknob moved once, a soft tick. Then it rattled violently.

Ben leaned back, pressing into the children, then raised his rifle. "Cover your ears," he said quickly.

The door blew off its hinges, and two hooded figures burst into the room. Positioned on one knee, Ben unleashed a blazing torrent of bullets. The children shrieked behind him, but then it was all over and back to quiet, except for his wheezing lungs.

"You guys okay?"

They were frozen. But the boy took a deep breath and nodded gravely. "Yes, sir, we're okay. Can we go now?"

"Yeah, let's go."

Ben led them out into a hallway. He stood there, stunned. The hallway was forty-feet long, and it ended with doors at both sides, the closest ten feet away. The entire ceiling was strung and lit with hundreds of large red Christmas bulbs and bleached white animal skeletons. The walls were painted black, and a soft goo slicked the floor.

It was clear of debris except for a couple of pallets leaned up against the wall, three empty five-gallon buckets, and an old industrial metal chair.

He ran over to the doors closest to him and yanked at the door handles. Locked.

I'm lost. Completely lost.

His chest hurt, and his left wrist throbbed like crazy.

Which way?

He glanced at the kids out of the corner of his eye. They were both watching him intently. He scowled at them.

But then the way was made known to him. *In a sense.*

The door at the other end of the hallway burst open, and at least three spear-wielding Witchers poured out, stumbling over each other like mad bulls charging to impale him.

Ben calmly raised his rifle and pulled the trigger.

Click.

Jammed.

He threw his left hand up and smacked his helmet three times. Then he unclipped a smoke grenade — his last one — and threw it down the hallway like a four-seam fastball.

Coughing fits erupted as the grenade exploded at the men's feet.

For good measure, Ben took out his pistol and fired three shots down the hallway to buy himself some seconds. A piercing howl answered.

He ran back inside the room and stuck his head out the window. On the far side of the alley, another window was smashed open.

The Stranger!

Ben pumped his fist then rushed back to get the kids, who were crouched behind the pallets.

"Okay, guys, I found a way out," he said quickly as he waved them to move back into the room.

They both shook their heads vehemently.

"Are you kidding me?" he cried. "This is our way out! Watch." He swept shattered glass to the side with his forearm and climbed through the window. Laying on his stomach, he turned around and extended his arms back inside the room. "See? It's easy. C'mon!"

He frantically motioned them to him, but they wouldn't move.

They're too afraid to come back in here.

Ben pulled his head out of the room and stood up in the alley. He looked up and around him.

Suddenly a gunshot ricocheted right off his helmet. Without thinking, he held his pistol up and pulled the trigger. Muscle memory. A Witcher fell through an open window and joined his comrade on the ground.

He touched the chink in his helmet. *I'm going to get killed — in fact, I should be dead right now.*

His face flushed with anger at the kids. *I can't believe this is happening.*

And then it hit him.

What do I owe these kids? And Fat Oswald. What do I owe him? Cameron is nice and safe hiding out in the bushes, yet I'm gonna die in this hole? For them?

He knelt down and gazed through the window. The children still sat out in the hallway, looking at him with moist, blood-shot eyes. Looked *through* him.

Ben scoffed in disgust, and then he left them to their fates.

He scampered across the alleyway and eased himself through the window that the Stranger had smashed.

As his boots touched the floor, an unforgettable feeling suddenly overwhelmed him.

He felt like his soul had been torn open, and a great emptiness was flooding his innermost being, and his heart was gripped by an aching sorrow that'd agonize him for all eternity if he left those kids behind.

Life is precious. . . .

Ben closed his eyes and let the guilt seize him and shake him to his core. He needed to feel it because he hated it, and he never wanted to feel it again.

He opened his eyes.

I'm going to save them, he told himself. *I was meant to save them.*

Clenching his teeth, he grabbed the top of the window pane, clambered out into the alley, then stumbled over to the broken window and into the black.

CHAPTER 17

SHOW YOUR FIRES

The children were still there. As he slipped through the window, Ben saw them recoil in anticipation of something wicked coming their way.

He charged toward the hallway and burst through the doorway just as a Witcher was reaching for Sammy's neck. Ben drove his shoulder into the goon, who crashed into the wood pallets.

The impact caused Ben to lose his balance, and as he fell backward, he pulled out his pistol and put a bullet in the other Witcher.

Like a felled tree, the armored brute toppled over and on top of him. *Seriously?* Ben groaned inside. He caught a whiff of the man and gagged.

Straining every muscle, Ben rolled the Witcher off him and staggered to his feet. Then he grabbed Sammy's and Claire Marie's arms and dragged them back into their cell.

"You kids are dumb, you know that?" he snapped as he ushered them to the window.

Checking to make sure it was clear, he lifted Sammy with an "Out you go!" Next came Claire Marie.

Ben covered his arms over their heads, and they ducked and stumbled to the other window, climbing in just as a line of gunfire peppered the ground.

He stopped for a moment to unjam his rifle and reload his pistol, then he grabbed Sammy's arm and motioned him down the hallway, followed by Claire Marie. He led them through several twists and turns, but in reality, he had no idea where he was going.

With frustration comes carelessness. He rounded a corner too quickly and came upon three Witchers ten feet away, squabbling among themselves. Without pause, they raised their shotguns and let loose.

Ben yanked the kids back as shards of cinderblocks exploded above their heads. Playing the odds, he took a right down a narrow, low-hanging passageway.

The Witchers were closing in, and Ben could hear them popping new shells into their shotguns and shouting profanities that, thankfully, were muted by their thick masks.

Rounding another corner, they stopped at a stack of rusted steel drums. He whirled around in a circle. That's it. No windows. Dead end.

Ben pulled the children down and motioned them to crouch behind two barrels.

The footsteps stopped. Silent as a tomb.

He wanted to call out for the Stranger, but he'd give away his position.

Keep cool, he told himself. *He'll come.*

Two minutes passed. Time was running out. The Stranger wasn't coming, and he needed to make a move.

They were pinned down — from a tactical standpoint, it was the worst possible situation for a soldier.

Ben double-checked his ammunition: one magazine left in his rifle; one on his belt; two clips for his pistol.

He dug around in his pack for more ammo, and clearing his throat, he called out: "Alpha, what's your location? I'm in quicksand!"

No answer.

"Alpha, I repeat: what's your location?"

No answer. Nobody's coming to help. It's all on him.

An explosion boomed in the distance, and the overhead fluorescent lights snapped off, flickered on, then buzzed off again.

Ben was about to pull the night vision goggles out when the lights fizzled to life. At the bottom of his pack was Tomàs's flash grenade.

He then spotted a half-broken broom on the ground a foot away.

He had an idea. Pulling the grenade out of his pack, Ben glanced over his shoulder and whispered, "Get ready, kids."

Standing up, he called out: "What's that, Alpha? Come out now? Copy that, I'm coming out now. Cover me!"

He stomped his feet twice then stuck the broom out into the hallway. A barrage of machine gun fire poured out, shredding the broom. He heard the click of an empty magazine.

Bingo.

Yanking the pin off, he hurled the grenade toward the Witchers.

Kapow!

The hallway lit up like a thousand Roman candles, and by the time the goons recovered their senses and reloaded, Ben had charged down the hall and emptied his magazine into their chests.

Then all was quiet except for a smattering of gunfire in the distance.

The kids were behind him, wide-eyed and trembling at this good bad guy who was rescuing them.

Ben read their faces, and he softened his features. He cocked his head at the hallway. "Let's go, kids."

Except he didn't know where to go. *Once again.*

"What about that way?" he asked Sammy, pointing down a dimly lit hallway that ended with a staircase, hoping that the boy would know.

The boy shook his head. But Ben felt a check in his gut.

"Let's see anyway."

They passed several rooms, already cleared out by one of the teams. Grotesque, armored bodies were everywhere. The lights fizzled out again, then flickered back on.

As he approached the stairs, he noticed that a door under the stairwell was ajar. Creeping up, he stepped into a large cavernous room lined with tall aluminum shelves and stacked with cardboard boxes and pieces of equipment.

He quickly scanned for an exit. None. He stepped back into the stairwell. But at that moment, in the deep darkness of the room, he heard a soft voice, lined with pain, cry out.

"Benedict. Help."

His heart froze. He knew that voice.

* * *

Ben moved through the aisles of metal shelves until he reached the last row, and there was Danna, hunched over a steel drum, her pistol in her left hand. On her right thigh, the fabric of her pants was soaked red.

Please, no.

He rushed over to her and propped her up with his arms.

"Let me sit," she whispered hoarsely.

Ben helped her slide to the ground and rest against the steel drum. That's when he saw Kaela laying on the floor two feet away — she wasn't moving.

"Ben," Danna said, reaching up and grabbing his face. "You gotta help them."

"Help who, Danna?"

She nodded behind her.

He looked past the steel drums. The eyes of four or five children glimmered in the meager light.

"You gotta get them outta here," she said with a cough. "They've all been kidnapped too."

"I can't leave you here," he cried. "Can you walk?" He looked over her leg. He knew the answer.

"Maybe you can come back and get me."

Suddenly the room shook violently. Several aisles over, a part of the ceiling fell through with a deafening crash, bringing with it a tumbling inferno. The thirsty fire at once engulfed the cardboard boxes stacked on the shelves.

Ben frantically looked around him. A toddler tugged on his pants legs.

"I'm hungry, papa," the toddler pleaded. "I'm hungry."

"He ain't your pa!" one of the older boys hissed. "*Shut up!*"

The toddler wailed.

Ben's chest tightened, and he glanced at Danna. *Think, think. Look around you. Something to move her. I can pull her in a cardboard box. Dumb idea. I can tie her around my pack and drag her on one leg. Stupid. Wait. There — a dolly. A mover's dolly. Yes!*

He pulled it out from a bottom shelf and yanked on it furiously to extend it. Laying it on its back, he pulled up the extendable handlebars until it clicked.

Whoosh! Another piece of ceiling fell through ten feet away. The children shrieked.

Danna was nodding off.

"No, Danna, c'mon," Ben said, tapping her face gently. Drops of his sweat plopped on her cheek. "Stay with me." He turned around. "Sammy, bring me that dolly."

"Y-yes, sir." The boy pulled it next to Danna.

"Okay, Danna, you need to help yourself up."

Danna, heavy-lidded and pale, nodded and grabbed the edge of the dolly.

"Sammy, give me a hand. 1-2-3, up!" Ben positioned Danna as comfortably as he could, then spun around and grabbed the toddler and settled her onto the dolly. "Get to go for a ride, okay?"

For a moment the toddler stopped crying, and a small smile cracked the corner of her mouth.

Ben slapped his cheek; his mind was clouding up. He turned to the kids huddled in the corner. They recoiled in terror.

"It's okay, guys, I'm here to rescue — er, *we're* here to rescue you," he said, gesturing toward Danna. "Now you're gonna follow me real close, okay?"

He unslung the rifle from around his back and popped in the last magazine. "Sammy and Claire Marie, you're gonna push Miss Danna, got it?"

Both nodded gravely.

"Kids, hold on to the dolly or Sammy's shoulder, just like this."

The kids jumped to their feet and scrambled toward them. "Don't leave us!" they cried as they huddled around Sammy.

A burning beam fell through the ceiling and smote the shelf above their heads. The shelf tottered, then fell forward.

"Go! Go!" Ben ran behind the kids and ushered them forward as the flaming shelf came crashing down. He shook his head and whistled. Stumbling ahead, he led them out into the hallway.

It was filled with smoke. But he had no choice.

Ben grabbed the dolly's handlebar and rushed down the hallway, stopping every ten feet to implore the kids to hurry and to stay low. The children scrambled after him, some crying, others screaming.

Then he came across a double door that hadn't been cleared by the other teams. He paused for a moment, looked both ways, then stepped up and pushed it open.

* * *

The room was pitch black, if not darker, as if light had ceased to shine in this desecrated corner of the world.

Ben led the children through the doorway, but a great uneasiness fell upon him, and the hairs stood up on the back of his neck.

He stopped and listened. Nothing. He took another step, but his blood suddenly ran cold and his muscles froze and he felt like he couldn't move.

He tried to talk, but nothing came out.

This is an evil place.

He jumped as a dozen hands fell upon him and wrapped around him. The children.

"Please get us out of here," one of the little boys pleaded. "Please get us out of here, please."

"Shh! I'm trying to! But you need to let go!"

Sammy, who was holding the door open to get Danna through, let the door slip, and it clanged shut, and blackness swallowed them whole.

Ben groaned. He reached into his pack and pulled out his night-vision goggles, fastened them around his helmet, and turned them on.

He looked at the door; it was smooth sided. They were locked inside.

He pulled out his tactical flashlight from his bag and clicked it on. "Come here, Sam," he whispered, grabbing the boy's arm.

Ben clicked off the flashlight and shoved it in Sammy's hands. The children cried out, but he resisted the urge to scold them. "Don't move, Sam, and don't let go of the dolly."

"Where are we?" Danna asked softly in the shadows. "How come it's so dark?"

"Getting you outta here. Just try to stay awake."

Facing the darkness, the first thing he perceived were the bones. Countless bones, splintered and interwoven like carpet at a funeral home for the living dead.

He looked up and saw dead animals hanging from the rafters, and —

Bones crunched.

Ben turned upon Sammy. "I said don't move!" he hissed.

Sammy's face was white with terror. "B-But I didn't move."

Ben slowly pivoted on his left foot and again faced the darkness.

Standing in the middle of the abyss was a large, wicked shape of a man, its arms outstretched toward them.

It wore a long, trailing black robe fastened at the chest by a barbed wire brooch. On its head was a gray metal helmet with twisted spikes that curved upwards like a bull from hell, and a mask shielded its entire face except for two bulbous red eye caps that throbbed to the rhythm of its foul heart.

On the other side of the door, Ben heard a thunderous crash. Amid the nauseating stench, smoke wafted into his nostrils.

The wicked creature stood erect, silent, and watching. It appeared unarmed.

"Aren't you gonna say something?" Ben called out, the sound of which echoed deeply across the vast expanse and gave him the chills. "Who are you?"

"I am the Witcher King."

Its voice was dry and scraping, like a twisted dagger being sharpened on the skull of the Red Dragon.

Its hands clenched into fists then snapped opened, fingers outstretched toward Ben. "You have *things* that belong to Adramelech."

Ben had never heard of that name before, but his knees buckled at the sound of it. "They're *people*, not things," he replied forcefully. He'd mustered up his toughest voice, but to him, it sounded like a whimper. "And they're coming with me."

Without a word, the Witcher King reached behind its back and slowly pulled out of a scabbard a long, vile-looking sword. It was rusted yet razor-sharp; the entire blade was forged with inch-long, triangle-shaped daggers, serrated like a chainsaw.

Holding the sword high above its twisted helm, the Witcher King advanced toward Ben.

Ben calmly pulled out his handgun, positioned himself in the Isosceles shooting stance, and waited.

Hearing the crunching and popping of bones as the Witcher King drew nearer, the children wailed in the darkness.

Danna shifted and said something, but Ben didn't hear what it was.

Twenty feet. Fifteen feet.

Just a little bit closer, Ben muttered to himself.

The Witcher King stopped and brought the sword to his side. Straightening up, he screamed: "And now, bloody star, show your fires! Let the Light see my black and deep desires!"

As if conjured up by a spell, a burst of sickly orange light blasted from the Witcher King's sword.

The children screamed and recoiled in blind horror.

Somehow Ben was thrown backward, and his gun inexplicably slipped from his fingers. A sickness washed over him, and he wanted to vomit.

With a blood-curdling howl, the monster lunged at him.

Ben fumbled around hopelessly in the bones, trying to find his gun; but the sword was about to cleave his skull, so he rolled twice to the side as the blade came slashing down.

Ben reached down to his right boot and pulled out a knife and drove it into the Witcher King's leg.

The monster stepped back with a roar, and Ben got back up on his feet.

They circled each other, the Witcher King with its crackling blade and Ben with his six-inch knife.

The monster began to chant in an unworldly tongue, and Ben felt like he was going to throw up again.

Suddenly a gunshot rang out, and the Witcher King staggered backward, clutching its stomach.

"Ben!"

He spun around. Danna was propping herself up — barely — with her gun in her hand.

"Catch!" She tossed the pistol underhand and collapsed back onto the dolly.

Ben caught the gun in his right hand, and his finger found the trigger.

He heard the sword whistling in the air as it thirsted for his neck, and he launched backward, feeling the wind sliced by the sword that was inches from his face.

Landing on his back, he raised the handgun and pulled the trigger, delivering armor-piercing, flesh-shredding bullets to the Witcher King's chest until the gun clicked.

The monster stood there, absorbing the slugs as if it was a possessed scarecrow stuffed with rot; then it tottered, the red eyes faded into the black nothingness of its soul, and it collapsed upon a pile of maggot-ridden animal remains.

Ben stood over the slain Witcher King.

The extinguished sword lay at his feet, and he thought about decapitating the monster. But that thought passed as soon as it entered his mind — *I am not a monster*, he said to himself — and he simply spat on the corpse and said: "Ha! 'Black and deep desire.' You ripped that line from *Macbeth*, loser."

* * *

As soon as Ben vanquished the Witcher King, an ear-shattering explosion hit the far side of the room, sending down a rain of animal carcasses, bones, and filth.

Light poured in through the door, and he now recognized that they were in the cargo bay – and, by the looks of it, the Witchers' temple.

A large shadow formed on the outside wall. Ben was about to pick up the sword when Oswald burst into the cargo bay with a machete.

"Sammy!" he hollered as he rushed to his son, faster than Ben thought was humanly possible.

Sammy met his dad halfway and leaped into his arms.

Several shots were fired outside. Then Cameron charged in and shouted: "The place is burning down!"

Ben stifled a giddy laugh. He tossed the night vision goggles in his pack and grabbed the dolly. "Let's go, kids."

With a grunt, he pushed the dolly through the bones and dead animals, taking care not to ram into the Witcher King's body.

An armored black dump truck was idling outside, and the Stranger and Jade were standing on the tailgate and lifting children into the truck bed.

"Danna's been shot," Ben shouted as he pushed the dolly out onto the dock. Drenched in sweat, he shivered.

The air was cold, and the stars sparkled above like frozen tears.

The Stranger jumped down from the truck, and he, Ben, and Cameron lifted Danna into the bed; then they helped the children up, followed by Oswald and Sammy.

"Ivan's driving," the Stranger said. "Jasper is upfront with him. Poncho didn't make it."

"Where's Kaela?" Jade asked. Several children had climbed on her lap and were resting their heads on her shoulders.

"She died," Danna said weakly. "Protecting us."

"Then let's not make her sacrifice in vain," the Stranger said. He smacked the side of the truck three times, and it rumbled forward.

Ben turned to the Stranger. "Where the heck were you? I turned around and you were gone."

"Long story, but I ended up finding them hiding in a closet." He pointed at the children with his thumb. "Oswald led us out and finished off two Witchers who were guarding the exit. *And* it was his idea to blow that door open."

"Way to go, Ozzy," Ben said with a grin.

Holding his son tightly, Oswald nodded gravely in acknowledgment.

At that moment, the dump truck hit a large bump then smashed through the gate and down the road. Danna let out a sharp cry.

Cameron unrolled his wool blanket and tucked it around her. "We gotta keep her warm," he said. "Otherwise she could go into shock."

"Is Miss Danna going to be okay?" a young girl asked timidly.

"Not now, kid," Cameron snapped as sweat formed on his brow.

"Here, let's lay her on her side."

"What about the bullet?" Danna groaned.

"We can't waste time looking for it," Cameron replied. "Doc Roylott can deal with that when we get back."

"You better give me some antibiotics."

"Yeah, yeah, I know."

"Lift her leg up," Ben grunted, shoving his pack underneath her leg.

Danna clenched her teeth and grimaced.

"Any sign of internal bleeding?" Cameron asked.

"There's no swelling around her leg," Ben replied; "and her pulse is stable, so we're looking good."

"*I'm* looking good, Ben," she rasped. "Not you. *Me*."

"Not if you have a peg leg," Ben answered. Cameron tossed him a special forces Israeli bandage, and he waved it in front of Danna. "So, you better be nice to me while I fix you up."

He spun the bandage around the gunshot wound once; then, to put pressure on the wound, he twisted it the other way and wrapped it around her leg; finally, he clipped the closure bar into place. Patting her on the shoulder, in a low voice, he said: "I think you're gonna be okay."

"*Think?*"

"You *are* gonna be okay."

Danna groaned.

"What?" Ben and Cameron asked at the same time.

"What are we gonna do with all these kids?"

Ben turned around.

Eleven filthy faces were staring wide-eyed at them. He imagined their teeth rattling as the dump truck tore across the gravel road.

Orphans. Just like us.

He gave them a small smile. "We'll take care of them."

CHAPTER 18
TORN

Four days they stayed at the Arx.

After two anxious hours, Dr. Roylott was able to remove the bullet from Danna's leg, and he announced after surgery that she would make a full recovery. Claire Marie reunited with her mother; and Sammy, filled with joy and admiration at his father's mighty deeds, hardly left Oswald's side.

The orphan children were given fresh clothing and were slowly being nourished back to health. But the horrors of the Witcher's fortress would not soon be forgotten. Indeed, Ben was startled more than once the first night by screaming children in the throes of nightmares.

By the second day, however, the sound of children's laughter filled the morning air. Their energy brought joy and delight to the Arx, emotions that seemed lost and forsaken forever. Many residents were parents who had lost their own children to unspeakable tragedies, and Danna predicted the children's arrival would repair the cracks in more than one heart. She was right.

Ben slept in past noon for the first time in over a year. He never got to sleep in at the retreat, which made him feel stunted and deprived of a constitutional right of a teenager. Especially because Mom had always let Cameron sleep in when he was Ben's age.

When he finally woke up, every muscle in his body ached. He'd never been sorer in his life, and his left wrist felt like someone had taken a sledgehammer to it. No doubt it was sprained. But he kept it to himself, and he quietly bandaged it while the others were distracted.

He spent that day limping around the vegetable gardens, sneaking a cherry tomato here and there, and marveling at Whit's ingenious Tower and all its complexities of pipes, people, and strange sounds.

His free time didn't last long, however, because the Arxians somehow learned of his repair skills. He soon had a line of fawning "customers" seeking repairs of solar-powered generators, hand-cranked flashlights, and other non-electrical devices.

Ben didn't feign inconvenience; he could barely mask the joy he got only from tinkering. The "Techno-wizard," that's what he'd call himself.

The night after the rescue, Cameron and Ivan geared up and disappeared into the moonlight. His brother said they had a job to finish. The following sunrise, a pillar of gray smoke swirled from the direction of the Witcher's fortress; and Cameron and Ivan returned shortly after dawn, ashen-faced with blackened hands.

They had taken a pickup truck from the compound, and the bed was filled to the brim with military-grade weapons: automatic rifles, grenades, pistols, and mountains of ammunition boxes.

"Here are your grenades," Cameron had told Oswald.

The Stranger spent a lot of time with Whit and the other leaders of the Arx, giving advice, drawing plans, solidifying defenses. Sometimes he would stop and play with the children, but Ben never saw him rest except at night, when he'd clean his weapons while softly humming a bittersweet tune.

The group ate together at every meal, setting up a makeshift buffet next to Danna's bed. It was during dinner on the third night when came the inevitable conversation.

"I thought we'd leave tomorrow," the Stranger said between mouthfuls of acorn bread. "At sunset."

Cameron nodded. "Yeah, me too. Now that we have the dump truck, we can make up for some of the wasted lounging around we've been doing."

Danna shifted uncomfortably in her bed.

Ben took a sip of water and cleared his throat. "So, are we just gonna drive all the way into the city now that Danna's hurt?"

"Well," Cameron started, but he stopped himself.

"What do you think we should do?" the Stranger asked Danna.

Danna handed her salad bowl to Ben and twirled her hair around her index finger. "I guess I don't know."

"What do you mean you don't know?" Cameron asked bluntly. "Can you walk?"

Ben shot his brother a dark look. "Can *you* think?" he barked. "She was shot four days ago. She's not going to be able to walk for weeks."

Cameron softened his face, and he looked down at his boots. "Sorry, I didn't mean it like that."

"Let's face it, guys," Danna said, propping her head up with a hand. "It's over for me."

Ben pressed his lips together in a slight grimace. He knew this would happen, but somehow, he felt like a freight train had hit him.

There was a heavy pause. Downstairs, two people were laughing, and a wind chime sang to the night breeze.

"Nobody's going to say anything?" Danna said, throwing up a hand.

"What's there to say?" Ben said. "Yes? No?"

"Anything would be nice."

The Stranger set his fork down and pushed his bowl away. "It'll be your decision," he said plainly. "We're here for you, but ultimately you need to decide what you think is best for both yourself, Izzy, and the mission."

Danna leaned back on her pillow and closed her eyes. "And for you guys, too," she said emphatically. "There's no way I can go anymore. I'll only slow you down. I mean, that's an understatement."

"Ben could build you a hover wheelchair," Cameron offered with a shrug.

"With built-in machine guns?" Danna replied sarcastically. "Let's be serious. I'm stuck in this dump."

"It's not all that bad here," Ben said mildly. "Now that Kaela's gone, they'll need someone to oversee security."

The Stranger nodded. "Whit's getting up there in years; and after talking with their other leaders, I'm not too confident in their ability to keep things going."

"*Tsk*, so you're saying I should help run things around here?" Danna asked. "A sixteen-year-old girl?"

Ben jerked up. "Sixteen? I thought you're fifteen."

"My birthday was last week."

"How come you didn't say anything?" Cameron asked.

Danna shrugged. "Kind of hard to celebrate a birthday when it's always somebody else's 'deathday.'"

"All the more reason to celebrate," the Stranger said. "Life *is* precious. Well, a belated happy birthday."

"Thanks," Danna mumbled, her cheeks blushing.

Ben ran a hand through his hair and thought: *Now she's two years older than me? I'm like the baby here.*

"So what if you're sixteen?" he said after a pause. "Age doesn't matter anymore. Especially after what we did at the Witchers' fortress."

"I think you'd do great," Cameron added.

Danna's face brightened.

The Stranger nodded. "I agree. I'll mention it to Whit first thing in the morning, tell him to give you some time to rest before getting started."

Danna shot him a quick look. "So, you're saying I should stay?"

"Not necessarily," the Stranger said slowly. "It's entirely up to you."

"No, it's not," Danna replied bitterly. "We all know there's no choice. And unless we find a tank and put together a small army, there's no chance of me seeing Izzy anytime soon."

Silence filled the room. After a moment, the Stranger got up, patted Danna on the shoulder, and walked out.

Cameron stood up and said: "Cheer up, kid. We're not gonna let you down, and you'll see Izzy before you know it." Then he followed the Stranger out the door, leaving just Ben with Danna.

"You okay?" Ben asked softly, leaning forward in his chair.

Danna gave a slight shrug. "Depends on your meaning of 'okay.'"

Ben's eyes wandered out the window, trying to think of something to say. He smiled. "You remember when we first met, don't you?"

Danna tilted her head back and groaned. "The picnic. It was so awkward!"

Ben chuckled. "At least you had your phone! I was just stuck there."

"What did you think of me?"

"Mean."

Danna laughed. "Yeah, I remember I was mad because my mom threw out my AR set the day before. I was 'waging a silent war of retribution,' as my dad said."

"I didn't know that! I just thought you hated me."

"Really? How come?"

"Because you probably thought I was a nerd."

"You *are* a nerd," Danna said. "I mean, c'mon, you actually brought that flying thing to the picnic."

"That was a prototype drone," Ben said in defense. He hated being called a nerd. "Half of my school would've died to have seen that thing fly." He caught himself. "Bad choice of words."

Danna ignored his comment. "And remember Izzy? She found those rabbits. My mom was flipping out because she said she was allergic."

"But it's not like she was gonna take them home!"

"She said the hair would still get on Izzy's clothes."

"Yeah, right," Ben said. He paused. "How come you were more talkative the next time we all got together?"

"Because my mom took away my phone and said that she wouldn't give it back until I talked to you."

Ouch.

"Aren't you *kind of* glad you got to know me?" Ben asked with a crooked smile.

"Yeah, but you didn't tell me that you were always such a troublemaker at school. I just can't put two and two together; it doesn't seem like you at all."

Ben shrugged. "I know. Sometimes I feel like two people wrapped in one." He glanced at Danna. "Why? If I'd told you about it, you'd have thought I was cooler?"

Danna smiled coyly. "Maybe. But we did end up having a bunch of stuff in common."

"Yeah, we both had weird English teachers, I remember that."

"But be honest," Danna said, cocking her head to one side. "You kinda had a crush on me."

Ben clicked his tongue. "Me? No way! My dad always talked about your family like you were like our new cousins or something." He raised an eyebrow. "Did you?"

"No way," Danna replied with a laugh. "You were too much of a—"

"Nerd," Ben said flatly. "Got it."

"I do like that about you now," Danna said with a little smile on her face. "In fact, your nerdiness has saved our skins more than once."

He scrunched his nose at her. "I guess. But if you're going to call me a nerd, then I get to call you a brat."

"Not fair. You can't call a sick girl names."

"Well, you better heal up quickly then!"

Danna fell silent.

"What?"

"It's Izzy," she finally said, sighing. "She probably thinks I'm dead."

"It's too dangerous to go back to the retreat. Like the Stranger said, you're better off waiting things out here for a while."

"Do you think she's safe? I miss her so much, it hurts."

"Of course she's safe," Ben replied confidently. "Safer than anywhere else in the world."

"Maybe. Don't you ever think there's someplace out there, someplace where people are getting things back together? The way things used to be?"

Ben crossed his arms. "I don't know why that's important as long as we have the retreat."

"You miss it there, don't you?"

"The retreat is everything to me," he replied.

"And HULC," Danna said. "Don't forget about HULC."

"Right."

Ben looked away.

"What?"

"I just thought you were gonna be with us until the end," he muttered.

"Well, this is kind of the end, but if you think about it, it's also a new beginning, and we get to be together for both."

"Yeah."

Danna perked up. "Which reminds me . . . hand me my shoulder bag."

Ben reached for the bag on the floor and set it on the bed.

She dug around in it then pulled out an old quarter. It was the one she'd found on the road after the cannibal attack.

"Here," she said, handing the coin to Ben; "I haven't had a gumball in ages. Bring me back one, promise?"

Ben slipped the quarter in his pants pocket. "I promise."

* * *

The blood sun sat low in the sky when the three said their goodbyes to Danna. A brisk, salt-tinged wind stirred from the west, causing ripples across the fields of greening grass.

It didn't take long to pack their things. The Arxians had washed their clothes; and Ben actually felt eager to get back on the road, if only to experience the journey wearing dry, mud-free pants.

And the sooner we get this over with, he thought, *the sooner we can get back home.*

Finishing their preparations early, they spent several hours going over maps and making plans. The Stranger pushed for Danna to be chosen as the next chief of security. Whit accepted the proposition without reservation; and after some grumbling from the other leaders about Danna being 'just a little girl,' they too came on board. Now Danna had only to heal.

The final farewell was short. Danna wasn't much of a sentimentalist, so Ben knew better than to dawdle. Even so, she couldn't hide her red eyes, and neither could he.

He knew how terribly she wanted to finish the mission, but also how terribly she wanted to see her little sister. She was stuck in the middle, at the Arx, torn apart.

Wasn't meant to be, as the Stranger had said.

A crowd gathered to see them off, unlike when they had left the retreat during the night. Several weeping children had to be pulled off a squirming Ben.

It took twenty minutes for Ivan to clear a path through the minefield; and once he gave the thumbs-up sign, Cameron let off a quick burst of the dump truck's horn and then they were off.

Ben would never again see the Arx.

High on the tower, on the balcony next to the great American flag, stood Danna, leaning motionless on her makeshift crutch. Her raven hair blew gently in the wind, half covering her porcelain face and her glistening dark eyes.

As the dump truck rumbled out of the yard and through the gate, Ben watched her in the side mirror, growing smaller until she was just a dark speck alongside a waving sea of red and white stripes.

A dull ache formed in his chest, and he felt like the whole world had come to a crashing halt, and then without warning, a new world had begun to spin in the opposite direction.

He'd see her again, that much was sure. *But what if I won't be the same person?* As hard as he tried, he couldn't push that thought out of his mind for a long time.

TO BE CONTINUED. . . .

J.D. Stone

**THE AUTHOR WOULD BE VERY GRATEFUL
IF YOU WOULD WRITE A REVIEW OF**

THE VAGABOND CODES
ON

J.D. Stone

amazon.com

THANK YOU!